"No, you do not see," sighed Bella, shunting aside her embarrassment and lifting her chin to face the duke squarely. "I was not at all popular, Diamond. No one wished to escort me anywhere. Even the younger ladies did not wish to be seen with me. It was because—because—"

"Because you were awed by everyone and everything and forgot that you are Lady Annabella Faire and not some silly little chit without an ounce of gumption."

"Well, yes, there was that. But there was also Miss Violet Harcourt. She was a diamond of the first water and caught Lord Weredon in the end. But she did not like me, not at all, and declared that no one who wished to be in her company—"

"Weredon's bride?" Derrinham interrupted. "That spoiled brat? She is a harridan, Bella, and a half-wit to boot. I met her in Surrey only six months ago. Why, she ain't got the sense of a plucked pigeon!"

"But she is very beautiful. Last Season she ruled the *ton.*"

"Bosh! She would have ruled no one had you stuck your chin out as you are accustomed to do and put the encroaching little baggage in her place!"

"But I could not! She was a Toast and I nothing but—"

"If you call yourself short and plain as buttered beans again, I shall pull this curricle to the side of the path, take you over my knee and beat the tar out of you!" exclaimed the duke in exasperation.

BOOK YOUR PLACE ON OUR WEBSITE AND MAKE THE READING CONNECTION!

We've created a customized website just for our very special readers, where you can get the inside scoop on everything that's going on with Zebra, Pinnacle and Kensington books.

When you come online, you'll have the exciting opportunity to:

- View covers of upcoming books
- Read sample chapters
- Learn about our future publishing schedule (listed by publication month *and author*)
- Find out when your favorite authors will be visiting a city near you
- Search for and order backlist books from our online catalog
- Check out author bios and background information
- Send e-mail to your favorite authors
- Meet the Kensington staff online
- Join us in weekly chats with authors, readers and other guests
- Get writing guidelines
- AND MUCH MORE!

Visit our website at
http://www.zebrabooks.com

ANNABELLA'S DIAMOND

Judith A. Lansdowne

Zebra Books
Kensington Publishing Corp.
http://www.zebrabooks.com

ZEBRA BOOKS are published by

Kensington Publishing Corp.
850 Third Avenue
New York, NY 10022

Copyright © 1999 by Judith A. Lansdowne

Zebra and the Z logo Reg. U.S. Pat. & TM Off.

First Printing: June, 1999
10 9 8 7 6 5 4 3 2 1

Printed in the United States of America

One

Lady Annabella Faire clung desperately to the saddle bow as the magnificent bay skyrocketed into the air, soared over the broad stone wall at the bottom of Meade's east meadow and splashed into the swollen waters of Twiney Creek. Whereupon Lady Annabella lost her grip, lost her seat and plummeted into the muddy depths. She struggled to the surface, gasping, and fought violently against the current that dragged at the heavy material of her riding costume. She sputtered; she screamed; her arms beat wildly against the waters.

"Thunderation!" a deep voice bellowed. "Stubble it, will you, Bella? It is three feet deep here at the most!" Immediately following, two strong hands came under her arms and tugged her upright. "Can you walk? I certainly hope so, for I am not about to carry you."

Lady Annabella, the plume of her hat wagging soddenly against one rosy cheek, turned, stumbling, to face her grouchy rescuer. "Diamond," she spluttered on a half whisper. "What are you doing here?"

"I was angling for trout, infant, but you have made that a futile exercise. I do not expect there is a trout left in the vicinity. Is there a groom trailing in your wake?"

"No, I—"

"I ought to have known not. You have not the least business, Bella, to go jauntering about the countryside without a groom in attendance. Not at your age. You have no more sense now than you had when you were a mut-tonheaded schoolroom miss."

"Oh!" spluttered Bella, refusing the arm he offered and slopping toward the nearest bank on her own. "And you, your grace, have no more manners now than you did when you were a wretched little schoolboy."

"Indeed," grumbled the duke as he waded across the creek toward the gelding which now grazed quietly on the opposite bank.

Bella watched, damply. Oh, but it was just like The Diamond to grumble about trout and the absence of a groom rather than offer sympathy or admit that he was pleased to see her after he had been away for what seemed like forever.

His hair, the deep gold of warm honey beneath the bright sun, curled just as unfashionably over his ears as it had always done. And his broad-shouldered form was just as straight and tall. And when he leads Castle back to me, thought Bella, his eyes will flash and sparkle like sapphires in candlelight as I have always known them to do. He never changes.

Hillary Holland Hallsworth, the Duke of Derrinham, had been her nearest neighbor from the day of her birth. The *ton* had dubbed him The Diamond, though no one had ever called him so to his face except Bella. She could remember to this day his dismay as the appellation had slipped into the air between them.

"My name, infant, is Hillary," he had growled, staring down his straight and very aristocratic nose at her from all the arrogance of his eighteen years. "And I am addressed as your grace as you very well know."

"I am s-sorry," she had stuttered, a bewildered ten-year-old, confused that he should not wish to be called Diamond, which she thought a marvelous name.

"Yes, well, I expect *you* may call me Diamond, Bella,

if it pleases you," he had relented, gazing steadily down at her. "I know that you imply no sarcasm by it."

And now I understand sarcasm, she thought, watching as he snatched up Castle's reins. They dubbed him that not because he is exquisite, but exquisite and so very hard. Anyone attempting to crush him would be shattered from the impact. "If only I could learn to be so hard," she whispered. "If only he would teach me."

Bella swiped at the unbidden tears that began to slide down her cheeks and sniffed.

"Bella, you are crying. Are you hurt, infant?" asked the duke as he led her mount up before her.

"N-no."

"You are not crying because I grouched at you? You have not become such a ninny as to take my crotchets to heart?"

Bella shook her head.

"What is it then? Tell me," urged Derrinham, placing a comforting arm about her shoulders. "What can I do to help?"

"N-nothing," sniffed Bella, wanting to kick herself for indulging in tears in The Diamond's presence. "I am just being a great baby is all. It is of no import, truly."

"Well, but it must be of some import or there would be no tears, Bella. There is nothing wrong at home? No one is ill?"

"No," sobbed Bella, the tears abruptly pouring in torrents down her apple-red cheeks. "I am—I must—I cannot—"

Derrinham, disconcerted, put his other arm around her and drew her to him until one wet cheek rested against the rough material of his hunting jacket. There ought to be something I can say to quieten the girl, he thought foggily, rubbing her back. "Bella, hush," he murmured. "You will make yourself ill with all this carrying on.

Nothing can be so bad as to require all these tears. Come sit with me and tell me what has happened."

He led her back to the wall, lifted her up upon it and swung up beside her with a muffled groan. Damnation, he thought, must I still be careful, even when I hoist a bit of a thing like Bella?

"Now," he said, carefully removing the sadly damaged hat with the damply dangling feather from Bella's light brown curls, "the sun will warm you up and dry you off while you cease this thespian display and converse with me in a civilized manner. You are not crying because you are dismayed at being unseated? Everyone has been unseated once or twice, infant, and Castle is a very large horse for such a dab of a girl as you."

Bella could not help herself and burst into sobs again.

"Now what did I say?" grumbled the duke, nervously destroying the limp feather barb by barb. "Bella, do try for some decorum," he ordered. "You have never been a wretched watering pot before. Do not be one now."

Bella took a deep breath and, staring intently at the toes of her boots, attempted to stem the tide of her tears. When finally she succeeded, she glanced up at Derrinham and gave him a watery smile. "I am sorry. It is just that everything is dreadful and I cannot do a thing about it."

"*Everything* cannot be dreadful, Bella. That is next to impossible. Tell me specifically what has set you off."

"I am to go to London tomorrow for the Season and—and—"

"Do not cry again!" ordered the duke with a deal of exasperation. "If you do, Bella, I shall climb down from this wall and take myself home. See if I do not. Now, what is so dreadful about a Season in London? I thought young ladies longed to spend the Spring gallivanting about Town."

"But I had a Season in London, Diamond, last Spring while you were away, and I did not take. I am short and plump and plain as buttered beans and not a gentleman in all of London wishes to come near me. I shall be a perfect quiz if I return. But Mama and Papa are determined not to understand!"

The duke's eyebrows rose. Admittedly he had not been to London in a while, but— "Short and plump and plain as buttered beans? You, Bella? What nonsense!"

"It is not nonsense. It is true. Every gentleman in London thinks so and most of the young ladies, too."

"Well, a group of deuced nodcocks inhabit London then," muttered the duke.

Though he had managed to tease a smile from Bella when he escorted her home, her unhappy countenance continued to pop unbidden into Derrinham's mind at the oddest times. During meetings with his overseer, in the midst of his meals, even in his dreams, Bella's sad little face rose unbidden before him.

"Botheration," he grumbled under his breath as a vision of Bella appeared in the midst of a discussion with his solicitor. "The infant is driving me to distraction!"

"Your grace?" asked Mr. Piermont.

"Nothing, Piermont. Do you return to town directly?"

"Yes, your grace, as soon as our meeting is concluded."

"Good, then you will do me the favor to carry a missive to Lord Billingsly. And you will open and staff Derrinham House. Sonnett and Shaughnessy will come with me, of course, but we will need a housekeeper, a cook and all the rest. I am no longer in mourning, Piermont, and I have a notion to take in the Season."

Lady Annabella, her brown hair coaxed into wispy curls about her cherub's face and her compact and gen-

erously curved little figure fitted nicely into an apricot
evening gown, descended from the Earl of Meade's Town
coach and paused uncertainly beside her mother at the
entrance to Almack's Assembly Rooms. It was Wednesday evening. And every Wednesday evening during the
Season, if a young lady were among the privileged few,
she attended the dancing at Almack's.

Bella had managed to avoid the humiliation of appear-
ing at that particularly intimidating place for two
Wednesdays in a row because her new ensembles had
not been completed. But this Wednesday she had no such
excuse. Her rosy face paled at the thought of ascending
those stairs and entering the marriage mart. Her white-
gloved fingers fidgeted restlessly with her fan and her
reticule. Her heart beat at such a rate that it seemed to
hum within her breast and a great lump grew and grew
and grew in her stomach. "Oh, Mama, I cannot!" she
exclaimed suddenly, causing Lady Meade to jump nearly
an inch into the air.

"You cannot?" asked Lady Meade as she fitted her
arm through her daughter's, drawing her up the steps and
toward the dreaded doorway. "Bella, I cannot understand
what has gotten into you."

Terror has gotten into me, thought Bella. They will all
be inside—the same fearsome gentlemen and disobliging
young ladies of last Season. And they will quiz me and
set me to blushing and mumbling and shuffling my feet.
Because, no matter how diligently I try, I will not do one
thing correctly. I will be tongue-tied and mortified and
will huddle beside Mama like always. And everyone will
laugh and call me The Hesitant Hedgehog again.

Bella's face flamed at the very thought of that dreaded
appellation. It was Lord Barrington had dubbed her so.
"Because," Miss Violet Harcourt had told Bella spite-
fully one evening, "you are a small, plump, brown crea-

ture who rolls herself into a prickly ball whenever anyone approaches."

"Smile, Bella," Lady Meade's voice intruded into Bella's thoughts. "Here is Countess Lieven to welcome us."

In the end, Bella sat demurely beside her mama watching from beneath lowered lids as other young ladies danced. Her fondest hope was that no gentleman would ask her to join him in a minuet or a country dance or—worst of all—a waltz, for she was certain to maim whoever took that gamble.

"She has returned," sighed the fastidious Lord Nesbitt, upon whom Bella had once spilled an entire glass of orgeat.

"Who? Whom? Who?" queried Lord Barrington, his head swiveling about.

"The Hesitant Hedgehog, James. There in the corner with her mama. After last Season I would have thought Lord Meade to have had sense enough to marry her off to one of the local squires."

"You do not expect she has improved since last year? No," sighed Barrington, answering his own question, "I expect not."

"What are you doing?" cried Nesbitt, catching Barrington's arm as that gentleman took a step in Bella's direction.

"I am going to ask her to dance. I was a thumping bounder to The Hedgehog last year. I am obliged to redeem myself."

"You are out of your mind, Barrington."

"No. One dance cannot prove a hardship and I shall feel better about myself. Do my duty by the gel. Get it over with."

Lord Barrington—a vision in a blue coat and black silk

knee breeches, his waistcoat decorated discreetly with one fob and his dancing slippers boasting silver buckles—started manfully off in Bella's direction with Nesbitt trailing in his wake, only to come to a sudden halt halfway around the floor. "Who the devil is that?" he murmured.

Nesbitt's gaze followed Barrington's and he gasped. "Miss May! Is she not a vision, Barrington? But what the deuce is she doing in London? Damnation!" exclaimed Nesbitt as a gentleman appeared at Miss May's side and bowed gracefully over Lady Jersey's hand. "The Diamond! The Diamond is out of mourning, Barrington, and back on the town!"

An excited hum arose amongst the chaperones and the mamas as they, too, noted the arrival of the elegant pair. Lady Jersey held Miss May's hand in her own and barely avoided braying with laughter at the upset the duke's unexpected presence caused. "How fortunate for all the hopeful mamas and chaperones that your companion could not accompany you, Miss May, and that your uncle could," Sally Jersey snickered as Derrinham left them to stroll deeper into the crowded ballroom. "Every mama here is advising her daughter of what a magnificent catch he is."

The only mama, in fact, who was not advising her daughter of exactly that stared perplexedly up at Derrinham as he bowed over her hand. "How nice to see you again, your grace," Lady Meade replied disjointedly to his "Good evening". "I had not the least notion—you never mentioned—I am certain Peter said nothing to me about your coming to London for the Season."

"No, I had not intended to come," replied the duke with a slight frown upon his astoundingly handsome face, "but Jane was in need of me and a gentleman cannot ignore a niece in need, can he? Good evening, Bella," he added with a curt nod in Lady Annabella's direction. "Dancing up a storm, are you?"

Bella met his eyes hesitantly. What was she to answer? She had not danced one dance all evening. Humiliated that The Diamond would now see her as the wallflower she was, her cheeks reddened and she lowered her gaze. And then she felt a movement beside her and saw a firm hand lift the empty dance card tied about her wrist and scrawl *Diamond* upon it. Twice.

"You will not object to favoring an old neighbor with a waltz or two, Bella," he told her gruffly. "I shall be back to claim you once I have seen Jane settled."

Lord Barrington paused in his perambulation of the ballroom long enough to be introduced to Miss May and then crossed to Bella and bowed politely. "May I hope that you are free, Lady Annabella, for the set that is forming?"

Hope that I am free? Of all the clankers, thought Bella. It is some wager among the gentlemen that brings him to stand before me. More likely than hoping I am free, he is hoping I have sprained an ankle so that he can collect his monies without suffering the fate of actually dancing with me.

Bella wished that she had nerve enough to kick the pretender in the shin. But she was much too intimidated to do any such thing and was just about to plead a headache when a pleasant voice called her name and Miss May came directly to her with Lord Nesbitt in tow. "Come and form a set, just the four of us, Bella. It will be such fun!" And then the elegant Miss May took hold of Bella's hand and tugged her out onto the dance floor.

"Oh, what a miscreant Lord Nesbitt is," murmured Miss May as the dance ended and she imperiously dismissed both of the gentlemen. "How dare he imply with those speaking eyes of his that we were going to stomp upon their toes. Not but what it would have served him right had I done so."

"He meant me," managed Bella in a breathy whisper. "He did not intend to imply that you would do so."

Miss May grinned, leading Bella back to her mama and taking a chair at Bella's side. "No, I think not. He was quite definitely quizzing the both of us. You must call me Jane, I think, for we are going to become enormous friends. May I call you Bella? I have already done so because Uncle Hill told me to do it, but I do think I ought to ask your permission."

"Yes," whispered Bella, astounded that this beautiful young lady would not only be seen sitting beside a frumpy wallflower, but wished to be upon a first-name basis with her as well.

"You will think I do not remember you, Bella, but I do. You were so kind as to attend my mama's funeral with your mama and papa. You are Uncle Hill's nearest neighbor and he has told me ever so much about you. I know we are destined to be bosom bows."

"Certainly destined to face the Season arm in arm," agreed The Diamond, who had approached unnoticed and now stood gazing down at them both. "If, that is, you will be kind enough to take Jane under your wing, Bella. This is our dance, I believe."

Bella, agog at the thought of taking such an astounding creature as the gloriously blond and beautiful Miss May under her own poor, drab wing, allowed the duke to lead her to the floor without the least protestation.

"Jane was to have had her Season last year, but she was in mourning for her mama, you know," murmured the duke, placing his hand upon Bella's waist and spinning her into the waltz. "And this year her papa has been sent to prepare for the congress in Vienna. She has spent more time trailing after Will in foreign climes than she has spent in England, and I thank my lucky stars that you are here, Bella, for she knows barely anyone. You will not mind having Jane about you from time to time, will you?"

"No, oh no, I should be delighted."

"You are a godsend," the duke smiled down at her. It was the oddest thing, but she felt as though she were swimming in the calm blue sea of his remarkable eyes and all fear of the ladies and gentlemen, of the dance itself, and of Almack's left her. "I promised Will to look after the girl. So I have come to London and opened Derrinham House for her. And then, this evening Janie's companion came down with something or other and could not play chaperone. What was I to do but offer her my own escort?"

"Of course you must."

"Precisely."

Lady Meade, surrounded by a number of envious cronies, could not keep from rejoicing. Annabella fairly floated in The Diamond's arms. She did not stare at her feet; her brow was not creased with worry; she was not rigid with fear. She was even laughing up at him now—a thing she had never done with any gentlemen who had partnered her. Bella was displaying herself to perfection. My girl is coming of age at last, thought the countess. This Season Bella will take, I am certain of it.

There was not one woman at Almack's that evening, excepting Miss May and Lady Meade, who did not envy Bella her place in the Duke of Derrinham's arms. He was as dazzling and as handsome and as self-possessed as ever he had been. And when he remained and waltzed with Bella a second time, the gossips began to buzz behind their fans and innumerable gentlemen's eyes began to blink as if accosted by a strong light.

"Well, there must be something more to The Hedgehog than any of us have had the wit to discover," Mr. Tottingham declared, leaning one shoulder against a pillar and sipping at a glass of orgeat. "Apparently she holds The Diamond spellbound. Just look at his face. The duke is beguiled by her."

Lords Nesbitt and Barrington nodded in silence.

Lord Barrington had never met his grace, the Duke of Derrinham, but he well knew the gentleman's reputation. The Diamond had first come on the town some eight years ago and had established himself in a matter of weeks as a Nonpareil. All of Society had been mad for him. He fenced like a master and spouted poetry with style. He was a dead shot with a dueling pistol and a Jehu with a whip and he was the finest pugilist the aristocracy had ever sprouted.

His skill at the Fancy, in fact, was unparalleled and Barrington had longed to make his acquaintance—to stroll into Jackson's boxing saloon and watch The Diamond in the ring and call him by name to urge him on. But just when he had become old enough to do so, the Diamond's sister had died, the duke himself had been injured and all of Barrington's hopes had come crashing down. Now, of course, they arose again and he determined to make The Diamond a close acquaintance, even if he must go by way of Miss May and Lady Annabella to do it.

"You do not mind that I called upon you for aid, eh, Janie?" asked the duke, sipping at a glass of brandy while untying his cravat with one hand.

"No, Uncle Hill, I do not mind at all. Papa was just wishing me off his hands when your message came. And I think it is kind of you to care about Bella. She seems a very nice person."

"Well, she was acting like a perfect ninnyhammer this evening, sitting there all huddled up against the wall beside her mama," muttered Derrinham, allowing Jane to help him slip out of his coat. "I cannot imagine what has gotten into her. Generally, Bella is an audacious little minx and full of the devil. I cannot comprehend why she has allowed a throng of fribbles to intimidate her. But between the two of us, Jane, we can get her to behave like her true self. If she can be brought to do just that, the beaux cannot help but think her a diamond of the first water."

Miss May urged her uncle into a deep wing chair, bent to remove his dancing slippers and placed a footstool beneath his stockinged feet. Then she set a branch of candles and the brandy decanter upon the table beside him and placed a well-worn book into his hand. "Most certainly they will think Bella a diamond of the first water," she smiled. "Especially if you are seen to take pleasure in her company. I think I shall take myself off to bed, Uncle Hill, if you will not be lonely."

"Of course I shan't be lonely. I have never been lonely in my life. And I will thank you, Janie, to cease treating me as if I am some doddering old fool. I am merely seven years your senior, you rascal. Convey my gratitude to Miss Davies, will you, and say that her aid is greatly appreciated and that she did an admirable job of it?"

Miss Lydia Davies, who had been Jane's governess and had subsequently become her companion, laughed when the duke's thanks were conveyed to her. "I did an admirable job? And to think, all that my job involved was to pretend to be ill and to curl up before the fire with a good book. I would have sought a position with your uncle long ago, Janie, instead of applying to become your governess, if I had known how little he required of a person, let me tell you. Did you discover his purpose in this subterfuge by any chance?"

"Indeed. And he is like to request you to be ill again, too. He is determined to lend his little neighbor—Lord Meade's daughter—some of his consequence without her thinking that he goes out of his way to do so. He has told her that he takes your place because he does not wish me to be disappointed at missing any portion of the Season."

"Oh, what a bouncer!"

"Yes, but Bella apparently believed him and I shall not disabuse her of the notion. She is very sweet and pretty but most unsure of herself and I think it is kind of Uncle Hill to take pity upon her. He will succeed in drawing her out and getting the beaux to chase after her, too," Jane added with a dazzling smile. "I could see light dawning in any number of gentlemen's eyes this evening and all Uncle Hill did was to waltz with the girl."

Two

The duke stared with blind eyes at the volume in his lap. Devil it, but he was a fool to have opened Derrinham House again. Of all the muttonheaded things to do. But it had been too late to hire a furnished house for the Season. And besides, how utterly stupid it would have looked for the Duke of Derrinham, whom everyone knew to possess a veritable palace in Great Stanhope Street, to avoid his own residence and hire another in its place. Yet that was exactly what he longed to do. More, in fact. He longed to build a snug little house for himself in Bloomsbury Fields and to let this ugly hulk rot away to nothing.

From the moment he had come to this monstrous residence in his eighteenth year, he had wished to be shed of it. Eerie voices and visions flashed like lightning through his mind when he wandered its halls. Nameless fears dogged him from room to room and a great sense of hopelessness attempted to overwhelm him.

But the house had belonged to seven Dukes of Derrinham before him and was part of the entail and he could not be shed of it. For six more years he had allowed himself to be haunted by unnamed fears each time he entered his own premises, and then midway into his seventh Season, his sister's death had thrown him into mourning and he had not returned to London since.

"I would not have returned this year either," he muttered, downing what remained of his brandy in one gulp, "if Bella did not require my support."

Resting his head wearily against the chair back, Derrinham closed his eyes and sighed. He was truly exhausted. He had arrived in London four days ago after stopping to fetch Jane and Miss Davies from the packet at Dover, and he had since awakened four nights in a row, leaning against the wall of the third floor servants' staircase, asleep on his feet.

Why bother to go to bed at all? Derrinham wondered. If I am going to go gallivanting all over this confounded house in my sleep, it is a good deal warmer to do so in my shirtsleeves than in my nightshirt.

"Your grace?"

"What? Oh, Sonnett. What is it?"

"It is nearing two o'clock, your grace."

"Is it? You ought to take yourself off to bed then, Sonnett. You are entirely too old to be wandering about at this hour."

"Yes, your grace. I did think I ought to point out, however, that Mr. Shaughnessy is still waiting to help you to your bed."

"Is he? Well, send him off to his quarters, Sonnett. I have decided to spend the night dressed and in this chair."

"We ought not to have come to this dreadful house," murmured Sonnett with a sigh. "It does nothing but plague you."

"Yes, but this is the first time I have taken to stomping about in my sleep. I thank you and Shaughnessy for coming with me. I do not think I could bear it without the two of you."

"You will never be without us, your grace," replied the elderly butler with a slight catch in his throat. "Not so long as there is breath in my body and in Mr. Shaughnessy's."

* * *

Lady Annabella discovered herself the following afternoon in the duke's coach, accompanying Miss May to Hatchard's Bookshop.

"He has read all of his volumes over and over until they are frightfully tattered," Jane was saying. "Some have even lost their covers. Can you imagine?"

Jane looked like Spring itself in a morning dress of blue-and-white-striped dimity with lace at the cuffs and around the hem, topped by a matching kerseymere spencer trimmed in white braid and a low-crowned, wide-brimmed bonnet covered in silk bluebells, lined with white silk and tied provocatively beneath her chin with blue silk ribands. "I intend to purchase the new edition of Blake's collected works. And I thought, perhaps, I might bring him a copy of Lord Byron's *The Corsair* as well. He has not yet read Lord Byron's work, but I think he will like that one very much."

"Poetry?" murmured Bella in a quiet voice. "I should never have thought it of him."

"No," grinned Jane, "he does not seem the type. But he is a lover of rhyme and meter nonetheless and Mama was used to say that he could recite it most eloquently— well enough to steal a lady's heart away. Oh, Bella, look! There in Madame Madelaine's window. It is the most charming bonnet. John," Miss May called through the trap. "John, do stop here for a moment."

The coach came to a halt; the footman lowered the steps and helped the ladies to descend; and Jane, with unbounded enthusiasm, tugged Bella into the shop. Bella stared at the bonnet as Madame took it from the window and then she laughed. "Jane, it is the most frivolous thing I have ever seen."

"Yes, a puff of nonsense! Bella, do try it on."

"Me?"

"Oh, yes, please? It is the most perfect bonnet for you."

Bella could not believe her ears. Perfect? For her? "But, Jane, I thought it was you who wished—"

"I wish for you to have it. It is such an audacious little thing. And this particular green will look delicious on you."

"Not to mention these cherries," laughed Bella, fingering the very real-looking fruit clustered upon the upturned brim.

Madame set the confection upon Bella's ordinary brown curls, and *voila!* a charming gaiety overcame Annabella and a spurt of total nonsense emerged from between her lips. "Oh, I say," she whispered, her brown eyes widening in amusement. "It is magical! It makes the whole world bright!"

"And it will charm the birds from the trees," grinned Jane.

"I certainly hope not! What should I do with charmed birds?"

"I have not the faintest idea, but I know what you will do with the bonnet. You will wear it down Bond Street of an afternoon and pierce gentlemen's hearts by the score. We will take it," proclaimed Jane grandly, opening her reticule on the spot and withdrawing her purse.

"But I cannot allow you to pay for it," cried Bella, astounded. "I have pin money of my own."

"No. It is to be Uncle Hill's present to you, Bella. He gave me orders to discover something that would make you smile. And this bonnet is just the thing."

"But why should he wish to buy me a present?" Bella asked as they left the shop with the bonnet safely wrapped and stowed in one of Madame's bandboxes.

"Because he missed your first Season, of course," offered Jane as they settled again into the coach. "He would have sent you flowers for your come-out at the very least had he been in London. But he was not. And I am glad, too, because the bonnet is much jollier than flowers and though it would be considered most improper for a gentleman to send it to you, no one will think a thing of it now, because they will believe it came from me."

When they reached the booksellers, Jane set off to procure the assistance of one of the clerks while Bella browsed quite contentedly among the shelves. To think that The Diamond liked poetry—not merely liked it, but was able to recite it. A tiny smile formed upon Bella's lips. Never once had she guessed at such a thing. She had always known, of course, that beneath his cantankerous exterior dwelt a noble and a very kind heart—but poetry? Sooner or later she would quiz him about that. She would not be able to restrain herself from doing so.

"Good morning, Lady Annabella," a voice murmured at her shoulder as she reached to lift down one of the volumes. "You are looking splendid this morning."

Bella, startled at the unexpected greeting in her ear, jumped and the volume she had been pulling from the shelf came bouncing down upon Lord Barrington's head.

"Oh, I am sorry!" gasped Bella.

Barrington grunted and bent to retrieve the book. Bella, nervous and unnoticing, bent to retrieve the volume as well and their heads clunked together.

"Oh, oh, my! I am so very sorry," Bella gasped, backing away and then bobbing undecidedly up and down. Should she retrieve the book herself or did the gentleman still intend to do so?

Barrington straightened and brushed a strand of soft blond hair from his brow. "Do cease bobbing about like a spastic sparrow, Lady Annabella," he ordered quietly, taking Bella by the shoulders and gently setting her aside. Then, with a quick glance to see that she stayed where he had put her, he bent down and snatched up the volume. With a flourish he gave it into her hands. "As I was saying, you look most fetching this morning. There is a becoming sparkle in your eyes."

Bella was flabbergasted. For Lord Barrington to single her out and speak so kindly after he had spent last Season avoiding her and calling her names behind her back set her mind to reeling. The volume in Bella's hand vibrated with nervous energy.

Barrington, a bemused expression upon his handsome face, thought to replace the book for her and took a step forward.

Bella, surprised, took a step back.

At once seeing the danger, Lord Barrington leaped forward to keep Bella from banging against the free-standing shelves. But he tripped over the toe of Bella's delicately embroidered half-boot and instead of saving both Bella and the shelving, crashed with her against them. Together they tumbled to the floor amidst cries of alarm, a multitude of books, and lengths of oak.

Bella wanted to die. Just shrivel away to dust where she lay beneath Lord Barrington's long, hard body. Beneath Lord Barrington's long, hard body? Oh, my goodness! She could feel every inch of him! Her cheeks flamed with embarrassment.

"Barrington, get off that girl at once," a strong masculine voice ordered gruffly.

Lord Barrington sputtered and attempted to roll aside but the silver button of his waistcoat had become entangled in the fringe of Bella's shawl. He attempted to gain his knees. Books skittered everywhere. He could not free himself from her.

"Bella," ordered the voice, which sounded more and more familiar to her, "you are hooked together. You must rise with him, minx. Come, let me help you."

A strong pair of hands slipped beneath Bella's shoulders and in a moment she was standing, her nose quite touching the lapel of Lord Barrington's coat. The Duke of Derrinham, maintaining a stern visage though he was forced to gulp back a whoop of laughter to do so, discovered he had to slip the shawl over Bella's head in order to set Lord Barrington staggering free of her. Then he whisked Bella aside, reached into the top of his boot and produced a most evil-looking blade.

"What will it be, Barrington, your button or her fringe?" the duke growled fiercely, his eyes bubbling with hilarity.

Bella, thoroughly flustered, saw the blade as the duke moved toward Lord Barrington, caught the duke's threatening tone but did not hear his words, and reached entirely the wrong conclusion. She shrieked and flung herself between the two gentlemen.

The duke stared down at her in amazement and then burst into laughter. "No, infant. You are under a misapprehension. I am not about to gut the fellow, merely relieve him of a button."

Annabella could not believe the spectacle she had made of herself. Huddled inside the coach with all the shades drawn, she castigated herself for her clumsiness and her foolishness and her total lack of wit. Even Jane, who sat silently beside her, must be wishing her at the devil.

"Do not be upset," Jane managed at last, attempting mightily not to giggle and putting a comforting arm around Bella's shoulders. "It might have happened to anyone."

Bella's eyes opened wide. "Might have happened to anyone? To anyone? Oh, I think not, Jane."

"Well—p-perhaps not to just anyone," replied Jane, struggling for a serious pose, but failing utterly. "Oh, Bella, you are the most amazing person! If only you could have seen the look upon Uncle Hill's face when he peeked into the shop to see what all the uproar was about and recognized you upon the floor beneath Lord Barrington! I have never seen him so totally flummoxed!" Jane's sweet laughter would not be held in check longer and chimed through the coach. "Truly, he looked as though he had swallowed a frog!"

"He did?"

"Precisely! And then, when he began to comprehend what must have happened, I could see him fighting to keep from bursting into whoops. I have not seen him on the verge of all-out laughter in a very long time and I thank you for it. I know you are mortified, but you were only the victim of Lord Barrington's clumsiness and so everyone will say."

"But it was I who caused it all," murmured Annabella, gazing at the floor of the coach. "I was overwrought. I could not understand why Lord Barrington should do more than nod in my direction and instead he spoke to me."

"He did?"

"He said I looked splendid and fetching."

"He did?"

"Yes, and that my eyes sparkled."

"Oh, oh my," giggled Jane. "And you repaid him by tripping him and bringing shelves of books down upon his head! Oh, Bella!"

Annabella could not help herself. Try as she would to remain humiliated and distressed, Jane's laughter was irresistible, and in a moment Bella was laughing as well, the very awkwardness of all that had happened taking on a most amusing aspect.

Lord Barrington, sadly rumpled and missing one silver button from his waistcoat, fairly strutted up Bond Street despite his dishevelment. The condition of his wardrobe did not once enter his mind because keeping step beside him was The Diamond and the sheer glory of actually being in the company of his hero was making him positively giddy.

"Whoa, slow down a bit, Barrington," Derrinham grinned. "No matter how late we arrive, Jackson's Saloon will still be there, I assure you. You are one of Bella's villains, are you not?"

"A villain? Me, your grace?"

"Yes, you. I have made certain inquiries and my sources lay the imaginative appellation Hesitant Hedgehog, at your doorstep. How could you have been so villainous as to label Lady Annabella a hedgehog?"

"No, but, she is very like one, your grace. Last Season whenever anyone approached her she curled right up into a tiny ball and you could fairly see the little spikes sticking out warning one to keep one's distance."

"Did it not occur to you that she was terrified of you and that bestowing that name upon her did not help matters?"

"Terrified? Of me?"

"Among others."

"Well, no. I did never think that. I knew she was shy, but I did never think she might be terrified. I was unkind to her last Season, though, and I regret it. That is why I asked her to dance with me last evening and I intend to take her driving in the park as well. Lady Annabella is particularly important to you, is she not, Duke?"

"You have deduced that, have you?"

"Everyone who was present at Almack's last evening deduced that, your grace."

"Yes, well, Bella has been my neighbor for all of her life. She is like a sister to me. Ah, here we are. Whoever thought the day would come when John Jackson would own his own saloon and teach the Fancy to a throng of eager young bucks? I can remember a match between himself and Mendoza the Jew at Hurlingame—"

"At Hurlingame? You were at Hurlingame, Duke?"

"Just so. I was fifteen. And they were both in prime twig. Twenty-eight rounds they went before either showed the least sign of not coming up to scratch. Jackson won, of course. He won incessantly in those days. He was splendid."

"He is still splendid," sighed Barrington, thinking how magnificent it would have been to have witnessed Gentleman Jackson in the ring facing up to Mendoza the Jew. "You box, do you not, your grace?" he queried, swinging in through the door to Jackson's Saloon. "I am quite certain I have heard so."

"Yes," nodded Derrinham. "You would not care to spar a bit with me, would you?"

Barrington soared into ecstasy. *Yes,* he imagined himself drawling to a room filled with envious friends, *invited into the ring with The Diamond. Top of the line, the Diamond. Never a fighter like him.*

Derrinham stripped to perfection and moved upon the canvas with infinite grace and agility. Every buck in the establishment ceased his labors to stare in wonder at the man. John Jackson, however, was not best pleased to discover The Diamond in the ring when he returned from a quick trip to Cribb's.

"An' what about yer back then, Duke, eh?" Jackson mumbled as The Diamond returned to his own corner after the third round to discover The Gentleman frowning there.

The Diamond cocked a haughty eyebrow at the old fighter.

"Oh, I know all about it, yer grace. Came to me, did Lord May, when it happened, wantin' to know did I have any ideas on how to make ye more easy. An' written to me since, too, so I know ye've not got rid o' it. Ye haven't any business to be dancin' around in the ring."

"I am fine, Jackson."

"Humph."

"I have sparred with May from time to time since."

"Aye, but Lord May ain't about to make ye dodge too quickly nor duck too sharp, knowin' as he does that it might well send ye into agony. This young buck, why, he's not the least idea."

"No, and do not you tell him either, John. I am tired of always being handled with kid gloves."

"But ye cannot wish to be pummeled by a buck as strong and handy with his fives as Lord Barrington. Not with him ignorant about yer back."

"And what makes you think, Jackson, that I am about to be pummeled?" responded The Diamond, a glare in his sapphire eyes. "Think I am over the hill, do you?"

John Jackson grinned woefully, gave a hopeless shake of his head and stood back to view the remainder of the bout. His thought was to step in and call a halt to it the moment The Diamond showed the least sign of pain but, much like the rest of the spectators, he found himself caught up in the wonders of The Diamond's feints and dodges and the subtle dancing of his feet. By the time John Jackson recalled himself to his purpose in watching the match, Lord Barrington was flat on the canvas with his cork drawn and The Diamond was kneeling worriedly over him.

"Damnation, but I never meant to do that," Derrinham muttered. "Barrington, can you hear me?"

"Uh-huh," replied his lordship groggily, boosting himself up on his elbows, "cer'ainly will."

Derrinham lifted an eyebrow.

"A bit woozy," Jackson murmured. "Ye leave him to me and get yerself cleaned up, eh?"

"His nose ain't broken, is it, John?"

"Aye, but I'll look to it. Get ye off, now, before ye catch yer death from all that sweat."

Derrinham nodded and climbed from the ring. He had not intended to land the viscount quite so violent a facer. But of a sudden, the memory of Bella's tears as she had sat beside him on the wall at Twiney Hill had flooded his mind. And the certainty that Barrington had been one of those responsible for those tears had abruptly released The Diamond's punishing right full force.

I ought not to have done it, the Diamond thought, drying himself with one of the boxing saloon's towels. The entire object of this exercise was to gain Barrington's friendship so that I could steer him toward Bella. And instead, I draw the man's cork! Devil it, what's wrong with me?

The duke stuffed his arms into his shirt with an excessive amount of vehemence at the thought, became entangled in one of the sleeves and jerked at it impatiently. "Oh, damn and blast!" he hissed as a massive blaze of pain shot through his back. He took a deep breath and clutched at the pillar behind him. "Devil, damn and blast," he sputtered on ragged breaths, willing the pain to cease and praying no one was taking notice of him, especially John Jackson who would not be at all loath to say I told you so.

The Diamond flung himself angrily down upon his bed, not even allowing Shaughnessy to remove his boots before he did so. "Just go, Shaughnessy, and let me die," he mumbled. "You are the wretchedest excuse for a valet any gentleman has ever been forced to swallow and the sight of you grieves me no end!"

"Indeed, your grace," nodded Shaughnessy, his fine green eyes filled with sympathy. "It is your back then. Perhaps a soak in a hot tub will help."

"The only thing that will help me, Shaughnessy, is a pistol ball to the brainbox."

Timothy Shaughnessy shook his head in consternation. His graying locks fell forward across his wide brow. "If the pain is so great as that, your grace, you must take some laudanum drops."

Diamond managed a painful grin. "It is not all that bad. I am merely being my customary cantankerous self."

"Right," nodded Shaughnessy with the cock of an eyebrow.

"No, but I was never one of your jolly good fellows, Tim. You know that I have been a duke since the age of five and I have never taken to it. It makes me brutally unsocial at times. To tell the truth, I would much rather have been a—"

"A what, your grace?"

"A prizefighter. Lord, how I hate this house," the duke spat out, abruptly sitting up. At the sudden movement, his eyes glazed and he went stark white beneath his tan. Shaughnessy rushed to the bellpull, gave it a mighty tug, then rushed back to the bed and urged Derrinham to lie back down.

"Thunderation, where is everybody? Does not that bellpull work? Samuel," he shouted loudly as he crossed to the doorway. "Samuel, we need you!"

"Boxing," Sonnett muttered, holding a glass of water into which several drops of laudanum had been mixed. "Of all the birdwitted, Bedlamite things to do! And with a buck half your age!"

"Barrington is not h-half my age! He is twenty-one if he's a day and that is merely five years my junior."

"Never mind. Drink this and lie still. I will not have you causing yourself more pain. It is the outside of enough that you strolled into that place, and that is all I will say about it."

The Duke of Derrinham took the smallest sip of the laudanum and then shoved the glass aside. "It is the outside of enough that I cannot be comfortable in my own house. That is what is the outside of enough. I expect I shall awake upon that blasted staircase again, shall I not?"

"No, you shall not," replied Sonnett with a speaking look at Shaughnessy. "You shall drink the rest of this and the pain will disappear and you will not stray so much as the breadth of a cat's whisker from your bed."

Derrinham's face registered disbelief but he took the glass from Sonnett and downed the remainder of the vile stuff.

"Now close your eyes, do," murmured Sonnett, removing the pillows one by one from behind Derrinham's shoulders. "Rest. It will not be long before you will be feeling your old self again."

Derrinham muttered something incomprehensible and closed his eyes as Shaughnessy tugged the draperies across the windows to block out the sun.

"We ought to have kept him in the country," whispered Shaughnessy as the duke surrendered to the drug and began to snore softly. "This house is a vile cancer seeping into his very bones. If he persists in coming here much longer, he will remember everything and what will we do for him then?"

Three

Bella swept down the staircase in a gown of *jonquille* muslin with a high waist and square neckline, puffed sleeves, and an overdress of sparkling white lace slit in a widening V down the front to display to perfection the lovely color beneath. Her soft brown curls circled a face flushed with excitement and Lady Meade rejoiced at the true happiness sparkling in her daughter's eyes.

"You look lovely, Bella, and you are smiling for once. I cannot tell you how pleased I am to see you beginning to appreciate the Season at last. It quite makes a mother's heart leap with joy when her daughter discovers delight in the very things she herself was wont to enjoy."

"I am quite looking forward to this evening, Mama," Bella admitted with a grin that coaxed forward the shy dimple in her cheek. "Jane has promised to attend the musicale as well. We are to sit together. And the duke escorts her. I shall not feel at all dowdy or out of place with them beside me. I do never feel odd or frightened, I find, in their company."

Lady Meade frowned uncertainly, not wishing to dampen her daughter's good spirits but quite positive that Bella had made some mistake. "The Duke of Derrinham? To attend a musical evening? Are you certain, Bella?"

"Indeed. Jane has assured me of it. Why, Mama? Does not the duke generally attend musical evenings?"

"He never has before," murmured Lady Meade thoughtfully. "Not, at least, to my knowledge. Though he does like music, does he not? He plays the flute himself if I recall correctly."

"Yes, Mama," grinned Bella, remembering all the afternoons that Diamond had slipped his flute from his pocket as they paused in their adventures about the woods or the fields or the groves and sat down to play for her alone. "He plays the flute and very nicely, too. He most likely looks forward to attending Lady Swithinby's musical evening. Most certainly he will attend."

And if the Duke of Derrinham had remembered the musical evening before he had allowed Sonnett to dose him with laudanum, he most certainly would at that moment have been assisting his niece into the Town coach and be on his way to the Swithinbys'. As he had not remembered, however, Jane, in a becoming gown of white sarsenet with silver spangles and three gorgeous flounces, left the house with Miss Davies as her chaperone in his stead.

His niece and her companion had been gone a full five minutes before The Diamond opened one bleary eye and groaned. They had been gone ten minutes by the time Shaughnessy made clear to him that Jane could not come to spend a few moments with him because she had gone to the Swithinbys'. And they had been gone a full twenty minutes before the Duke of Derrinham had dragged himself from his bed and cursed passionately enough to convince Shaughnessy to help him don his evening dress.

"I do not think this is at all a good idea, your grace," Shaughnessy ventured, assisting him into his coat.

"I do not give one damn, Shaughnessy, what you th-think," mumbled Derrinham.

"Begging your pardon, but you are not yourself, your grace."

"I ain't? Who am I then?"

"What I mean to say—well, look at your neckcloth."

Derrinham stared into the looking glass, his pupils large with the residue of the drug, and blinked languidly at himself. "What's wrong with't?"

"It is tied in a knot, your grace."

"Eh?"

"Knot," said Shaughnessy loudly and slowly.

"I am not deaf, Shaughnessy. Not what?"

Shaughnessy sighed. "Your neckcloth is tied in a plain knot and not in any recognizable style."

"Is it? Well, I find I do not care, Shaughnessy. I shall go whether the knot's reco'niz'ble or whether the knot's not."

"I truly do not think that you ought to set foot out of this house tonight, your grace."

"I truly d'not care what you think, Shaughnessy."

"Now, that is the laudanum speaking," Shaughnessy commented, straightening the lace at The Diamond's cuffs. "I shall choose to ignore it. If you must go, allow me to get you a new neckcloth. I will do the tying of it for you myself."

"No, 'sfine. Late a'ready. Promised Bella I'd be there."

"You did?"

"Uh-huh, no, Jane, promised Jane."

The luster in Bella's eyes dimmed when Jane appeared at the Swithinbys' with Miss Davies and not The Diamond at her side and her stomach began to ache and all the energy and enthusiasm she had carried with her departed on the instant. Her lovely new gown notwithstanding, she became abruptly aware that she was the same plain wallflower who had attended similar entertainments all last Season and she was certain that not one gentleman among all those who attended would find her the least bit interesting.

Settled upon a charming gilded chair in the midst of other gilded chairs and surrounded by her mama and Jane and Miss Davies, Bella sought to make herself invisible and gave thanks that the entertainment would soon begin and that she would not be expected, tonight, to hold any lengthy conversations or consort in any way with the likes of Lord Barrington and his friends.

"You look lovely, Bella," Jane whispered in her ear. "Just see all the gentlemen glancing in your direction."

"Do not tease, Jane," Bella whispered back. "I know upon whom those glances are bestowed and it is not myself. If you were not beside me, not one head would be turned in this direction."

"Oh, that is not true at all," replied Jane with a tiny pout. "You are stunning in that gown and I only wish Uncle Hill might be here to see you."

"Why did he not come? Is it because Miss Davies is recovered? Will he not escort you at all anymore?"

"Lydie is feeling a deal better, but she is certainly not up to rushing about every evening," fibbed Miss May in a rush. "Most certainly Uncle Hill will still be called upon to provide me escort. But he is indisposed this evening. His back, you know."

"His back?" Bella's finely etched eyebrows moved toward each other in a puzzled frown.

"You do not know about Uncle Hill's back? It happened the night my mama died. Mama and Papa and Uncle Hill all attended the masque at Danfurth House the night it burned to the ground. Uncle Hill escaped uninjured but went back inside to attempt to rescue those who had become trapped. He did locate Papa and carried him out, but when he went back in again a great beam fell upon him, breaking his shoulder and knocking him backward down the staircase. The fall injured his back. He might have died as well that night if someone had not seen him come tumbling down and rushed in to drag him out into the street."

The color drained slowly from Bella's face. She had known that The Diamond had had an elder sister—Lady Diana, who had left Twiney Hill to marry Lord May two full years before Bella, herself, had been born. She had even attended Lady May's funeral with her parents—but she had heard nothing of a fire. She had assumed that Lady Diana had died from an illness.

"Sometimes Uncle Hill's back is so painful that he can do nothing but take laudanum drops and go straight to bed. Which is exactly what he did this afternoon. He was not yet awake when Lydie and I left the house," concluded Jane softly.

"Oh, poor Diamond," murmured Bella. "I had no idea."

The young ladies were called to order directly as Lady Swithinby strolled to the front of the room beside the pianoforte and announced that the musical evening would commence with the rendition of several compositions written by Mr. James Hook and played upon the pianoforte, the violin, the flute and the cello by the Misses Binghampton and Master Geoffery Binghampton.

The Misses Binghampton were three sturdily constructed young ladies of fourteen, sixteen and eighteen and Master Binghampton, who played the cello, was a tiny young gentleman of seven years whose prowess with the instrument had aroused a great deal of interest among the *ton*. Greeted by polite applause, the quartet of Binghamptons launched themselves into music—the remarkable little Geoffery smiling widely as he bowed his cello, proud to appear among the adults in a most adult ensemble of bottle green coat, buff inexpressibles and a neckcloth tied *en cascade*.

"Zounds, a gnome!" exclaimed a voice at the rear of the chamber just as the Binghamptons began the second composition.

Any number of heads turned to see who had spoken. Bella's head was one of them and she gave the tiniest gasp. "Jane, your uncle," she whispered, her eyes regaining their luster at the mere sight of Derrinham.

"Where the devil did it come from, Swithinby?" the duke continued, the timbre of his voice carrying over the music. "What sort of bait did you use to capture the thing?"

Lord Swithinby, chuckling, acknowledged the pleading glance his wife aimed at him from her chair near the front of the room and whispered quietly into the duke's ear. He received a surprised glance from the wide sapphire eyes in return. "It ain't a gnome? But of course it is, Swithinby. Just take a look at it."

"No, your grace, it is not. Take my word for it," laughed Lord Swithinby. "Come with me, eh, and we will have us a coze in m'study. Sample my cognac."

"Cannot. Obliged to remain, Swithinby. Deuced energetic with that saw, ain't he? Why have you set a gnome to sawing wood in your drawing room? Deuced fat log for such a little fellow."

Lord Swithinby grinned and explained again that Master Geoffery Binghampton was not a gnome. "And we are not in my drawing room, Derrinham. This is the music room. You are at m'wife's musicale, Duke, and the little Binghampton lad is playing upon a cello."

"It's a Binghampton and not a gnome? What's a Binghampton? No, you are hoaxing me, Swithinby. I know a gnome when I see one. And you can hardly hope to keep him a secret, man, if you persist in setting him out in the middle of the room to saw a cello into firewood. Only look at all of the people staring at him already.

They have even brought up chairs to watch the thing, Swithinby."

Despite Lord Swithinby's attempt to keep their conversation low, both gentlemen were possessed of voices which carried exceptionally well—a virtue in the House of Lords but a definite detriment in the midst of Lady Swithinby's musicale. The guests, to give them credit, kept their backs straight and their chins upright. And after the duke's first exclamation, they had returned their gazes to the young performers, though several of the gentlemen stifled guffaws by seeming to choke and a number of the ladies swiped surreptitiously at tears of mirth as the conversation continued.

"Oh, dear," giggled Jane softly. "Uncle Hill is still quite befuddled by his medicine."

Miss Davies nodded slightly, her fine gray eyes alight with laughter and her smiling lips covered by her fan.

"I'd step on the thing if I were you. Squash it. Put a merciful end to that awful moaning it makes. Poor gnome sounds near death as it is."

The Misses Binghampton, polite young ladies that they were, had carried on through the disturbance with notable aplomb. But Master Geoffery, who was closest to the duke and understood near every word he muttered, was very close to tears at being labeled a gnome and having his music called sawing. When the words 'squash' and 'death' reached his seven-year-old ears, he could control himself no longer and dropping bow and cello, he rushed sobbing into his mama's arms.

"He's gonna squash me, Mama," Master Geoffery squeaked in a loud, frightened voice. "That gen'leman's gonna kill me dead!"

The Misses Binghampton, ceasing to play at their brother's hasty defection, fluttered about and tittered with embarrassment.

"Oh, great goodness," sighed Bella, attempting to hide

her laughter behind a frown. "He is disrupting Lady Swithinby's entire evening." And with that, she stood and made her way to the back of the chamber, took The Diamond's arm and escorted him out into the corridor. "For shame, your grace," she scolded. "You have destroyed Lady Swithinby's entertainment and frightened the wits out of that poor child."

"No. Have I, Bella?" asked Derrinham, staring fuzzily down at her through dilated pupils. "What child?"

"The one you referred to as a gnome."

"No, but I didn't. I referred to a gnome as a gnome. I ain't ignorant, Bella."

"Perhaps not, but you are very, very foxed."

"I have not had a drop all d-day."

"It is the laudanum," offered Jane as she and Miss Davies and Lady Meade all stepped out into the hallway. "You ought not to have come, Uncle Hill. You are not well."

"Balderdash! Fit as a fiddle!"

"You must apologize to Master Binghampton," Bella said, her eyes alight with amusement at the bewildered look on the duke's face. "And you ought to apologize to his sisters as well, for you put a quick end to their performance."

"Oh," muttered Derrinham, not quite convinced that he had done any such thing. "All right, if you think I ought, Bella, lead me to the little b-blighter and I will have a go at it."

Jane, her blue eyes sparkling, took Miss Davies and Lady Meade each by an arm and urged them into step behind Bella and the duke. "We do not want to miss Uncle Hill's apology," she declared on a giggle. "I think we will regret it if we do."

Bella, her hand planted firmly upon The Diamond's arm, reentered the Swithinby music room, which was alive with discussion, and urged the duke toward the front of the chamber and the child sobbing in Mrs. Binghampton's arms.

"Do not cry anymore, Master Geoffery," she said, stooping down to the boy's level. "His grace will not hurt you."

Master Geoffery peeked up from his mama's arms, saw Derrinham standing beside Bella and let out an earpiercing shriek. He pried himself from his mama's grasp and dashed toward the door. Derrinham, stunned, stared at the tiny figure darting around chairs and between people and stated in his most penetrating and exasperated tone, "B'gawd, but it is a gnome, Bella. An' just see how it tries t'escape. Looking for a toadstool to hide beneath, no doubt."

Lady Swithinby, who up until that very moment had held out some hope for a return to proper decorum, burst into most unladylike chortles of laughter and buried herself in her husband's embrace. Swithinby whispered in her ear and made her laugh even more. Lord Barrington, who stood grinning madly in the midst of several other young gentlemen, reached down as Master Geoffery squiggled past, seized him by the coattails and hoisted him up into his arms. "Do not be frightened, rascal," he grinned. "His grace will not hurt you. He has already had his bit of blood and bone for today. Mine. Just take a gander at my poor nose."

"He did that, sir?" asked Geoffery, his cheeks streaked with tears, his eyes wide and his voice still filled with sobs.

"Indeed."

"Did he think you were a gnome, too?"

"No, sir. Did it in Jackson's Boxing Saloon. The duke is a reg'lar Nonesuch, y'know, and he cannot be beaten when it comes to the Fancy."

"Him, sir? An old gentleman like that?" Master Geoffery asked, setting all the bucks off into unbridled mirth again.

"He is not an old gentleman," declared Bella, drawing up beside Lord Barrington and the boy with her arm snugly through Derrinham's. "He is a gentleman in the very prime of his life."

"He is?" asked Master Geoffery in disbelief.

Derrinham peered down at the child. "Just give 'im over to me, Barrington, and I willn't draw your cork again," he grumbled, with a suspicious twitching at the corner of his lips. "Take him off and pop him into the oven, I will; have m'self baked gnome for a midnight snack."

Bella, watching Geoffery's eyes widen, gave Derrinham's arm a furious shake. "Do not tease," she ordered. "Apologize to Master Binghampton at once or I shall pop *you* into an oven!"

Barrington shifted his gaze from Derrinham to Bella at her words and met a pair of laughing but determined liquid brown eyes that were like to set any man's peace and serenity afire.

How exquisite she is, he thought. Why have I never seen her like this before? Her chin is high; her cheeks are flushed; that is an adorable dimple flashing in her cheek. Glory, but she is even more fetching than I thought her this morning at Hatchard's.

Derrinham, not misreading the dawning awareness in Barrington's eyes despite the laudanum, transferred Bella's grip from his own arm to that gentleman's, set Master Binghampton upon the floor, and taking his hand, strolled off with the boy.

"You ain't goin' to squash me?" asked Geoffery softly, eyeing the duke with some trepidation.

"I reckon not, gnome. Bella does not appear to think it a good idea. I admire your coat. Dressed to the nines, ain't you?"

"Yes, sir," replied Geoffery. "I could fix your neck-cloth for you if you'd like."

"No, I think not. Do not want any gnome prints on it."

Geoffery giggled. "You are in your altitudes, ain't you, sir?"

"Chirping merry, I expect," nodded the duke thoughtfully. "Too much medicine and not enough food." He came to a halt before the boy's mama and leered at Geoffery. "Some gnome pie would straighten me right up," he muttered.

Mrs. Binghampton flashed him an exasperated look and he grinned charmingly at her.

"It is all right now, Mama," declared Master Geoffery bravely. "The gentleman is only teasing. He is thoroughly disguised."

"But he does apologize for causing such a fuss, do you not, Uncle Hill?" inserted Jane, coming up beside him. "He has taken a deal of medicine, you see, Mrs. Binghampton, and should not be out of the house at all, but he wished to hear Master Geoffery and the girls play and came regardless."

"A vile mistake," mumbled Derrinham, an eyebrow cocking expressively at Jane's out-and-out clanker.

"And I am quite certain," inserted Miss Davies, "that were the young people to begin again, we should all be most pleased to hear them, would we not, your grace?"

It took a good five minutes before all of Lady Swithinby's guests had settled themselves for the continuation of the musical evening. Derrinham was ushered to a chair between Jane and Bella, both of whom swore to keep him under strict supervision.

Lord Barrington abandoned his friends at the back of the chamber and found a chair to the right of Bella's mama. Throughout the performance his gaze constantly strayed to wisps of brown curls and the dimple that peeked out each time the duke grumbled beneath his breath. By the time the Binghamptons had completed their performance, Lady Meade was in transports of delight over the viscount's attentive glances at her daughter and she was drawn to whisper hopeful phrases in Miss Davies's ear.

Following the Binghamptons, Lady Anne Traine, the daughter of the Earl of Barthby, sang a most melancholy ballad in a rich alto voice. The Duke of Derrinham took Bella's hand in his and placed it upon his knee.

Bella knew she ought not let him do so the very instant he did. But she did not give a fig. No, she did not, not even if Lord Barrington was glaring at them. The Diamond was her duke, after all. She had known him from the very day of her birth and had been chased and bullied and teased by him for as long as she could remember. And if it gave him patience or fortitude or ease to hold her hand upon his knee, then it was her duty to allow him to do so, regardless of what others might think.

Derrinham, restless, gave her hand a squeeze. And though he kept his gaze fastened upon Lady Anne Traine, Bella could tell from the way in which he played with her fingers encased in their white silk gloves that he was not paying a bit of attention to the song.

"Are you feeling poorly, Diamond?" Her curls brushed softly against his ear as she whispered. "Do you wish to leave?"

"Only this immediate vicinity," he replied in a voice more hushed than he had managed earlier. "Is there a supper involved in this enormously distracting evening?"

"It is to commence as soon as Miss Covington performs her solo upon the harpsichord."

"Drat, we must sit through the odious twanging of a harpsichord yet?" He gazed down at her, a smile twitching at the corners of his lips, and Bella knew very well that he was being crabby merely for his own entertainment.

"May I escort you in to supper, Bella?" The words were out of The Diamond's mouth before he thought and he could not call them back. Damnation, it was the laudanum again! He had clearly seen signs of appreciation and envy on Viscount Barrington's face and here he sat inviting Bella to remain at his own side throughout supper. Derrinham cursed himself silently.

"I should be proud to accompany you to supper," Bella whispered. "Now shush—Miss Covington is about to begin."

In the end, the duke redeemed himself in his own eyes by escorting both Lady Meade and Bella to supper and giving Jane and Miss Davies into Barrington's care. That way, the viscount would come to share the table with them. And Derringham was most careful to take the seat across from Bella and leave the one next to her for Barrington. Which would have proved an excellent maneuver if only the laudanum had not made Derrinham feel atrociously above par and incredibly impish.

As it was, he could not forgo gazing mirthfully across the table into Bella's eyes and discoursing upon the immensely sad tale being told to him by his lobster patty who, it seemed, had been coerced by the Swithinbys' cook into a press. "Promised he would be a lobster stew," Derrinham intoned sadly, one ear toward his plate. "But that wily cook tricked him. And as for the vanilla cremes," he added, lifting one of the sweets up before Bella's eyes. "They were promised that they would be caramel."

This set Bella to giggling and she blushed so prettily that Derrinham had half a mind to take her out onto the tiny balcony beyond the French doors and keep her there all to himself. Devil it, he had more than half a mind to do it.

He gazed into her laughing brown eyes, winked audaciously and reached across the width of the table to pop the vanilla creme between her lips. "Put the poor thing out of its misery, Bella, do," he muttered. "I cannot bear to hear another complaint out of it." And once she had chewed and swallowed the offending creme, he rose, begged a moment with her, and swept her from beneath Lord Barrington's nose out onto the balcony.

Lady Meade rose to go after them, but Miss Davies's hand touched her arm. "She will come to no harm in his grace's company, Lady Meade," murmured Lydia Davies softly. "And the air will help to clear the duke's head. No one will think your Bella compromised to spend a moment alone in the company of an old friend and neighbor, most especially when we may see them perfectly well from where we sit."

"No, of course not," agreed Lady Meade, a perplexed frown upon her brow. "He is not dangerous, do you think?"

"No, not at all," Miss Davies smiled encouragingly. "He is only a bit nonsensical because of his medicine."

"I think he has gone completely 'round the bend," grumbled Barrington, "and if they are not back in two shakes of a lamb's tail, I shall be most pleased to go out and retrieve Lady Annabella for you, Lady Meade."

The perplexed frown upon Lady Meade's face softened into a smile at Lord Barrington's words.

Four

Derrinham House rasped and whimpered and grumbled through the quiet of the night. The last of the coal fires, on the grate in the duke's bedchamber, popped and sputtered and hissed its way into ashes as the Duke of Derrinham, under the influence of another dose of laudanum drops, slept soundly. Like the dead, thought the man staring down at him. He sleeps like the dead.

Long, slim fingers caressed the handle of a ten-penny blade. One quick thrust directly through that unsuspecting heart and the deed would be done. The promise would be kept. The past avenged.

The man groaned quietly. For an entire year and more he had been able to go forward with his life, to forget that the Duke of Derrinham existed. Whenever he had strolled down Great Stanhope Street to see Derrinham House closed and shuttered, the knocker gone from the door, he had imagined the residence moldering and rotting inside, being devoured by its own evil until at last it would collapse inward upon itself and be no more. But the house had not moldered and rotted. And the Duke of Derrinham had returned. And, once again, his promise loomed over him in all its ghastly glory.

He raised the blade, stepped forward and bent over the sleeping form. And then he straightened and stepped back. Had he heard a footstep in the adjoining chamber? He held his breath and listened intently. Yes, a footstep and another. The carpet-muffled sound grew louder, closer. He ought to have known that Shaughnessy would choose to sleep upon a trundle bed in the dressing room when the duke was ill. He cursed himself for not having thought of that and nimbly hid the weapon amongst the folds of his robe. He turned and strode toward the door he had left ajar and hurried into the hall.

It is fate, he thought as he made his way toward the servants' staircase. Fate. But there are more days and more nights to come. And on one of them, fate will smile upon me. On one of them all will fall out perfectly and the Duke of Derrinham will pay for the sins of his father. He will pay most dearly.

Bella came down to breakfast to a most pleasant surprise. "Oh, Mama," she cried delightedly, "what lovely flowers!"

Lady Meade, her eyes sparkling with triumph, nodded. "For you. You must read the cards that accompany them, Bella. This," she said, passing the cards into Bella's hand, "came with the roses and this one with the wildflowers."

"The roses are from Lord Barrington? From Lord Barrington, Mama? Whatever has gotten into that gentleman? He calls me his *dearest* Lady Annabella and he thanks me for a most memorable evening. The wildflowers are from his grace! How beautiful they are. Why there are jonquils and daffodils and tug-at-hearts—"

Lady Meade laughed. "Yes, dearest, I am not blind. They are most beautiful. And what does his grace say?"

"He begs my pardon for his odd behavior last evening and hopes that I will consent to drive with him this afternoon in Hyde Park. Oh, Mama, may I? I shall wear my new bonnet!"

"Of course you may, Bella, but do you wish to do so? It would not surprise me if Lord Barrington pays you a morning call and entreats you to accompany him to the Promenade."

Bella's glance strayed from the duke's wildflowers to Lord Barrington's roses. Why would Lord Barrington send her roses when he had despised her so last Season? And what on earth would she do, perched beside that gentleman in his phaeton in the midst of the Promenade? What would they say to each other? Would she even find the courage to converse at all? And why would he think to ask her to drive with him in the first place? No, most certainly Mama was mistaken about that. Lord Barrington would not be caught dead driving her about in public.

"No, Mama," Bella said, "I shall not depend upon Lord Barrington. May I send a note accepting his grace's invitation?"

Lady Meade nodded, excused herself and strolled off to seek a word with her husband in his study.

"Just on my way out, Mary. Auction at Tattersall's. Some good coach horses to be had. And I thought, perhaps, a little mare for Bella."

"Yes, Peter, whatever you decide. I have not come to discuss horseflesh. I need your advice, my dear, about our daughter."

"About Bella? I think not, Mary. Don't know anything about gels. Leave that to you, don't you know?"

"But you do know a good deal about the Duke of Derrinham."

"The Diamond?"

"Yes. You did not request him to come to Town and to court our Bella, did you, Peter? It is not as a favor to you that he appears at her side wherever she goes?"

The Earl of Meade's eyes grew wide and he sat back down in the leather chair he had recently vacated. "The Diamond is paying Bella court?"

"Well, he did waltz with her at Almack's and apparently he manages to stumble upon her wherever she goes, and last evening at the Swithinbys' he took her out upon the balcony and held her in conversation for a full five minutes. He claims he has come to Town to watch over his niece, but anyone can see that it is our Bella his eyes are constantly upon. And now Lord Barrington has begun to display an interest in Bella and will quite likely stop by to ask her to drive with him this afternoon, but Bella chooses instead to drive with his grace."

"Viscount Barrington?" the earl asked, his eyes sparkling. "Well, well. Might I assume that there are others who will rise to the bait as well, Mary?"

"Rise to the bait?" Lady Meade murmured. "What do you mean, Peter, rise to the bait?"

"Well, it is obvious, m'dear. Did not Derrinham escort our gel home the day before we departed Meadowlark? Told him, our Bella did, that she dreaded a second Season. Like a brother to Bella, Derrinham. Never a thing he would not do for her."

"Yes, he has always been kind to her, but I do not—"

"Come, Mary, think. Before he went into mourning, whenever he came to London a throng of bucks followed wherever he led."

"Yes, of course, Peter, because he is a Corinthian and a Nonpareil, but what has that to do with—"

"Well, who is to say that they will not follow him this year as well, Mary? Set himself the task of drawing other gentlemen's attentions to our Bella, The Diamond has. Let him drive her through Hyde Park and the clubs will be abuzz with it. You must expect any number of morning callers tomorrow, Mary, I assure you. Bless Derrinham! Always knew he loved our Bella like a little sister. Now he is proving it beyond a doubt."

Hyde Park at the height of the Promenade seethed with color. Forming a vibrant Chinese dragon, barouches, stanhopes, curricles and phaetons curled along the row. The ladies in their pale and bright, beautiful and daunting carriage dresses spun their silk and muslin and lawn parasols in the brilliant sunlight and bestowed their equally brilliant smiles upon friends and acquaintances. The gentlemen in formfitting inexpressibles of dove and buff and pearl tucked neatly into gleaming top boots and Bluchers and Hessians with spurs jingling and gleaming, with embroidered waistcoats peeking temptingly out beneath coats of blue and green and claret, with top hats and curly-brimmed beavers cocked rakishly upon their curls, grinned and nodded and waved to one another while they drove their lustrous, prancing chestnuts and grays and blacks and bays with reins threaded through strong, competent fingers. To those unaccustomed to such splendor, the Promenade was an awesome and intimidating spectacle. At least, Bella had thought it intimidating last Season. But this afternoon at the Duke of Derrinham's side she relished the shifting colors and the pulsating grandeur and her eyes glowed with happiness.

"Care for this sort of nonsense, do you?" muttered the duke, his own curly-brimmed beaver pushed back on his head to expose a seductive expanse of honey-blond curls. "Nonsensical, I think."

"Oh, do you? Then why did you invite me?" Bella replied, turning from the sights around her to meet his sapphire gaze. The bright red cherries bobbed and glistened on the upturned brim of her new bonnet and Bella noticed at once how The Diamond's attention flew to them. It is because they are so very gay, she thought. And she felt a warmth rise to her cheeks as the duke raised one gloved hand and flicked a finger at the fruit.

"Truly, Bella," he murmured, "that is the most outrageous bonnet I have ever seen."

"You do not like it, your grace?"

"I—well—those cherries," he said, his eyes once again

catching hers. "I vow, Bella, those cherries are dangerous."

"Dangerous?" Bella stared at him, perplexed.

"Indeed. I cannot keep from glancing at them. They will distract me at a most inopportune moment and we will run slap into another vehicle." His eyes laughed at her and she grinned back, her shy dimple peeking out enticingly at him.

"Are you having a good time, Bella?" he asked softly.

"Oh, yes, a very good time. It is all so wonderful."

"Did you not join the Promenade last Season?"

Bella's fingers tightened upon the handle of her parasol and she gazed away from him in embarrassment. "Well I—only once, actually. With Mama and Papa. In the barouche."

"I see."

"No, you do not see," sighed Bella, shunting aside her embarrassment and lifting her chin to face the duke squarely. "I was not at all popular, Diamond. No one wished to escort me anywhere. Even the young ladies did not wish to be seen with me. It was because—because—"

"Because you were awed by everyone and everything and forgot that you are Lady Annabella Faire and not some silly little chit without an ounce of gumption."

"Well, yes, there was that. But there was also Miss Violet Harcourt. She was a diamond of the first water and caught Lord Weredon in the end. But she did not like me, not at all, and declared that no one who wished to be in her company—"

"Weredon's bride?" Derrinham interrupted. "That spoilt brat? She is a harridan, Bella, and a half-wit to boot. I met her in Surrey only six months ago. Why, she ain't got the sense of a plucked pigeon!"

"But she is very beautiful. Last Season she ruled the *ton*."

"Bosh! She would have ruled no one had you stuck your chin out as you are accustomed to do and put the encroaching little baggage in her place!"

"But I could not! She was a Toast and I nothing but—"

"If you call yourself short and plump and plain as buttered beans again, I shall pull this curricle to the side of the path, take you over my knee and beat the tar out of you!" exclaimed the duke in exasperation.

Bella's jaw dropped. How could he—why would he—why had he—remembered word for word what she had sobbed out to him all those weeks ago? Her eyes widened and she looked up to see him glaring angrily down at her.

"You will not say so again, do you understand, Bella?"

Bella nodded slowly, the cherries on her hat bobbing. It was the oddest thing how that militant light in his eyes and that stubborn jut of his jaw, which Bella knew as well as she knew her own face, suddenly set her heart to beating rapidly. A distinct warmth suffused her entire body. She gave a tiny gasp.

"Bella, what is it?" Derrinham, his angry glare changing rapidly into a worried frown, urged his horses to the side of the path and brought the pair of shining blacks to a standstill. "Bella, answer me! Toby, take the horses!" he called to the little tiger who had already leaped from his seat at the rear of the curricle and was dashing toward the horses' heads.

Derrinham jumped to the ground, hurried to the other side of the vehicle and, reaching up, lifted Bella down into his arms. His back twitched, but he paid it no mind. Her parasol tumbled to the ground, but he ignored it. She gasped once again and a flush rose high on her cheeks.

"Diamond what—what—?"

"Hush, infant. You are overcome by the heat is all. It is exceeding warm this afternoon and the sun much too bright."

"Diamond, put me down. Your back! I am not in the least ill. I promise I am not."

"No, of course you are not," agreed Derrinham softly, carrying her to a shady bench beneath one of the oaks and setting her safely upon it. "You are merely over-heated. No, go away, Tottingham," he added as a gentle-man appeared beside him. "All she requires is shade and a cool breeze. And take the others with you. I can care quite competently for Lady Annabella on my own."

Bella's cheeks flamed as she realized that several gen-tlemen, including Mr. Tottingham, had reined in their mounts and gathered 'round to see if they might be of some assistance. She stifled an embarrassed groan, but then giggled as the duke sighed and mumbled that all he required to set his mind at ease about her was the inter-ference of an entire brood of coxcombs.

"So, you are feeling better already," he murmured, tak-ing a seat beside her and putting his arm protectively about her shoulders.

"How do you know?"

"Because, in my vast experience, young ladies seldom giggle upon their deathbeds."

"Should—should you have your arm about my shoul-ders, Diamond?" Bella asked quietly. "Everyone is look-ing."

"Then they will get an eyeful, will they not? What? Do you think they will say you are compromised? Do not be gooseish, Bella. You came near to fainting. Of course I must lend you my support for a few moments." He grinned and Bella thought how very handsome he looked. "Besides, I am the very nearest thing you have to a brother and I am much too old for you besides."

"But you are not my brother," Bella protested, rapidly doing sums. "And you are only—only twenty-six. That is not too old."

"Oh, well, then—" the duke chuckled, removing his

arm from about her shoulders and clasping his hands tightly in his lap like some frightened little clerk.

"Do behave," laughed Bella. "You are making a perfect spectacle of yourself."

"Perhaps," agreed Derrinham, carrying on with his interpretation of a shy suitor by a nervous twitch of his nose, a suppressed cough and a fleeting glance in her direction, "but I do not wish to appear in any way improper, my lady. I shall not think to touch you again."

"Oh," sighed Bella softly, lifting one hand to her forehead.

"What? Are you feeling worse, Bella?" The Diamond's arm was instantly about her and he was attempting to untie the ribands of her bonnet with one gloved hand.

"Ho," grinned Bella impishly. "So much for the Duke of Proper."

"Little minx," muttered the duke, but he did not release her and his fingers fiddled with the ribands until they were undone. "There, take your bonnet off and let the breeze cool your brow."

"You just want the cherries out of your sight. Admit it."

"No such thing. Do you know, my sister Diana had a hat with cherries on it once. You never met Diana, did you? No, of course you did not. She was already married and had given birth to Jane by the time you were born and—and dead—by the time you were out of the schoolroom."

"Was she very beautiful, Diamond, your sister?"

"Exquisite. When I was a lad I thought her the most beautiful lady in all the world. Jane is very like her."

"I—I—Jane told me about the fire. I did not know. I am so very sorry, Diamond, that you lost your sister in such a dreadful manner. It cannot be easy for you to return to London even after a year and more. B-because of the memories, I mean. Why, every day you may look out your window and see where Danfurth House once stood."

"The memories, yes," nodded the duke slowly. "But that is neither here nor there, Bella. I have returned to London and I intend to enjoy myself immensely, no matter what."

"You do?"

"Indeed. And I intend to see that you—that Jane and you—enjoy yourselves as well. I should not say so, but Miss Davies's illness has proved most fortuitous. It has provided the impetus for me to return and thrown me into the whirl again immediately."

"It is most kind of you to escort Jane about, Diamond. Most gentlemen would be loath to do so."

"They would?"

"Oh, indeed. But Miss Davies is feeling much more the thing, is she not? I expect you will not be called upon to escort Jane any longer."

"Yes, well, it is a most perverse illness," muttered the duke, glancing toward his horses. "Apparently, it comes and it goes and it comes again. Who the devil is that?" he added, his attention caught by a woman who had approached his team and now stood conversing with his tiger.

"I am sure I have no idea," murmured Bella. "Perhaps she is a friend of Toby's?"

"I think not. Toby is merely twelve and has never been to London before in his life," replied Derrinham, rising. "I am going to discover what she wants, Bella."

"I am going with you," Bella replied directly, rising from the bench and taking his arm.

The young woman looked up as they approached. She wore a walking dress of blue sprigged muslin and a wide-brimmed hat was tied with white ribands beneath her chin. Her eyes were a dazzling blue and they appeared to study the Duke of Derrinham most thoroughly as he neared.

"May I be of some assistance?" his grace queried, coming to a halt beside his tiger.

"I was merely admiring your team," replied the young woman in a husky voice. "They are quite beautiful. I have a fondness for horses," she added—quite unnecessarily, Bella thought. "You brought them from Ireland, your groom tells me. You are his grace, the Duke of Derrinham?"

"Yes."

"I am Miss Winstead. I did not intend to keep you from your enjoyment of the afternoon, your grace," she added with a glance at Bella. "You must forgive me. I intended merely to gain a closer look at these lovely beasts. Good day to you, Duke," she said with a slow smile. "It has been an honor to make your acquaintance." And then, without another word, she strolled away.

"Well, I'll be," muttered Derrinham, staring after her. "Only intended a closer look at my cattle, eh? What do you expect that was all about, Bella?"

"Perhaps she is an old acquaintance and hoped you would remember her?"

"If we are already acquainted, why did she not say as much? And she is unaccompanied. Extraordinary that she should approach strangers unaccompanied. Toby, what did she say to you?"

"Wishin' ta know whose horses was they, yer grace, an' where they comed from. That was all."

"I see. No harm in that, I expect. It grows late, Bella. Your mama will wonder what I am about to keep you out so long, and she will comb my hair with a butcher knife for doing it, too."

"Never," smiled Bella. "Mama has always stood in awe of you. Do you not remember when you brought me home covered in mud from head to toe because we had been off seeking treasure along the Dappled Run? She never said one word to you about it."

The Diamond laughed. "True. I always wondered why she did not. Sonnett said a great deal about it when I got home. Yes, and Shaughnessy as well."

Derrinham helped Bella back up onto the box, sent his tiger scurrying for his perch and took the reins. Miss Winstead, he thought as he turned his team toward the west gate. Why the devil does that name seem so familiar when the young woman does not? Though there is something about her eyes and the curious tilt to her lips. And the way she cocks her head just the merest bit to one side when she speaks. Who the deuce does she remind me of?

He puzzled over it in silence for the longest time, paying not the least attention to his team or to the people they passed. And then he had it—Diana. She had reminded him of his sister. A deep and searing anguish washed over him at the thought that he had not immediately recognized whom it was the woman resembled and he groaned softly.

"Diamond, what is it?" asked Bella. He had not said a word since he had given his horses the office to start. She had guessed his mind to be engaged with something of importance and had been loath to disturb him. But quite of a sudden the burning sapphires of his eyes had frozen to blue ice and he had made that mournful sound low in his throat.

Bella tugged anxiously at his arm. He had driven right by Mr. Tottingham and Lord Derfield without so much as a nod and given Lady Smithfield the go-by as well. "Diamond, do pay attention and say something, please. You are frightening me."

"Huh?" Derrinham glanced down at the young lady beside him and came near to drowning in a pair of chocolate eyes brimming with tears. "Bella, do not!" he ordered in a low rumble. "If you cry one tear, Bella, I shall set you down at the side of the path and drive off without you. What? You doubt me? I am irascible, you know, and notoriously lacking in manners."

"Oh, you are not," grinned Bella, swiping at her eyes with the backs of her hands. "You are simply stiff-rumped and crotchety and a regular grumblemumbler. I thought—I thought something dreadful was wrong with you, but it cannot be too dreadful for you are grumping now like a crusty old curmudgeon."

"No, Bella," he drawled, the ice of his eyes melting and his hand carrying one of hers to rest comfortably upon his thigh. "There is nothing dreadfully wrong with me. I was caught up for a moment in memories, nothing more."

He studied her for a moment from the corner of his eye as he turned the blacks into Park Street. With her pink cheeks and her wide eyes and that perfect confection of a bonnet perched on her curls again, she was the most fetching child he had ever seen.

No, he reminded himself, she is no longer a child. She is a young lady and a very pretty one, too, though she seems capable of hiding that from every gentleman in London but myself. Although, Barrington is beginning to take note. Devil it, but I am a fool to be putting Bella through her paces and displaying all her charms to London's beaux when I might very easily keep her charms all to myself.

The thought struck him from out of nowhere and he became so nonplussed that his hands tightened on the reins, sending his blacks into a dither before he loosened his grip and directed the team around a farrier's wagon. Keep her charms all to himself? By thunder, was he losing his mind?

He had known Bella from the day she was born. They had raced about Twiney Hill and Meadowlark together from the first moment she could walk. Wherever he had led, Bella had followed. He had cradled her between his knees while sledding down snowy slopes and held her upright upon her first pair of ice skates. He had taught her to swim and to fish and to climb trees. She was the little sister he had never had and he the big brother she had lacked. He could not possibly be considering Bella as—Gawd! Keep Bella's charms all to himself? It was those damnable cherries on that outrageous bonnet that were to blame. He had always had a weakness for bright red cherries.

Five

"I saw him," Miss Winstead whispered in awe. "He spoke to me, Michael. In Hyde Park not more than forty-five minutes ago."

"Who?" asked Michael Winstead with a frown. "Who did you see, Emily?"

"Him. The little duke. Oh, Michael, he is so very handsome! His hair is the color of honey and his eyes are like sapphires."

"Pah! What do you know of sapphires?"

"I have seen sapphires, Michael."

"Emily, what were you doing in Hyde Park? Mrs. Glendenning was not to take you there anymore."

"She did not take me," replied Miss Winstead with flushed cheeks. "I went on my own. I hired a hackney and was driven to the west gate and then I strolled about for the longest time. I saw the most beautiful pair of blacks, and I knew immediately they must be his."

Michael Winstead's face flushed with anger. It took every ounce of self-control he could muster not to shout at his sister, but he did not. Emily could not be held accountable. She did not in the least understand what harm there could be in strolling about Hyde Park on her own. And most certainly she did not understand the danger that lay in revealing herself to the duke. Try as he might, he could not make her understand it. "You must not go again," he said in a most controlled voice. "It is not safe, Emily, to stroll through Hyde Park without a companion—and the Duke of Derrinham is not your friend."

"Well, of course he is not my friend, Michael. He does not even know me. But he is a very fine gentleman and most polite."

Mr. Winstead took his sister's hands and led her to the ancient fainting couch before the hearth and sat down beside her. With tender care he untied the ribands of her bonnet and set the thing aside. A wealth of raven black hair fell from beneath it. "You must not go to the park alone again, Emily," he repeated softly. "And you must set aside this need to know the Duke of Derrinham. Papa would not like you to do either."

"Papa is dead, Michael."

"Even so, he would be most displeased with you. What did you say to the duke, Emily? What did he say to you?"

"I only spoke of his horses and he did as well. There was a young lady with him. She was quite lovely, Michael. Is she his wife do you think?"

"No, his grace is not married."

"Not yet? My goodness, he is so very exquisite. It is a wonder he did not marry the very first year he came on the Town."

"James is not here?"

"He has taken his half-day, your grace," explained Sonnett quietly. "There are five other footmen. Why must it be James?"

"Oh, I don't know, Sonnett. Because he is the first footman, perhaps? Or because he is the eldest of the lot? I expect either reason serves to give me more confidence in him. It would be different, you know, if I actually knew any of them."

"Mr. Piermont, your grace, hired them all and I am certain his judgment can be depended upon."

"Yes, you are correct, Sonnett. Send one of the others, then. Whomever you think. Say this must go directly into Sir Cyril Blythe's hands."

"Sir Cyril Blythe, your grace?"

"Yes," mumbled Derrinham from behind the table in his office as he pressed his signet ring into the wax to seal the missive. "It must go to Number 10, St. James's Square, I expect."

"You have no call to be contacting Sir Cyril Blythe. Not for any reason," Sonnett replied, realizing how perfectly audacious he sounded, but not caring in the least. "The man is an abomination and you can have nothing to say to him."

"I have questions to ask him, Sonnett. I have had questions to ask him for years. I did not do so because I did not wish to upset Diana. But Diana is gone now and I will have my answers."

"I knew we should not have come to London!" exclaimed Sonnett in agitation. "You have not given Sir Cyril one thought in well over a year! No, and you would not be writing to him now if we had not come to this confounded place! And if Lady Diana were alive, she would do anything to prevent you contacting that man and Lord May with her!"

"Well, Diana is not alive, Sonnett, and Will is in Vienna, and you are nothing more than my butler, so stubble it!"

"Nothing more than your butler, am I, your grace?" murmured Sonnett with a shake of his head. "After all these years, I am nothing more than your butler? Well, that is what I shall be then. And as your butler I refuse to send any of my footmen on such a fool's errand."

"You what?"

"I refuse."

"You cannot refuse!"

"Indeed I can and I do. I shall send all of the footmen off on errands of my own making at once and you, your grace, may consign your blasted missive to the fire boy."

Jane could not think why her uncle was roaring louder than the Tower lion as she and Miss Davies entered through the front door, but his bellow virtually thundered down the hallway.

"Goodness," Jane breathed.

"Goodness, indeed," agreed Miss Davies, standing awestruck beside her charge. "What has gotten into the man?"

"I cannot guess, but I am going to find out. In his office, I think," Jane added, as Shaughnessy, disdaining the servants' stairs for those closest to hand, came dashing past her.

Shaughnessy nodded and continued his run.

"Jane, where are you going?" gasped Miss Davies as Jane hurried up the staircase and down the first floor hall.

"Do you not wish to know what has happened, Lydie? I most certainly do," Jane declared as she tugged her companion into a tiny chamber known as the sewing room where she crossed quickly to the fireplace and settled into a chair before the hearth.

"Sir Cyril Blythe, your grace?" came Mr. Shaughnessy's voice, out of breath but as clear as a bell up the chimney.

Lydia Davies's fine gray eyes widened and she stared openmouthed at Jane, who put a finger warningly to her lips.

"You cannot possibly mean for me to deliver a missive to that particular gentleman."

"Do not tell me, Shaughnessy, that you intend to be

insubordinate as well. I have swallowed all the rebellion I can stomach from Sonnett."

"Rumph!" came Sonnett's grunt, bounding up the chimney into the sewing room.

"Do not harrumph at me, Sonnett. You are beyond anything fortunate that I have not thrown you bodily out of that window!"

"You may throw me from that window or from the roof," grumbled Sonnett, "but nothing will induce me to aid you to contact Sir Cyril Blythe."

"You cannot possibly wish to do this thing, your grace," offered Shaughnessy. "Sir Cyril is a perverted old man. No one of any sensibility would be seen to associate with him."

"I do not wish to associate with him, Shaughnessy. I merely wish to discover what he knows that no one else will tell me."

"There is nothing he knows that you have not been told," offered Sonnett and Shaughnessy in a rush.

"What could have put such a thing into your mind?" queried Shaughnessy. "Did Lady Diana not explain to you the very first time you came to London that Sir Cyril would set bait for you and attempt to reel you in?"

"Yes, and Will backed her in it. But I am eighteen no longer and I will have words with Blythe! He has intimated a certain knowledge."

"But we have all been answering your questions since you were old enough to ask them," sighed Shaughnessy. "Do you think we have been lying to you all these years?"

"I prefer to think not," muttered the duke so quietly that Jane barely caught his voice. "I prefer to think that Diana and Will did not lie, either, that you all merely declined to mention a thing or two. There was a young woman," he said then, a bit more loudly. "A young woman in Hyde Park this afternoon. Said her name was

Miss Winstead. And I remembered. Blythe spoke all those years ago about a Winstead and how I should know what had occurred between that family and my father. None of you, not one, has ever mentioned a Winstead."

"Balderdash!" exclaimed Sonnett loudly. "Your mother and father never knew a Winstead! I was butler then as I am now and never once was a Winstead admitted to this establishment!"

Jane left her chair and huddled against the chimney bricks as the voices lowered again, but try as she might, she could not make out the remainder of the conversation.

"They have opened the French doors and wandered outside," she sighed at last. "Drat! Blast and drat! Did you hear, Lydie? Uncle Hill said something about Miss Winstead again at the last. Could you make it out?"

Miss Lydia Davies, her face flushed, stood up, removed Jane from contact with the chimney piece and firmly escorted that young lady back along the first floor corridor into the drawing room. There she settled her charge firmly upon a red-and-white-striped settee, rang for tea, and only then moved to the seat beside Jane and stared at her thoughtfully. "Whoever taught you to listen at chimneys?"

"Papa and Uncle Hill when I was very small. Well, they did not teach me to listen at them, precisely, but they did explain how some voices I had heard had floated up the chimney and were not ghosts at all. Lydie," she added on a soft intake of breath, "Uncle Hill wishes to meet with Sir Cyril Blythe!"

Miss Lydia Davies was not one to quibble over the propriety of eavesdropping when more important things were at hand. She nodded and took Jane's hands into her own. "Yes, and that is precisely the person that your papa warned us against when he agreed we should come to your Uncle Hill in London."

"And he did not only warn us against the gentleman, Lydie, but he said we were to keep Uncle Hill far from Sir Cyril. He said Sir Cyril was *dangerous* to Uncle Hill."

"Yes, but he did never say *how* we were to keep the duke from Sir Cyril. Apparently Mr. Sonnett and Mr. Shaughnessy are attempting to do just that and are not getting very far at all."

"I wonder who this Miss Winstead can be?" murmured Jane. "Did not Uncle Hill say it was because of a Miss Winstead that he meant to speak with Sir Cyril? Perhaps we can discover where this Miss Winstead lives and urge her to tell Uncle Hill what he wishes to know. Then Sir Cyril will be of no interest to him."

Lord Barrington discovered himself to be uncommonly nervous as he escorted Lady Meade and Lady Annabella into his box at the Royal Opera two evenings later. Any number of people watched in amazement as he settled Bella into one of the seats and Lady Meade into another. He could feel astonished stares stabbing him between his shoulder blades.

Let them stare, he told himself. If I wish to attend the opera with Lady Annabella, that is my own affair. To Bella he drawled a few well-rehearsed phrases about how beautiful she looked, then came to an abrupt halt.

She actually does look beautiful, he thought dazedly. Her eyes are shining and her light brown curls are newly cropped and glistening. Her cheeks are a beguiling pink and her lips are cherry-red and ripe for kissing. Gad, Barrington thought in wonder, how could I have ever thought her unattractive? She is glorious. The thought made his ears redden at the very tips.

Barrington's studied praise had made Bella most uncomfortable. She glanced anxiously at her mama, only to discover that lady engrossed in conversation with Lady Rothfield in the adjoining box. She could not expect any aid from that quarter, then, for those two ladies had been friends for years and would most likely converse to the exclusion of everyone else the entire evening. And quite likely Lord Barrington would say something else sooner or later. Really she must think of something to say in response. She could not sit in silence and ignore the gentleman for the entire length of the performance.

Why the deuce did he invite me to the opera in the first place? I would have turned him down at once, thought Bella, if only Mama had not interrupted and accepted on my behalf. But a tiger does not change his stripes, she told herself, and I shall not trust a word the man says. He is most likely out to discover a new appellation for me since Hesitant Hedgehog appears to have gone out of style. "Possibly, The Dreary Dairymaid might take," she murmured, her glance going to Lord Barrington for a moment and then flying hurriedly back to the proscenium.

Barrington fairly gaped at her. "I—dreary dairymaid? I do apologize, Lady Annabella," he said sheepishly, attempting to collect his wits. "I daresay I have been woolgathering and have missed some significant portion of your conversation."

"I said," replied Annabella softly, "that it is quite possible that The Dreary Dairymaid might take, your lordship."

"That is just what I thought you said."

"Well then, you were not woolgathering. Oh, the opera begins! I know it is gauche of me. But I love the music." With that, Annabella turned her attention toward the stage and left Lord Barrington to gaze at her in bewilderment through the entire first act.

When at last the act ended, Lord Barrington inquired whether Annabella and her mother would care for some refreshment and went off to fetch them some oranges, still pondering the significance of a dairymaid. Oh, most assuredly he had missed something. And the minx that Lady Annabella was fast becoming in his mind refused to enlighten him. He determined to confront her upon it immediately upon his return, only to discover when he reached his box that Miss May had taken his seat and was whispering seriously into Lady Annabella's ear while Miss Davies and Lady Meade had strolled off into the corridor.

"Trouble, Barrington?" asked a voice behind him. "The ladies have deserted you, eh?" The Duke of Derrinham smiled sympathetically. "Ran into Meade at White's. Said you had called to take his ladies to the opera."

"You followed me here?"

"Not at all. Followed Bella," replied the duke. "May I have one of those?" he added, taking an orange from the sack Barrington carried. He reached into his waistcoat pocket and produced a tiny blade, carved the fruit and began to peel it from its skin hungrily. "Missed m'dinner," he offered nonchalantly. "I have had the devil of a day so far, Barrington, let me tell you."

Oblivious to Lord Barrington's return and to the Duke of Derrinham's unexpected presence, Jane continued her whispered conversation with Bella. The young ladies were huddled so closely together that blond hair and brown virtually combined, producing a most delightful picture. "Sir Cyril Blythe?" Bella asked, aghast. "Oh, Jane, certainly not!"

"Indeed. Uncle Hill is determined. Not only did he send a message—to which the ancient libertine has not replied, thank goodness—but he actually went off in search of the man this very afternoon."

"Well, even I have heard of Sir Cyril Blythe," whispered Bella. "But I cannot think why Diamond should wish anything at all to do with him. You misunderstood the matter, Jane."

"No, I did not. It is because of Miss Winstead."

"Miss Winstead?" Bella pictured quite readily the young woman who had spoken to the duke in Hyde Park. "Miss Winstead said barely anything to Diamond except to praise his horses."

"Apparently, when Uncle Hill first came on the Town, Sir Cyril Blythe attempted to form an acquaintanceship with him and mentioned some secret about a Winstead. Meeting this Miss Winstead has jogged Uncle Hill's memory and now he is determined to hear what Sir Cyril wished to tell him all those years ago."

"Well, but I cannot see how there is anything at all that you can do to stop him."

"No, I do not think that I can actually stop him. But I can make Sir Cyril quite unnecessary to him, Bella. If I am able to discover this Miss Winstead's direction, perhaps she might be convinced to answer all of Uncle Hill's questions and he would have no need of Sir Cyril. Did she say nothing to give you any hint of where she might reside, Bella?"

Bella was at a complete loss. Quite likely this Miss Winstead knew nothing whatsoever of any interest to Diamond. There must be any number of Winsteads in London. Who was to say that this particular Miss Winstead had anything at all to do with the duke or Sir Cyril? "Jane," she whispered at last, "we cannot continue this conversation here. If we are to do anything to keep Diamond from Sir Cyril, then we must work out a proper plan."

"We?" gasped Lady Jane. "Oh, Bella, I knew you would help!"

"Yes, but we cannot decide what is to be done here and now. We must discuss it further. Tomorrow. You will come to visit me for the afternoon. No one will protest if you come without Miss Davies if it is only to have a coze with me, will they?"

"Of course not. And your mama will be at home, after all."

"Whose mama will be at home?" Derrinham asked softly.

"Uncle Hill!"

"Diamond!"

"Do you realize, opera lovers, that the second act is about to begin and almost everyone has returned to their rightful places? Lord Barrington, I think, Jane, would like his seat back. Come, I shall escort you and Miss Davies back to my box." He winked at Bella and, taking Jane's hand, led her away.

"Whose mama will be at home?" he asked again as he gave his other arm to Miss Davies.

"Bella's. She wondered if I might not pay a call tomorrow afternoon. Without Lydie, you know, because we only mean to spend time in Bella's chamber gossiping and trying new hairstyles and the like. Do you think I may, Uncle Hill?"

"I do not see why you may not if Lady Meade is amenable to it. I shall send you in my Town coach and Miss Davies may have the day free to do as she pleases. You will not mind, Miss Davies, to lose your charge to someone else for an afternoon?"

"Not at all," smiled Miss Davies.

"Fine. Settled then." He ushered them into his box, saw them seated and then took one of the chairs behind them. The music had already begun and he turned his attention immediately to the stage. He appeared so intent upon viewing the performance that Jane and Miss Davies directed their attention to the stage as well and did not once ask what had brought his grace to the opera in the first place.

When he noted that he was going to be granted peace

for at least the remainder of the act, Derrinham's gaze left the stage and traveled to Lord Barrington's box. He saw Barrington whisper in Bella's ear and sighed.

I ought to be rejoicing over it, he mused grumpily. Have I not come to Town purposely to see that Bella receives her fair share of attention and to find the infant a husband if I can? And Barrington is a good catch. Meade would be pleased with an alliance there. And any number of those gentlemen ogling her from the pit are eligible as well. Devil it, but she does look fetching this evening.

Derrinham squirmed uncomfortably in his chair and tugged at his neckcloth. What the devil is Barrington about, whispering to the girl all the time? he thought angrily. The man brought her to the opera—why does he not allow her to listen to the music? Bella likes music. At least, she always liked to hear me play my flute when we were children. But she is two years out of the school-room now; perhaps she likes music less and the attentions of gentlemen more these days.

Miss Winstead eyed Sir Cyril with some apprehension. It seemed to her that she had known this gentleman all of her life and still he made her inordinately anxious each time he appeared in her parlor. He did not, of course, make Mrs. Glendenning nervous. No one, it seemed, ever overwhelmed the superior Mrs. Glendenning, who was even now sipping politely at her tea.

"I cannot believe my luck," said Sir Cyril with the merest bit of a sneer. "I have had a missive from the Duke of Derrinham. He wishes to speak with me as soon as is convenient."

Mrs. Glendenning looked across at him with a warning frown. "How fortunate," she murmured. "I had heard the duke was in Town, but I took leave to doubt it, myself. Perhaps he wishes to contact you in order to gain an introduction to Miss Winstead."

Emily's lips parted to advise her two visitors that she had already made the Duke of Derrinham's acquaintance and that he was quite as handsome and polite as she had always imagined him. But then she thought better of it, for she had not the least wish to let on to Mrs. Glendenning that she had gone to Hyde Park without her, so she lowered her eyes and sipped at her tea in silence.

"He is older now, Bessie, and without his sister's influence. He is without the least fear and will come to me at last. I have been avoiding him these past two days in an effort to make him more eager for my company."

"Miss Octavia Delacey says that the little duke is most handsome and drives the most beautiful team of blacks," offered Miss Winstead shyly. "Mr. Bremmerman pointed him out to her upon their drive in Hyde Park. Oh, I do so wish that we could go to Hyde Park again, Mrs. Glendenning. I was used to enjoy it so, and you enjoyed it as well, I think."

"We will go again one day, Emily," replied Mrs. Glendenning with a nod of her head. "It is merely that your brother and I discussed it and we thought it would be best to cease for a while. I am not feeling quite the thing, you know."

Actually, Emily thought, she looked quite robust for a woman of her age. And whatever her complaint, it had not kept her from rushing over from next door to play chaperone the moment Sir Cyril had mounted the front stoop.

"I did expect to discover Michael at home this evening," offered Sir Cyril with a speaking look at Mrs. Glendenning. "Things must be quite busy at the shop."

"Oh, oh, no. Michael is not at the shop," Emily provided on a frightened intake of breath. "He has—has—

accompanied Mr. Hobson and Mr. Bridges to the theater this evening."

"Is that so? He has been out and about quite a bit of late, has he not?" asked Sir Cyril with what Miss Winstead could only consider unwelcome curiosity. "Well, when next you see him, I hope that you will give him my sincerest regards, Miss Winstead, and say that I should be most happy if he would present himself at Pickering Place on Wednesday next. Will you do that for me?"

Emily nodded and sipped her tea. Very soon now Sir Cyril would depart and Mrs. Glendenning with him and she could be at ease again. She was never at ease when Sir Cyril was about, but tonight his presence was most overwhelming because she had been forced to lie to him for Michael's sake. And she was not at all certain that the elderly gentleman had not seen right through her and recognized her lie on the instant.

Michael was not at the theater. No, he was working. He had left his position at Rundell and Bridges and taken a new position which kept him from home day and night except for one half-day every two weeks. He had assured her that this was merely a temporary situation and that soon things would be as they had been. But he had instructed her quite clearly not to reveal to anyone that he was gone so very much from home. Not even to Mrs. Glendenning. And most certainly not to Sir Cyril.

Six

"Well, I did ask Lord Barrington if he, perhaps, knew a Miss Winstead," Bella replied softly, sitting with Jane before the hearth in her tiny sitting room. "But he does not."

"We shall ask others," declared Jane, "until we discover someone who does know her and can give us her direction."

"But there must be any number of Winsteads in the City of London, Jane. How do we know that this Miss Winstead is the person we ought to seek?"

"We do not," sighed Jane, "but she is a place to begin."

"And what will we ask her if we find her?"

Jane's lovely blue eyes sought Bella's brown ones. "We shall ask her, Bella, whether someone in her family has been involved in some way with the old Duke of Derrinham or Sir Cyril Blythe. We shall ask everyone we know, everyone to whom we are introduced. Someone must know Miss Winstead. She does not, certainly, live in a cave like a hermit." Jane's fingers began to pleat the folds of her bishop's blue walking dress. "We cannot allow Uncle Hill to meet with Sir Cyril, Bella. Truly we cannot. Papa warned me the very moment we received Uncle Hill's missive requesting me to join him that if I came to London I was to strictly avoid Sir Cyril Blythe and to prevent Uncle Hill from ever coming into contact with the man."

Bella stared at her, wide-eyed. "Your uncle Hill's missive requesting you to join him?"

"Oh! I did not intend to say that," mumbled Jane, turning her gaze quickly away from Bella and staring into the hearth.

"But I thought you came to London of your own accord and that Diamond only came to help when Miss Davies became ill."

Jane had the good grace to blush guiltily as she turned her gaze back to Bella and laid one hand atop Bella's own. "I am so sorry, Bella. That was a great bouncer. Uncle Hill sent a message to Papa in Vienna asking if Miss Davies and I could join him in London. He wrote all about you and what you had told him about your last Season and said that he wished to lend you his support this time around and that my becoming your friend would give him an excuse to appear at your side and bring you into fashion."

"B-bring me into fashion? Diamond?"

"Yes. And he can, you know. He has already begun to do so. Did you not notice the incredible number of gentlemen's eyes directed toward you last evening?"

"No, I did not. Bring me into fashion? Why would he even think to attempt such a thing?"

"Because he wishes you to be happy, Bella. He could not bear to see you turned into a mouse and a watering pot, he wrote. He said that he would go to London regardless of whether or not I joined him, but that it would seem less suspicious to everyone if I were there to provide him a ready excuse for his actions."

"Well, I never!"

"Do not be angry with him, Bella. Please do not. And do not be angry with me, either. I do so like you and I would wish to be your friend whether or not Uncle Hill had asked it of me."

"Angry? I am not angry, Jane. I am purely flabbergasted. Diamond has always stood in the place of a brother to me. But I never intended my silliness to bring him all the way to London! Whoever would have thought it of him? Did your papa tell you why Diamond was to be kept apart from Sir Cyril, Jane?"

"No."

"Well, I think we are going about it all backward. It will take us forever to locate Miss Winstead again. If we wish to discover what there is to know and then tell Diamond so that he will not need to speak to Sir Cyril, then we ought to go directly to the person who will be able to tell us everything. We ought to go and speak with Sir Cyril ourselves."

"Oh, Bella, no!"

"Yes. That is the only certain way. We must approach Sir Cyril ourselves and do so before The Diamond does."

To say one intended to approach Sir Cyril and to do so, Bella discovered, were two entirely different things. The man might well be a ghost, she thought despairingly. *He is nowhere and everywhere all at one and the same time.*

People, she discovered, were quite willing to pour forth gossip into her ears about him, but no one seemed able to point her in his direction. He lived in a moldering old mansion in Pickering Place that had been let to fall to ruin. He lived in a veritable palace in Pall Mall that quite outshone Carlton House. He lived in a set of rooms in Curzon Street that were most ordinary and unpretentious. Apparently, he lived everywhere and therefore, for Bella's purposes, nowhere. She was fast becoming frustrated. Diamond had managed to contact Sir Cyril. Where had he sent his message?

"Number 10, St. James's Square. But why the deuce you should wish to know any such thing, I cannot imagine," grumbled Lord Barrington as he sat between Bella and Jane in the long drawing room of Derrinham House. "It is a gaming establishment. The Pigeon Hole. Rumor has it that the old libertine owns stock in the place. Have no idea if it's true. But that would be the place."

"What place?" Mr. Tottingham queried, taking a chair across from the three of them. "Good afternoon, Lady Annabella, Miss May. You are both looking quite lovely, I must say."

Bella, her entire mind focused upon reaching Sir Cyril before Diamond did, forgot to so much as lower her eyes or blush at the compliment. "We are discussing Sir Cyril Blythe," she replied. "We have been told he resides in Pickering Place, Pall Mall and Curzon Street. And now— St. James's Square."

"No, he does not actually live in St. James's Square," Barrington mumbled, frowning across at Tottingham.

"Do not glower at me, Barrington," grinned that gentleman. "I came to pay a morning call and I intend to do so. These two young ladies do not belong exclusively to you, you know. You cannot possibly wish to contact Sir Cyril Blythe," he added, looking first at Bella and then at Jane. "Your reputations would be torn to shreds at the first hint of an encounter. The man is anathema and to be avoided at all costs."

"Of course they do not wish an encounter with the villain," asserted Barrington. "They have merely heard so much about the man that they are curious as to what is truth and what is fiction. His place of residence, for instance."

"Yes, I can see how his place of residence might prove confusing. He has so very many. Did you think people were hoaxing you, my dears, when they all gave you different directions?"

"That is exactly what they thought," inserted Lord Barrington before Bella could so much as part her lips to reply. "Not that it is in the least your concern, Tottingham."

"What ain't Tottingham's concern?" asked a third gentleman. "Good afternoon, Lady Annabella, Miss May. Fine day, ain't it? And you are looking perfect goddesses," added Mr. Anders with an odd smile. "I wondered if perhaps you might care to take advantage of the fine weather and drive with me this afternoon, Lady Annabella?"

Lord Barrington and Mr. Tottingham glared at Anders, who was the third son of the Earl of Willonshire and a completely dedicated Corinthian and spent his days and nights in sporting pursuits to the exclusion of all else including young ladies.

"Of course she don't want to go driving with you, Anders," grumbled Tottingham. "She is going driving with me."

"With you?" exclaimed Barrington. "Oh, I rather think not, Tottingham. I am taking Lady Annabella driving."

Jane's laughter was almost bell-like. "Am I to be left all alone then? Oh, dearest me. And to think, it is my very best friend has made me a wallflower."

Bella could not believe what she was hearing. Why, last Season not one of these gentlemen had approached her unless they had been compelled to ask her to dance by one of their hostesses. Really, she could not understand it. Jane had said that The Diamond intended to bring her into fashion, but this was ridiculous. What had he done but dance with her at Almack's and sit with her at Lady Swithinby's musicale and drive her once in Hyde Park? Certainly there was more to bringing someone into fashion than that. Bella grinned at Jane, causing the shy dimple in her cheek to make a most appreciated appearance, and then looked at each of the gentlemen in turn. "You are all quite mad, you know. You have come to visit Jane and instead of her, you are petitioning me to drive with you."

"Yes, so will you?" laughed Mr. Anders, his brilliant green eyes sparkling down at her. "Drive with me, I mean, because I am the maddest of the lot."

"She will not. This afternoon at precisely four o'clock Lady Annabella and Jane shall be with me," announced a fourth voice, which Bella recognized immediately. "However, if any of you gentlemen should care to join us in a canter along Rotten Row, you are most welcome to do so. Your papa and I have been to Tat's, Bella, and have found you the finest little mare," the duke added, raising the other gentlemen's eyebrows by his familiar use of her Christian name. "He wishes you to try her paces. I told him that Janie and I would be pleased to accompany you."

The duke would ride the big black he called Arnold. He had a passion for blacks, much as his father before him. But what a stupid name to give such a magnificent animal, the man thought as he entered the stall. Arnold. "May as well call the thing Cholmondeley," he muttered. "What a waste to put such an animal in the hands of a man who names it Arnold."

He thought for a moment, gazing at the beast as it reached down to him and nuzzled at his shoulder, that perhaps he was mistaken to do this thing. The truth was, he was not a man who killed people lightly. He had, in fact, never before killed anyone at all. And if only Hillary Holland Hallsworth had had the good sense to stay far from London and out of his reach—but there, he had not. He had returned to Town, bringing the evil of the dukes of Derrinham with him. And there was only one way to put an end to that evil. He must destroy this villain who was the last of the line. Of course, he was not truly the last of the line. There was his niece, Miss May. She shared his blood. But surely, oh most surely, the May blood had diluted and conquered the Hallsworth blood and he need not accost the girl. His heart faltered at the thought. He could not murder a young lady. Never.

Clumsily, because his hands were somehow unmanageable, he took the hat pin from his lapel and slipped it awkwardly into the saddle blanket. Then he took the ten-penny blade from the inside pocket of his coat and cut into the saddle cinch. It was not a deep cut. The groom who saddled the beast would not notice it in the least. And the cinch would not give way immediately the great horse began to buck. But, providing the duke remained in the saddle, which he would because he was what they all called a Nonesuch and a Nonpareil and his pride would not allow him to give way to his mount, the cinch would break eventually and send him hurtling to the cobbles.

And his head will crack open upon the cobbles and that will be an end to it, thought the man as a shudder ran through him. And I may get on with my life knowing that I have done my duty.

He placed the saddle back on its hook and tucked the blade safely away. Then, with a quiet groan, he gave the horse's nose a pat and let himself quietly out of the stall. He gave a great sigh of relief when he managed to exit the stables without any of the grooms having so much as noticed his presence. With long, hasty strides he reached the kitchen door of Derrinham House, pasted a most bored look upon his face and took himself inside.

* * *

Bella gave her papa a smacking kiss upon his cheek. "Oh, she is so very beautiful, Papa. I cannot thank you enough."

"Well," the Earl of Meade smiled fondly, "I cannot have my only daughter forced to meander along the Row on some old nag, can I? What would people say?"

"But she must have cost a fortune, Papa," murmured Bella, gazing with great admiration at the little gray mare.

"A mere pittance," supplied the earl, his eyes alight with laughter at the joy upon his daughter's face. "You will not be shy, Bella, with such a mount beneath you, eh? You will outshine every other young lady in the Park."

Bella was about to explain that she could hardly out-shine all the beautiful young ladies in the Park, but just as she opened her mouth to do so, the duke and Jane cantered into the stable yard. Her papa, with a wide grin, gave her a swift kiss and a leg up. "What is it bothers your horse, Derrinham?" he asked as the three turned their horses' heads toward the street.

"Have not had him out in more than a week," the duke replied, as Arnold circled and danced beneath him. "Merely fresh, I think, and needing a run. He will be deuced disappointed to be held to a trot along the Row."

The streets leading to Hyde Park were already begin-ning to clog with vehicles and the going was slow. From time to time The Diamond readjusted his weight in the saddle. "Arnold!" he exclaimed at last. "If you cannot settle and keep a decent pace I shall be forced to whip the daylights out of you!"

"Yes, I can just imagine you doing that," grinned Jane. "It is much more likely, Uncle Hill, that you will go down on your knees before him and beg him to have some discretion."

"And he will eat your hat while you are doing it, too," added Bella, her eyes sparkling with laughter.

"First my hat and then my hair," chuckled the duke. "What are you going to call that creature, Bella? At Tat's she had only a lot number. Came from Greenbriar in Scotland. Might have been in the Scottish Grays if she had had more weight to her."

"I shall call her *Enchanté.*"

"*Enchanté?* Great heavens," grinned Derrinham. "Does that mean you think she is enchanted then?"

"No," replied Bella. "It means that I am not so prosaic as to name her Arnold."

"Unfair, Bella. Arnold is a perfectly fitting name for this particular horse."

"Why?"

"Yes, Uncle Hill," joined in Jane. "Tell the tale."

"It is not a tale. He is the image of the elder Mr. Piermont of Piermont, Piermont, Jersey and Beck, Solicitors and——"

"Do not tell me," giggled Bella. "The elder Mr. Piermont's Christian name is Arnold."

The duke nodded as gurgles of laughter rose from both young ladies. The delightful sound attracted the glances of a number of gentlemen as they entered the Row.

Could not have planned it better, thought Derrinham, taking note of the interested stares. Bella looks a diamond of the first water with her eyes sparkling and her cheeks rosy and giggling merrily away. And the way she sits that little filly adds to her allure. We shall be mobbed by suitors if we are not careful.

They were, in fact, in little less than three minutes, surrounded by a number of gentlemen. Lord Nesbitt took up a position beside Miss May. Lord Barrington and Mr. Anders flanked Bella to either side and Mr. Tottingham and Mr. Wainwright brought up the rear. The Duke of Derrinham was forced to ride behind the lot of them or chance knocking up against the rail, because Arnold, rather than ceasing to act like a perfect nodcock, had increased his skittishness.

"Do not listen to a word Barrington says," protested Mr. Anders with goodwill. "I can dance, and very creditably, too."

"Ha!" exclaimed Barrington. "In a boxing ring, Lady Annabella, he dances like a champion. I cannot deny that. But the man has never set foot upon a dance floor in his entire life."

"I have!" replied Mr. Anders on a chuckle. "I set foot upon a dance floor at my sister's come-out and I slipped and fell and broke my arm. That was the end of my dancing career."

"Oh, no," giggled Bella. "How dreadful for you, Mr. Anders."

"Not dreadful at all. I was seventeen then. Gave up all thought of becoming a dandy on the spot and became a Corinthian instead. Boxing and racing and gaming and driving four-in-hand are a good deal more safe than attempting to tread one's way through a *contra-danse*. And besides, the dandies are much too dull for my taste. Corinthians never have a dull moment. Or if they do, they discover a cure for it at once."

"I cannot imagine you ever having a dull moment, Mr. Anders," agreed Bella with a wide smile.

Barrington could not decide as he studied her whether it was the gray mare or the green velvet riding habit or the high-topped beaver with one white plume which she wore upon her curls, but whatever it was, the sight of Lady Annabella Faire was taking his breath away. And she was taking Anders's breath away as well. He could tell from the gleam in that gentleman's eyes and the quaint conversation going forward from between his lips. Really, it was the outside of enough! Last Season he might have had Lady Annabella all to himself. And this

Season, when he found his heart beating faster at the mere thought of her, every deuced Corinthian in Town had decided to come after the gel. It was The Diamond's doing. Word had got 'round and every Corinthian in London wished to discover for himself what the Nonesuch found so intriguing in the gel.

Barrington gave a great sigh as he spied three more of his acquaintances making their way up the Row. I expect they are come to determine for themselves what power Lady Annabella wields, he thought in frustration. I expect I should join Nesbitt beside Miss May. "What the devil?" he muttered abruptly, turning in the saddle. "What goes on?"

The Duke of Derrinham, in an effort to gain more control over his mount, had shifted his weight in the saddle again, but this time he had shifted the hat pin in the saddle blanket directly into Arnold, and Arnold's fidgeting had turned to something more. With a great snort and a frightened whinny, the big black bolted over the rail and onto the verge where he began to buck violently, his head lowered, his ears back, his rear legs kicking a full five feet into the air.

"Diamond!" Bella screamed upon seeing it, and turning her mare about on the instant, leaped the fence as well, leaving each and every one of the Corinthians staring after her in shock. Once she had come within an acceptable distance of the furious Arnold, she directed the little mare around him and approached the horse and rider head on.

The Diamond knew with a certainty that the best possible thing he could do to calm Arnold was to dismount, but that was a good deal easier said than done—unless, of course, he chose to let go and allow himself to be flung clean over the horse's head. He chose instead to attempt to dismount by kicking one foot out of a stirrup and then stepping down hastily from the other. Take a tumble, he thought, but at least it will free Arnold of my weight. He had already kicked free of the stirrup when he looked up and saw Bella and the gray mare carefully advancing upon him.

"Bella, go back," he bellowed. "Take her back."

With a shake of her head, Bella continued to advance. It was pure luck, she thought, that the great black beast was bucking across the verge in a fairly straight line and not in circles. That would give her an opportunity to reach out and seize a chin strap and tug Arnold's head upward and that, for an instant, would cause him to cease his gyrations. She could see that Diamond had already kicked free of the right stirrup and knew what he had in mind to do. And it is the right choice, too, she thought. But Arnold may well kick him when he stumbles—perhaps in the back. The thought of The Diamond doing more damage to his back made her more determined than ever to seize that chin strap, if only the little mare would not panic and run.

But *Enchanté* appeared to have every confidence in her rider and responded without the least protest to the signals of Bella's heel and toe and her touch on the reins.

"Do not step down until I have pulled his head up," Bella called loudly.

"Be careful," the duke called back. "This is not old Pagan."

Bella smiled. She had not thought of old Pagan for years. Then she leaned forward in the saddle, caught at Arnold's leathers and tugged upward with all her strength, at the same time signaling the little mare to back away. For a moment Arnold stuttered in his gyrations and Diamond swung his leg over the horse's back. It is going to work, Bella thought happily. He will be able to clear before Arnold bucks again.

And then, as all of The Diamond's weight rested for

a moment upon one stirrup, the saddle broke away and sent the duke crashing to the ground.

Bella might well have screamed at the unexpectedness of the thing and the sudden likelihood that the duke would be trampled beneath the black's iron-shod hooves, but she did not have the leisure to do so. Instead she loosed Arnold's chin strap and spurred the little mare forward between the great beast and the place where Diamond struggled to rise from the verge. And in a breath of a second, Diamond was up behind her on *Enchanté* and they were dashing toward the Row.

"Stop now, Bella," she heard him say in her ear. "Let me down. She cannot carry us both any farther. Besides, Arnold has ceased his carrying on."

Bella brought the mare to a halt and Diamond slid to the ground. "Help me down," Bella commanded. "I am going with you."

"The devil you are," exclaimed the duke. "What if he should take it into his head to begin kicking again?"

"He will not, Diamond. He is settling."

Derrinham grasped her about the waist and set her firmly upon the verge and together they hurried back to where Arnold stood snorting and whimpering and attempting to bite at the place on his back where the saddle had been.

Before they reached the big black, Lord Barrington and Mr. Anders, Lord Nesbitt and Mr. Tottingham and Mr. Wainwright and Jane, had all jumped the rail and reaching them, dismounted.

"What the deuce happened?" asked Barrington, a bewildered look upon his handsome face. "Are you all right, Duke? Excellent maneuver, Lady Annabella. I should never have known how to go about helping him."

"Nor I," admitted Mr. Anders while the rest of the gentlemen mumbled the same.

"That is because you never rode old Pagan," laughed

Bella, feeling overwhelmingly joyful now that The Diamond was safe.

"No, they have not one of them had that privilege," chuckled Derrinham. "You must tell them all about old Pagan one day, Bella." And then he was strolling confidently up to Arnold and taking the horse's reins in his hand and running his long, lean fingers along the horse's back. "I'll be damned," he muttered as the others approached. "Something has pricked him, and deeply, too. It has drawn blood."

"Possibly a hat pin," offered Barrington, holding the offending article in one hand and the saddle and blanket in the other. "How do you suppose that came to be in his blanket?"

"Someone put it there," muttered Mr. Anders, taking the saddle from Barrington and staring intently at it. "And this cinch has been cut part way through as well. Devil it, Duke, there is some villain out for your blood."

Seven

"No! Never!" Lord Barrington's face grew quite red, and though he refrained from shouting, his hoarse whisper forced Bella to shush him by placing a finger softly upon his lips.

"My mama will hear you. She has very sharp ears, my lord."

For the veriest moment that it remained, that lace-gloved finger upon his lips drove all rational thought from Barrington's mind. He forgot that they stood in the tiny rose garden at the side of Meade House. He forgot that Lady Meade sat upon a stone bench not more than twelve feet from them. He even forgot what it was that had put him into such a pucker. Never had a young lady placed a finger—such a gentle finger—upon his lips before. It made his insides twist and his breath come in short gasps.

"You claim that you wish to be The Diamond's friend and my friend as well, my lord. A true friend would rush to assist me in such a serious matter as this."

"Well, but," stuttered Barrington, attempting to bring his mind back to the topic. "I cannot—we—it is—"

"I expect I must ask Mr. Anders then," sighed Bella.

At her words a veritable fire ignited in Lord Barrington's hazel eyes. A fierce scowl swept across his countenance.

"Well, but Mr. Anders is an out-and-out Corinthian.

Everyone says so," murmured Bella, astounded by the change in Lord Barrington's visage.

"I am a Corinthian as well," spluttered Lord Barrington, "and I have known you a great deal longer than has Mr. Anders."

"That is true," Bella said with a tight smile, "but it does not speak to the matter at hand."

"The matter at hand is outrageous."

"Indeed. The very thought that anyone should attempt to do away with the Duke of Derrinham is most outrageous."

"Yes, that, too," grumbled Barrington. "However, I was referring to my escorting you to Number 10, St. James's Square. It is a gaming hell, Lady Annabella, and no gentleman would think to expose any lady to such a place."

"But how am I to speak to Sir Cyril? And it is more important than ever that I speak to him. Someone has actually made an attempt upon the duke's life and Sir Cyril may well know who it was. He would be the type of person to know a murderer, would he not?"

"Precisely the type," growled Barrington. "Anders will not escort you to The Pigeon Hole, either. If you ask it of him, he will give you the same answer as I."

"He will?"

"Indeed."

Truly, when her great chocolate eyes looked at him in just that way, Barrington was certain he could be convinced to do anything the lady desired. But he must not allow her eyes, nor the little disappointed pout to her lips, nor the rosiness of her cheeks nor the seductiveness of her full little figure in that totally adorable sprigged muslin garden dress to overwhelm his common sense. That would lead them both into certain disaster.

"I could go myself," Barrington offered quietly.

"How kind of you, my lord," murmured Bella, knowing that it was indeed kind but most unsatisfactory. "But if it is such a dreadful place, I cannot ask you to enter it on our behalf. Jane and I will simply be forced to reconsider what it is we can do."

Lord Barrington accepted her words with a relieved nod. He truly detested the idea of entering The Pigeon Hole and even more the idea of speaking with Sir Cyril. Warnings against that particular gentleman and his cronies had been drummed into Barrington's head ever since he had first begun to speak of going on the Town. Innumerable stories of young gentlemen brought to ruin at Sir Cyril's hands had literally dripped from between his mama's lips until the drips had become a flood and his lordship come near to drowning in the torrent.

But I would have gone, he admitted to himself dazedly as he left the Meade establishment and wandered off toward White's Club. I would have done it if Lady Annabella had required it of me. I cannot think why, but I am certain I would have.

Jane reached out from behind a potted palm in the Treavers' ballroom, grasped Bella's hand and tugged her behind the thing. "It is the best I can do. Privacy is not to be had anywhere tonight, let me tell you, Bella."

"I know," replied Bella with a nod. "I have been hoping to draw you aside all evening, but each time I began to do so, some gentleman came to lead you off to the floor."

"Yes, or to lead you off to the floor, Bella. You have become quite the object of the gentlemen's eyes, dearest. Uncle Hill would be so very happy for you."

"He did not come tonight, did he?" Bella asked. "He was not injured, Jane, when Arnold bolted?"

"Not injured, no. But he is at odds with his back again. From being jolted about so. He will not be up and about for at least two days, Mr. Shaughnessy says. That is why I prayed you would attend this ball. It will be our best opportunity, Bella, these next two days. Uncle Hill cannot possibly discover what we are about, tucked up in his bedchamber. And the house will be at sixes and sevens as well, because Mr. Sonnett has called upon Bow Street and they have sent a Runner who intends to interview everyone. The mere thought of it has raised such a hub-bub among the staff that even Lydie has been called upon to settle people's nerves. We must conceive of a plan and carry it through as soon as possible, Bella, before anyone finds time to take notice and stop us. Uncle Hill has had a missive from Sir Cyril that says he will be pleased to meet him at his house in Pickering Place on Wednesday."

"How do you know about the missive? Are you quite certain?"

"Quite. Uncle Hill abandoned it upon his bedside table. I brought him some books this afternoon and visited until he drifted off to sleep and then I peeked at it."

"Jane, you should not have done."

"I know, but how else was I to gain the information? I have been peeking at his messages ever since I first heard that he was determined to meet with Sir Cyril. My papa would think it quite my duty to do so, I am certain. It was he, after all, who told me to keep Uncle Hill away from that gentleman. Did you speak to Lord Barrington?"

"He adamantly refuses to escort us to The Pigeon Hole but he will be happy to go himself on our behalf."

"If that is not just like a man," mumbled Jane. "Well, I for one have no intention of allowing him to go in my stead."

"No, and neither have I," agreed Bella. "But, Jane, perhaps no one need go to The Pigeon Hole. We know now that Sir Cyril resides at Pickering Place. He would not have summoned Diamond to him there if he did not."

The frown that for a moment had puckered Jane's brow cleared at once. "Of course. And Pickering Place is a perfectly acceptable neighborhood. We must merely discover some excuse to take us driving in that direction."

"But we must discover an excuse to do so without my mama or your Lydie beside us," added Bella. "They will neither of them countenance our paying a morning call upon Sir Cyril Blythe."

Miss Winstead sneaked quietly out of the kitchen door of her little house in Curzon Street and kept to the shadows until she reached the tiny alley. Then she hurried through it until she emerged safely at the far end where she tugged her brother Michael's hat low over her brow and walked off with long, determined strides as she had often seen him do. In Michael's clothing, with his boots upon her feet and her hair tucked nicely up beneath his hat, Miss Winstead was quite certain she looked every inch the gentleman and that no one would think to accost her as they might well accost a young woman walking the streets alone at such an hour of the night.

Emily knew quite well that it was wrong in her to wish to do this thing. Her father would cry out against it had he still been alive and Michael would most certainly do the same. But it was not as if she would cause anyone the least bit of trouble. No. She merely wished to wander down Great Stanhope Street until she reached the magnificent facade of Derrinham House and then to take up a position across the way from it.

And perhaps I will see him drawing up before his door in one of his coaches, come from some fine ball or the theater or the opera. And he will descend into the street and glance in my direction. And his eyes will flash and he will tip his hat to me, she thought happily as she hurried along. And I will nod, just as I have seen all the gentlemen nod to one another. And no one will be the least harmed by it. And perhaps he will stroll across the cobbles to discover if I am one of his acquaintances and he will recognize who I am and invite me into his house.

It was what she wanted more than anything in all the world—to be recognized by this Duke of Derrinham and invited into his house. For as long as she could remember, it had been her dream. Her mama had often whispered to her in the night tales of Derrinham House and the little duke to whom it belonged. He is five years older than I, Emily thought, remembering. Five years is not so very much older. And I am certain we must have a great deal in common. We would find so very much to discuss. Much more than horses, she added silently but with a tiny giggle. How odd it had been to speak to him of his horses that afternoon in Hyde Park—and he not once knowing who she was. There had not been even a glimmer of recognition in those incredible sapphire eyes.

"And that is very sad," she whispered into the night around her. "That he did not know me that afternoon is very, very sad. But perhaps if he sees me again, just standing outside his house in Michael's clothes, he will know me."

By the time she reached Great Stanhope Street, her heels were very sore from rubbing up and down against the back of Michael's boots; her hands were perspiring inside his gloves; and her head was beginning to itch from the unaccustomed weight of her brother's beaver hat. But all of that was as nothing when she turned the corner and spied the windows of Derrinham House ablaze with lights midway down the block.

Derrinham set aside the volume and rubbed wearily at his eyes. It was outrageous, but the more he read of

The Corsair, the more he envisioned Bella upon her little mare confronting the furious Arnold. Her face had fairly blazed with excitement; her eyes had sparkled and flashed and danced like bubbling wine in the sunlight.

"And I am a perfect nodcock," he mumbled. "What the devil has gotten into me?"

"Pardon, your grace?"

"Nothing, Shaughnessy. Just passing through, are you?"

"Indeed, your grace. Returning your boots to the dressing room. Is there anything you wish? A cup of tea perhaps?"

"No, unless you can provide me with a new head."

"Now your head aches as well as your back?"

"No, Shaughnessy. My head hurts not at all. But it has apparently become stuffed full of the most incredible notions."

"Well, and one cannot blame you for that, your grace," Shaughnessy replied bracingly. "An attempt on a man's life might easily fill his head with incredible notions. And then to have that wretched Runner about all day disrupting the entire staff."

"Oh, that. I had almost forgotten."

"You had almost forgotten Mr. Farraday, your grace? But that is remarkable, because I am quite certain that I and every other person in this establishment shall see that man's face in our dreams tonight."

Derrinham thought to correct his valet and explain that it was not only Mr. Farraday, the Runner, that he had forgotten, but the entire idea that there had been an attack upon himself. But then he thought better of it. Shaughnessy would not in the least understand. He did not understand it himself. But the fact that someone had attempted to do him damage had faded like a puff of smoke into the night sky. All he seemed able to remember was Bella. Every single thing about Bella. From the look on her face to the tilting of her toes against the little mare's sides.

He was running mad. That was it, of course. Why, he had known Bella almost from the day she was born and never once had she occupied such space in his mind. It was almost as though he were—drawn to her in some way.

"Well, and I'll be deviled," muttered Shaughnessy, pausing in the midst of drawing the draperies across the final window. "And didn't the man say he would *not* stand lingering about and drawing attention to this house and its occupants? And by thunder, there he is peering up at our windows."

"Who?"

"That Mr. Farraday, your grace. Good heavens, he is taking a seat upon Mr. Palmer's stoop!"

"What? Mr. Palmer's stoop? Never, Shaughnessy. No Runner worth his salt would make himself so very conspicuous."

"Nevertheless, your grace, there he be."

Curious, Derrinham eased himself out of the bed, his back giving only the slightest twinge, and made his way to the window. "Well, I cannot guess who that gentleman might be, Shaughnessy," he offered, "but it is not our Mr. Farraday. Our Mr. Farraday is a good deal more rotund than that fellow there, I think."

"Perhaps, your grace, and perhaps not. There is not so much light that shines upon him there. One cannot perfectly tell."

"No. I expect one cannot. And I expect we ought to hope it is our Mr. Farraday, Shaughnessy, because if it is not, then it might well be the scoundrel who has taken it in mind to rid the world of me."

Mr. Shaughnessy's face turned the most peculiar color of fishbelly-white and he closed the draperies in a great rush.

* * *

The coach, when it finally came, had lights that sparkled like diamonds and a man in livery upon the box and a groom as well and two footmen at the rear. Oh, it was most remarkable. And the team that pulled it pranced and snorted in the misty air and arched their necks quite like all the horses in all the nursery tales she had ever heard. Miss Winstead's weary eyes opened wide at the sight of it. For a moment she quite thought that she had nodded off upon the stoop and that now she was in the midst of dreams. But she had not nodded off. She pinched herself to be certain of it.

It was the Duke of Derrinham. She shivered, chilled by her lengthy exposure to the fog and the brisk night air. And then a most audacious thought entered her mind. It was the same audacious thought that she had not been able to resist that day in the park. She would gain her feet and stroll over to the coach and introduce herself to the duke as brazen as could be. And this time, this time, she would introduce herself as she ought, not simply as Miss Winstead, for he obviously had not at all recognized her name.

She was just rising from her seat upon the stoop when one of the footmen leaped down from his perch and hurried around to open the door on the far side of the vehicle. Oh, if she did not hurry, she would miss his grace altogether!

Emily scrambled to her feet and dashed into the street.

"What the devil!" exclaimed the second footman, seeing the figure of a man rushing toward them. "James, a footpad! See to the ladies quickly!" And with that he abandoned his perch and went flying at Emily. The groom on the box, equally as tense as the footman because of the recent assault upon his grace, leaped from his perch to the cobbles.

Emily was stunned. She came to an immediate halt. Two ladies were hurrying up the steps and into the house on the arm of one of the footmen while two very large men were running directly at her. She abandoned all her bravery on the instant and turned and ran directly down the street, away from the men who chased her.

When at last she could run no more, Emily halted and stared back over her shoulder. There was no one there. She was so very relieved to discover that fact that she immediately sat down upon the nearest stoop and began to cry, her tears coming upon great, gulping sobs and feeling like sleet against her cheeks. Why had the duke sent his men chasing after her? Did he hate her so very much then? As much as Michael had said he would?

It was the most amazing opportunity and he knew it to be so. Fate. It was fate. Accosted by a footpad right outside their very door only a few hours ago, and now this. The Duke of Derrinham huddled immediately before him on the servants' staircase just below the door to the third floor, muttering mindlessly to himself. Who would blame him for thinking to protect the household and confronting an intruder in the dark stairwell, striking out at him?

The man reached into the pocket of his robe and took the ten-penny blade into his hand. Very quietly he moved down the steps to where the duke had crammed himself against the wall as though cowering in fear. Gripping the knife in a tense, anxious hand, he leaned down to tug the sleeping Derrinham into a standing position so that he would be certain to plunge the weapon in accurately and kill the duke with his first effort.

"No, please no! Do not!" gasped The Diamond, his arms abruptly flailing toward the man. "Stop it! Stop it! Do not! I will kill you! I will kill you myself!" And then the duke's eyes blinked open and his whole body shuddered and most suddenly he was staring in disbelief up into the man's eyes.

By the light of the single candle that rested above them on the stairs, Derrinham pulled himself into awareness and strove to recognize the pale face that glared at him in the shadows. "Who? What?" he stammered, shaking himself more fully awake. "James, is that you?"

Once again it was not to be. His stomach turned and twisted and ached. The knife slipped from his grasp to the step below. He cursed himself under his breath for being such a coward and a bungler. But he could not do it. He could not do it with those eyes looking at him in such astonishment.

"Where? Where am I?" asked the duke in a hoarse whisper.

"On the servants' staircase, your grace. Just below the third floor. You have been walking about in your sleep, I think."

"Yes, yes, I do sometimes," murmured Derrinham, his eyes still wide with amazement. "It is this house. Something in this house causes me to do it."

"Indeed, your grace?"

"Yes, but I do not know what it is. I am—I was—I did not intend to disturb you, James," he managed. "Thank you for waking me. I shall let you get back to your bed now."

"First I shall see you to yours," replied the first footman, stepping back up the staircase to retrieve his candle and then coming back down to grip the duke's elbow, steering him around the knife that barely glittered on the step below.

"I can find my own way, James," declared the duke, disgusted with himself and wishing to escape the footman as quickly as possible. He must think me a veritable corkbrain, thought Derrinham. Or worse yet, a great baby who flees from noises in the night. I shall never be able to look him in the face again without seeing the accusation there.

"I shall at least light your way," declared the footman, keeping step beside him. "Would you care for anything? Some brandy, perhaps? I should be happy to fetch it to you."

"No, thank you, James," muttered Derrinham as at last they reached the door to his chambers which stood open wide. "Did you think I was an intruder?"

"Indeed, your grace, at the first."

"That is why you had the knife?"

The first footman blanched. He had thought his weapon had gone completely unnoticed. "Yes, your grace," he managed in a quiet but firm tone. "That is exactly why I had the knife."

"Well, you ought not have come into that dark hall with but one candle and a blade," declared the duke softly. "You might well have been murdered, James. If you think there is an intruder you ought at the very least arouse someone to accompany you. I could never forgive myself were you to lose your life protecting this ugly old place from anyone. They are welcome to steal everything in it if they wish, so long as none of my people are harmed. Thank you," he added, entering his chamber and lighting a candle at the flame James carried. "Now take yourself off to bed and do not forget to retrieve your weapon."

For the longest time the Duke of Derrinham sat in an armchair before the cold hearth in his bedroom and stared at nothing. I should not have come, he thought despairingly. From the very first this house has brought me nothing but nightmares. I should pack up first thing in the morning and return to Twiney Hill. "I only came to help Bella," he whispered, running a hand through his hair. "And apparently she requires my assistance no longer. No one will call her The Hesitant Hedgehog now. Barrington is head over tail for her and Anders was willing to forsake the mill at Topeley Green to take the girl driving. And there are any number of others who are looking up and taking an interest." And Jane will be perfectly content to remain here under Miss Davies's care. She don't need me about to look after her, he added in silence.

But there was a nagging emptiness in the region of his heart when he thought of abandoning the field. He would not see Bella again until the Season had ended. And most likely she would be engaged to marry one or another of the gentlemen by then. Or she might even be married to someone by then and never return to her father's estate. The mere thought of that came near to overwhelming him. Never to see Bella again—his dearest Bella—the Bella who had trailed after him for so many years, had always grumped right back at him the moment he fell into his crotchets, always teased him out of his doldrums and gave him a perfect setdown every time he deserved one.

Truly, it was the most formidable thing, the thought of losing Bella. It would be much like losing his sister, Diana, all over again. Only it will be even worse, he thought despairingly. It will be even worse, because Diana was so much older and absent a good portion of my life but Bella—Bella has always been somewhere about me from the time I was eight.

He attempted with a grunt and a whispered curse to call himself to order, but he could not. The truth was that he was a selfish, spoilt man and he had not the least wish to lose Bella forever. But what was he to do? For all the years of her life, he had stood in the place of a brother to her. A brother would do all in his power to make her happy. And he wanted Bella to be happy. Truly he did. But to gain her happiness at the price of his own—he was not at all certain he could be so very noble.

He had been blind not to know that that was how it must be in the end. Blind and stupid. He had set out to make some other gentleman fall in love with Bella and had done a good job of it, too. And now he regretted every effort he had made. Now his very soul ached with the thought of losing her. What was wrong with him, anyway? Perhaps, he thought, perhaps it is the laudanum makes me think and feel such odd things. Perhaps I will feel differently in the morning.

Eight

It was all very flattering and exciting and did, indeed, when she stopped to consider it, set her head to spinning. Mr. Anders had begged to escort her to Drury Lane and Mr. Tottingham had applied for the privilege of accompanying her to the Fieldings' al fresco breakfast and a certain Mr. Davidson, whom she had met only days ago, had asked to take her riding along Rotten Row. Even Lord Nesbitt had apparently relented toward her, for he had invited her to make one of his party at Vauxhall Gardens. And any number of other gentlemen now chose to gather around her at the balls and *soirées* and routs. Her mama was in alt and always smiling these days. And though Bella found it a most pleasant change from the humiliation and loneliness of last Season, still, something about it all did not feel quite right.

Perhaps she could not truly revel in all the masculine attention she was drawing of late because Diamond's safety was constantly on her mind? Bella pondered the question quite seriously over tea and toast with marmalade that morning as she sat across from her mama at the breakfast table.

Yes, she thought. Most likely that is the very reason. Well, at least this afternoon some of my worries will be laid to rest. Thank goodness that Lord Barrington has agreed to abandon the Promenade and drive myself and Jane to Pickering Place instead. I do hope Mama does not discover our little subterfuge before we have done the thing.

If only Sir Cyril Blythe will speak with us. Though how we are to discover the correct Winstead without letting on that we are seeking the person for the purpose of destroying Diamond's need to meet with the man himself, I cannot think. Still, we will develop a plan of some sort along the way. Lord Barrington is very good at plans, I think. And once we have the information and are able to contact this Winstead person, I shall be able to lay all of my fears for Diamond aside and quite enjoy the remainder of the Season.

It was all Bella could do not to spend the entire morning lingering near the front door, waiting for Lord Barrington and Jane to arrive. There were no morning calls to be paid, no shopping to be done, and Bella could not at all concentrate upon her stitchery or sit in one place long enough to read.

"Bella, whatever has gotten into you?" asked her mama at last. "You are fidgeting about like a hound in honey."

"It is nothing, Mama. I am only impatient for Lord Barrington to come and fetch me for the Promenade."

Lady Meade's eyes lit up at once. Now this was her Bella! The shy, solemn, frightened child who had suffered through last Season was gone for good, she was certain. God bless you, your grace, she thought with a distinct fondness for the duke. You have worked magic for our girl.

It was amazing, really, Lady Meade reflected as she beamed upon Bella and then turned back to her embroidery. Who would ever have thought that the poor little Duke of Derrinham, after all the scandal and the horror of his childhood, would have grown into such a fine and considerate gentleman? Oh, he was gruff and grouchy at times, of course. But just look at what he had done for Bella out of the goodness of his heart. "We were right to agree to bury the thing for good," she murmured to herself as she selected the perfect shade of green for an oak leaf. "It was best for the *ton* and best for the duke. Thank goodness everyone has kept their silence."

"What, Mama?" asked Bella, tilting her head one way and then another before the bevelled glass in the morning room. "I am afraid I was not paying the least attention."

"Oh, nothing, my dear," replied Lady Meade quickly, realizing only then that she had spoken aloud. "Lord Barrington will be here shortly, Bella, and I am certain he will find that confection most alluring."

Bella did wonder as she stared into the bevelled glass if the cherries upon her hat brim would have the same effect upon Lord Barrington as they had had upon The Diamond. If they did, perhaps they would serve to turn Sir Cyril up sweet as well. Sir Cyril Blythe, after all, could not possibly be as black as gossip painted him. No one could be as black as that. Bella pinned some hope upon the cherries to soften the old villain and perhaps to distract him from pondering over the reason that she and Jane hoped to locate a particular Winstead.

We must discover all that we can about this Winstead person and quickly, too, she told herself. Diamond will go to visit Sir Cyril else, and Jane's papa said that that would be dangerous. Perhaps this Winstead person is the one who attempted to—to—oh, it is so very hard to think of anyone at all attempting to take Diamond's life! But if Sir Cyril is at home we shall settle all this afternoon. I am certain of it. "And Diamond will be safe," she whispered to the pretty young lady in the looking glass, "and I shall get on with my Season and feel much differently about Lord Barrington and the others, I am sure."

When Lord Barrington at last appeared, he was dressed to the nines in a double-breasted morning coat of blue superfine with large silver buttons over a gold waistcoat embroidered with silver apples. His hair was combed into the windblown style and his cravat tied *en cascade*. His hazel eyes glowed as Bella came down the staircase to take his arm, the cherries upon her hat brim jiggling merrily.

"I cannot think this is the best way," Barrington murmured as he settled onto the banquette across from Jane and Bella and directed his coachman to drive straight to Pickering Place. "It would be much better if I went to speak to the man alone and you ladies remained in the landau."

"No, it would not," replied Jane stubbornly. "The duke is my uncle and I am the one charged to keep him away from Sir Cyril."

"And I have promised to assist her in it," added Bella.

"Still, neither of you ought to be calling upon that old scoundrel. I am not at all certain that even my presence will protect your reputations should word of this visit get out."

"Who will even know that we have gone to pay the man a call?" asked Bella innocently.

"Sir Cyril," replied Barrington.

"Ha! As if we fear anything that he will say!" Jane exclaimed with a determined tilt to her chin.

"Well, you should," advised his lordship, noting the color that rose high upon Miss May's sculpted cheekbones. "You ought to know better than anyone that appearances are everything, Miss May. Your father is a diplomat and that is one lesson he ought to have taught you."

"There is nothing whatever wrong in our visiting Sir Cyril Blythe in Pickering Place with you to lend us countenance," replied Jane. "I am quite certain there is not."

Derrinham could not believe his eyes. He had been on his way to indulge himself in the joy of visiting Madame

Tussaud's figure museum—a joy which he had never shared with even his closest friends, but one in which he indulged himself every time he came to London—when he had glared ahead into the bright sunlight, blinked, and glared again. "Well, I'll be deviled," he muttered and angrily urged his horses forward until he was directly behind Barrington's parked vehicle. "Hold 'em, Toby. I shall return in a moment," he called to his tiger as he leaped from his curricle and rushed across the flagway and up a short flight of steps to a bright red door.

Ignoring the knocker, he pounded upon the solid oak with his fist. Surprisingly, the door opened almost immediately, and there in the grand hall before him, just beyond the butler, stood Jane and Bella and Lord Barrington, gazing back at him over their shoulders with individual expressions of astonishment.

"What in the name of all that's holy do you mean by bringing Bella and Jane to this place, Barrington?" the duke exclaimed hotly, striding past the butler, spinning Lord Barrington around, and only just managing to refrain from giving the viscount a facer. "You said that you were taking them to drive in the Park. This is most definitely not Hyde Park!"

"N-no," stuttered Barrington.

"No. Nor is it a place any of you have business being. Jane, Bella, go out to my curricle at once!"

"Absolutely not!" exclaimed Jane, stamping one foot upon the floor. "We will not even consider it until you release Lord Barrington's lapels, Uncle Hill."

"Jane and I are going nowhere," Bella declared.

"Fine," growled the duke. "Stay and watch me blacken both this rascal's daylights for him then."

Sir Cyril's butler, Twimbly, harrumphed quite loudly, but apparently the duke chose to ignore the sound. Twimbly closed the door and harrumphed again.

"Do cease making those sounds," tossed Bella at him.

"A bit of harrumphing is not going to make the least impression upon Diamond and will only serve to urge him on."

"Yes, quite," agreed Jane with a nod. "Uncle Hill, do climb down out of the boughs. It is not Lord Barrington's fault that we are here. He did not at all wish to come."

"He did not?" Derrinham's gaze left Barrington and traveled to Jane, but his hands remained fastened to Barrington's lapels.

"No, he did not. Bella talked the poor gentleman into it."

"Bella? You talked Barrington into bringing you here? Here?"

"Well, I could not convince him to take us to The Pigeon Hole," Bella declared hotly. "Luckily, Jane—"

"The Pigeon Hole?" The Duke of Derrinham's eyebrows rose so high as to almost disappear beneath his curls. His hands released Barrington's lapels and took up residence on his hips and his eyes widened considerably more than they had already.

"What the devil is going on down there?" asked a querulous voice from the top of the stairs. "Twimbly, what are you about to open my door to a gang of ruffians?"

All eyes looked upward. The duke's lips straightened into a thin, determined line. Barrington brushed at the strands of hair that had fallen into his eyes to get a clearer view. Jane gave the tiniest of squeaks and Bella took a step backward to get a better look. "You are Sir Cyril Blythe?" she asked.

"Indeed."

He was not at all a tall man. And he was very thin. His hair was steel gray and his eyes, as much as Bella could see of them, were dark and squinty. His face sagged in places and wrinkled in others. Dressed in a pea green coat and fawn breeches, he looked more an aging leprechaun than the demon rumor named him.

"Derrinham," he said, his eyes drawn to the duke. "You are days early for our appointment. And you have brought friends. How kind of you to think to brighten an old man's life."

The sound of his voice, unlike his harmless appearance, sent a chill deep into Bella's bones.

"I have not brought anyone," The Diamond replied. "I was driving down the street and saw them enter this house. I came to escort them out again."

"Escort them out again? I will not hear of it. I cannot think why it did never occur to me, but it will be most entertaining, Derrinham, to meet your friends."

"We are engaged for Wednesday, Blythe," responded the duke. "I shall return then alone. Go," he urged Barrington who stood frozen, staring upward. "Take Bella and Jane from here at once. I shall follow in a moment."

"No, no, no, no," droned the gentleman at the top of the stairs. "I will have you all for tea. Bring them up, Twimbly."

The duke opened his mouth to protest, saw the fear in Jane's eyes, and turned to peer over his shoulder. The butler was holding an enormous horse pistol trained upon his back.

"You would not dare, Blythe," he observed coolly. "Not at all the hospitable thing to do."

Sir Cyril Blythe laughed. "Correct, dear boy. And I am nothing if not hospitable. Especially to you, your grace. You cannot think how surprised and gratified I was to receive your note. Come up. Come up. All of you."

Sir Cyril Blythe's house in Pickering Place is not at all moldering or falling to ruin as it has been rumored to be, Bella thought as she took The Diamond's arm and ascended the curving staircase. "That is a Hogarth," she whispered, pointing to one of the paintings that adorned the stairway wall.

"Quite," nodded the duke. "What are you three doing here?"

"I—we—Jane overheard you insisting that you wished to contact Sir Cyril. And then, she accidentally read his message telling you to come to Pickering Place."

"Overheard? Accidentally?" The Diamond gazed back over his shoulder at his niece ascending the staircase on Lord Barrington's arm, her chin lifted in spirited determination.

"Very well, Uncle Hill," Jane declared. "I eavesdropped and I peeked. But it was all for your own good. Papa gave me strict orders before I departed Vienna that I was to keep you far from Sir Cyril Blythe and I promised that I would."

The four followed their host into a drawing room of white and gold and seated themselves upon chairs upholstered in rich brocade. "Tea, Twimbly," intoned Sir Cyril, taking a stand before the marble fireplace. "And be quick about it."

They all waited in uneasy silence until the tea tray arrived and the butler again departed.

"It is most unfortunate," droned Sir Cyril, directing Jane to pour out, "that it is not Wednesday. Michael will be here Wednesday. But you will return then, Derrinham, will you not? This afternoon I shall merely take advantage of the opportunity to come to know your niece. Lady Diana's child, is she not? Of course she is. You were possessed of only one sister."

"Michael who?" asked Derrinham.

"Michael Winstead, of course. You did write that you wished to hear what I once promised to tell you concerning the Winsteads, did you not?"

Bella, having handed the tea around, returned to her seat beside Jane and studied Sir Cyril thoughtfully. He

did not look at all like a leprechaun now as he studied
The Diamond. He looked like a gleeful troll. She could
almost see him jumping up and down in some moldy
old ruin of a castle and clapping his hands in joy while
tiny animals lay dead at his feet.

There is something stinks about him, she thought.
Something rotten deep inside. One can see the dissipation
in the broken vessels of his face and the yellow of his
teeth and the muddy brown of his eyes, but there is something much, much worse beneath. I was wrong. The gossips are close to the truth. He may well be a demon from
the very depths of Hades.

Junius Farraday doffed his hat and ran his fingers
through his hair in agitation. Someone had come close
enough to the duke to know which horse he would ride
and which gear he would use and to insert a hat pin
inside his saddle blanket and cut his cinch, which meant
he had come very close indeed. Yet not one of the staff
had noticed any stranger at all near the stables. Nor did
it seem likely that any of the servants themselves held
any enmity against his grace. Most of them, in fact, had
come into his employ but recently, hired by his solicitor.
And his solicitor, thought Farraday, appears a very careful gentleman. Still, if a person could get so close to
Derrinham once, he would likely do so again and the
next time—the next time—he might well succeed in
snuffing out the duke's light forever. And Junius Farraday
did not take kindly to the thought of seeing The Diamond's light abruptly snuffed. No, he did not.

Everyone at Bow Street thought that he had petitioned
Sir John to be sent out upon this case because, like Ran-
dall and Johnson and McCarty, he admired The Diamond
and the courage he had shown during the fire at Danfurth
House, but that was not at all the reason. No, it was not.

His determination to be the one to aid The Diamond arose from a very different time and place.

To this very day Junius Farraday could see the lad running to him out of the night and could feel the lad's hands, slick with blood, tugging at his own great mitt and dragging him toward that horrid house. Old Bobbie Oakes had drunk himself silly and had been dozing inside his box when the child had come. And seeing only Junius Farraday, the boy had thought him the Charlie and pleaded for his help. And he had gone with the boy, too, he had, because it would have taken forever to raise Oakes from his sleep.

And now the lad was in trouble again. And he, Junius Farraday—whom The Diamond did not remember—he, Junius Farraday, was no longer some mere mortal stripling mistaken for the Watch, but a Bow Street Runner. And he had a better knowledge of what to do about things this time. And he would do everything he knew how to do, too. Everything.

Junius Farraday stared up at the veritable palace across the cobbles from where he stood leaning against an iron rail in Pickering Place and muttered. He had known the minute he had seen The Diamond's curricle racing up the street that there was trouble brewing, but he had not expected The Diamond to go stomping into that particular establishment. Mr. Sonnett and Mr. Shaughnessy had both assured him that The Diamond's appointment with Sir Cyril was not until Wednesday, and Farraday had planned to have a private word or two with the old knight before then and to discover if the butler's and the valet's fears of Blythe were based upon anything at all substantial. If they were, he would certainly go to The Diamond himself and warn him of it. But there it was. Somehow the two old gentlemen had gotten it wrong, and The Diamond was likely meeting with the man at this very moment.

* * *

"I cannot conceive why you are so overjoyed to see me, Blythe," the duke sighed, sipping at his tea. "No more than I could conceive why you dogged my heels my first Season in London. And though I shall be most interested to discover the reason for it, I doubt these young ladies or Barrington will find it at all amusing, so we shall not speak of it until Wednesday as we planned, eh? Now, as for urging us up here at the point of a pistol. Have you run completely mad?"

"Mad? Me? Never," replied Blythe. "It was merely a joke, your grace. There is no pistol holding you here now, is there? No, of course not. I was a great friend of your father's, you know. You do not remember me?"

"No. Diana spoke of you from time to time."

"Ah, the lovely Diana. Now *she* remembered me. I did never express to you my sympathy for your loss." The muddy brown eyes left Derrinham and turned upon the two young ladies. "Her daughter looks much like her. And Lady Annabella—you are Meade's daughter, you say?"

"Yes," replied Bella, staring the old scoundrel straight in the eye. "And my papa will not at all like to hear that your butler has pointed a pistol at me."

"No," grinned Sir Cyril. "I expect he will not. No more than he will like to hear that you came to this place. And Barrington, your mama will not be at all pleased with you, will she? A regular harridan, your mama, and quite despises me. She is mistaken in my character, however. Quite mistaken. Ah, I know just the topic for discussion," Blythe added with a snap of his fingers. "It comes to me when I think of all your mamas and papas whom I remember very well. Let us speak, my darlings, of The Society of Lost Souls."

"The what?" Bella stared at the man over her teacup.

"The Society of Lost Souls, my dear. A quaint little gentlemen's club. I cannot believe that your papa has never told you of it. It no longer exists, more's the pity. But you might find a discussion of it most interesting. I have always found it to arouse my curiosity."

"Oh, I do not think so," murmured Jane. "It was a horrible thing and is best forgotten."

"No, no, on the contrary, my dear. Only ask your uncle. It was quite a wonderful club, really, until things got out of hand."

"Never heard of it," drawled the duke.

"Never heard of it? Are you certain, your grace? Your father was one of its founders, you know."

"Never said a word about it to me," responded Derrinham with a stiff smile. "He died when I was five, Blythe. How many gentlemen do you know discussed their clubs with five-year-olds?"

"Only one, your grace. Only one. Here, what's that?" Sir Cyril Blythe rose from his chair and hurried toward the doorway. "Twimbly, what the devil is all that ruckus?" he shouted into the corridor. From beneath the drawing room, raised voices and a most unusual pounding sound could be heard in the front hall.

"Now," murmured the duke, rising, "would be an advantageous time to take our leave. Bella, come. Barrington, give Jane your arm. I do not trust this man as far as I can spit."

"Indeed," nodded Barrington as he stood and escorted Jane to the doorway.

The Duke of Derrinham grasped Sir Cyril's shoulders and without the least effort moved the man aside so that Jane and Barrington might exit. "I thank you for your hospitality, Blythe," he said with a cool smile, taking Bella's hand tightly into his own. "But apparently someone else is attempting to gain an audience with you, eh? I shall return on Wednesday without these children and we will discuss the Winsteads and The Society for as long as you wish."

Jane stopped, tugging Lord Barrington to a halt upon the staircase. "Why, that is Mr. Farraday, the Runner," she whispered, staring. "Why ever is he pounding that stick upon the parquet?"

"To give old Twimbly a hard time, it seems," whispered Barrington in return.

"Go!" urged the duke from behind them. "Out of here now before something else absurd happens and we are persuaded by the point of another weapon to accept more of Blythe's hospitality."

"I'll be d-deuced," mumbled Barrington as his coachman pulled the landau out into traffic. "The Society of Lost Souls. And I always thought it was just a great deal of nonsense that Nanny recited to the nursery set to keep us in line and shivering in our shoes."

"Likewise," nodded Jane. "I cannot think that the man was speaking seriously. You do not believe that there actually was such a thing, do you, Lord Barrington? Much less believe that my grandpapa was one of its founders?"

"No," Lord Barrington replied with a shake of his head. "Sir Cyril has attics to let. Everyone knows that to be the case. He has gotten reality and fairy tales all jumbled together."

"What is it you are speaking of?" asked Bella, her glance carrying beyond Jane and Lord Barrington to the duke, who had pulled his curricle into traffic directly behind them. "I am certain I have never before heard of such a society in the nursery or elsewhere."

"Which is one of the problems of being a country girl," said Jane with a shake of her golden curls. "Had you been raised in London for any period of time, Bella, you would know of The Society of Lost Souls."

"A tale told by night to frighten babes," explained Lord Barrington. "I am certain that if that moonstruck old knight had not mentioned it, I would never have given it one more thought for the remainder of my years."

"Blood and guts," murmured Jane on a bit of a giggle.

"What?" Bella's glance flew to her at once.

" 'And blood and guts devour raw, to feed their minds, to find their souls.' Do not tell me you have never even heard the rhyme, Bella?" Jane said before reciting in a breathy whisper:

> *Beware the mists on London Bridge*
> *'Tis all, my lad, ye need to know*
> *And take ye home on wary feet*
> *Before the hour of three shall toll.*

Barrington finished in an eerie, guttural tone.

> *For there and then their feast begins*
> *The lost, the damned, the wretched, all*
> *And blood and guts devour raw*
> *To feed their minds, to find their souls.*

"Oh, what a dreadful poem," declared Bella with a shiver. "How do you both come to know it?"

"It is called 'The Society of Lost Souls' and our nurse was accustomed to recite it to myself and my brothers at bedtime," grinned Barrington. "To put the fear of God into us, I think."

"It was Uncle Hill himself taught it to me," smiled Jane, reaching across to give Bella's hand a pat. "He was thirteen at the time and read it in some book. And when I recited it for Mama, I thought she would have an apoplexy right on the spot. But it is only a rhyme and nothing more."

"Unless, of course," added Barrington, his smile fading somewhat, "Sir Cyril was not hoaxing us and The Society of Lost Souls truly did once exist."

Nine

"I do not care in the least," declared Miss May as she and Bella stood staring at a china pug dog in one of the shops along Bond Street the following afternoon. "Uncle Hill may ring peals over me until the cows come home. It will not make one bit of difference. There is nothing he can say to stop me."

"I expect he was most angry," sighed Bella.

"Oh, extremely. But I do not give a fig, because now I know how dreadful Sir Cyril Blythe truly is and I shall try even harder to prevent Uncle Hill's meeting with him on Wednesday. At least we now know which Winstead it is we need to find. We must locate this Mr. Michael Winstead, Bella, before Wednesday. If he will come to Derrinham House to speak with Uncle Hill, there will be no need whatsoever for Uncle Hill to keep his appointment with Sir Cyril."

Bella nodded. "But whom shall we ask about him, Jane?"

"Everyone we know," replied Jane, her glance wandering to Miss Davies and Lady Meade, who were conversing only a few feet from the two young ladies.

"Well, we must begin immediately then," smiled Bella. "It is already Friday. Look there," she added on a little gasp. "Just entering Rundell and Bridges. That is the very young lady."

"Which very young lady?"

"Miss Winstead—the very Miss Winstead who addressed Diamond in the Park. What wonderful luck. We shall begin our search by asking questions of her."

"Which is exactly what I suggested more than a week ago," giggled Jane. "And which you convinced me would be little more than useless."

"Yes, well, that was before I discovered what an awful person Sir Cyril truly is. I doubt he would tell us the truth even if he could. Come, Jane, there is a particular snuffbox you are interested in purchasing to add to your Uncle Hill's collection. It will be his birthday soon."

"Uncle Hill has a collection of snuffboxes?"

"No, but your Miss Davies does not know that and neither does my mama."

The entrance of the four ladies into Rundell and Bridges caused Miss Emily Winstead to turn her head for the briefest of moments, and recognizing Bella, she inhaled a tiny gasp.

"What is it, Miss Winstead?" queried Mr. Willis, who was at that moment just setting Emily's mama's pearl necklace down upon the countertop. "Are you not feeling just the thing? Do have a seat, my dear. Cannot have Michael's sister fainting in our shop, now can we?"

"Oh," sighed Emily, pulling herself together immediately. "I am not feeling faint, Mr. Willis. It was merely—merely the thought of needing to part with Mama's pearls."

"You need not part with them forever," smiled Mr. Willis condescendingly. "Merely for a day or two until the clasp can be fixed. I cannot think how it came to break, but most assuredly it is one of our own and we will stand behind it."

"Mr. Willis, do you know the ladies who have just entered?" Emily asked with a glance toward the little group.

"No, not at all. But then, I am generally in the back

with your brother and rarely see our customers. Is Michael feeling the least bit better?"

Emily turned back to stare wide-eyed at the man.

"He has been ill near three weeks and Mr. Rundell has quite determined to send his own physician to attend him if he does not come about soon."

Emily felt the veriest fluttering in the pit of her stomach. She knew she was not highly intelligent, but she was not a birdwit either. Something was very wrong. Michael had lied to her. He had not left his position at the jewelers' shop and taken a new position! "He is—he is—not as poorly as at first," murmured Miss Winstead haltingly. "Truly, I do not think he will require the attentions of Mr. Rundell's physician. I shall come back on Monday, shall I, Mr. Willis? For the pearls?"

"Indeed. And do give Michael my best. We miss him here. He is the best jewel cutter in all of London."

"Yes, yes, I will tell him he is sadly missed," agreed Miss Winstead, stepping toward the door.

Bella, standing with her mama just behind Jane and Miss Davies, noted that Miss Winstead had completed her conversation with the clerk and called out to her. "Miss Winstead! Imagine meeting you here! What a wonderful coincidence! Mama," she continued, taking Miss Winstead's arm. "You have heard me speak of Miss Winstead, no doubt."

Lady Meade, who could not at all remember her daughter speaking of such a person, nevertheless nodded politely.

"You will not mind, Mama, if Miss Winstead and I have a coze for a moment, will you?"

"No, no, go right ahead," acquiesced Lady Meade.

"You do remember me, do you not, Miss Winstead?" whispered Bella as she literally dragged Miss Winstead to the side of the showroom. "I was with the Duke of

Derrinham in Hyde Park when you stopped to comment upon his horses."

Emily nodded. "You had cherries upon your bonnet."

"Yes, I did. I am Lady Annabella Faire. My papa is the Earl of Meade. I hope you will not think me forward, but there is something I must ask you."

"Wh-what?"

Bella noted a slight flush rise to Miss Winstead's cheeks as the remainder of her face paled. "You do think me forward," Bella sighed. "Oh, I knew you would. But do not be frightened, Miss Winstead, I am not moon-mad, I assure you. I only wish to know if you are related to a Mr. Michael Winstead?"

"Michael?"

"Indeed. That is the name I have been given. Of course, there are most likely any number of Michael Winsteads in London."

"No, there is only my brother that I know of and my papa. But my papa has passed on."

"I see." Bella's hopes rose, but she could not for a moment believe that she and Jane could be so lucky as to have located the correct Winsteads on the first attempt. "And might your papa have been acquainted with the seventh Duke of Derrinham?"

Emily nodded shyly.

"How wonderful!" exclaimed Bella. "You are the very person Jane and I have been searching for. It is most important that you speak to your brother, Miss Winstead, and ask him to send a message to Derrinham House requesting an interview with the duke before Wednesday. His grace is most interested to discover the relationship between your two families and unless your brother comes to him, his grace must go to Sir Cyril Blythe to discover the information. And we—his niece Jane and I—that is Jane looking at the snuffboxes—we do not wish for the duke to go to Sir Cyril because he is not at all a nice man."

"No, he is not," whispered Emily, surprised at herself for saying so. She had always been rather frightened by Sir Cyril, but she had never before thought to tell anyone else that she did not like the man. "He is most intimidating."

"I should say so," agreed Bella. "Will you speak to your brother, Miss Winstead?"

"I—are you certain the duke will wish to invite Michael into his home?"

"Why, yes. Most certainly." Bella studied the girl with a perplexed frown. "Why would he not?"

"Perhaps he holds our family in abhorrence."

"In abhorrence? Why ever would he do that?"

"I do not know," sighed Miss Winstead, her great blue eyes looking sad and confused. "Perhaps because my papa wished to kill his papa?"

Bella stared at the young woman nonplussed. "Your papa wished to—but why? He did not kill the old duke, did he?"

"Oh, no, though a good many people suspected that he had. But Sir Cyril stood as witness for him in the court. Papa and Sir Cyril were together at the very time it happened."

The Diamond's papa had been murdered? Bella's heart flew to her throat. She had never once thought—well, but she had never thought about The Diamond's mama and papa at all. She had always known they were dead. She had never questioned how their deaths had come to be.

"I must go now," Miss Winstead murmured. "I shall tell Michael if I see him, but I do not know if I will see him before Wednesday. Do you think," she added on a tiny breath. "Do you think that I might be invited to Derrinham House? That I might be of assistance?"

Bella could not think what to say. The yearning for

the answer to be yes was so very evident in that young woman's wonderful eyes.

"No, I expect not," sighed Miss Winstead before Bella's lips could form a reply. "I do not know very much at all about what happened. And even if I should be invited, Michael would not allow me to go."

Miss Winstead was gone out the door before her words were spoken and they barely floated back to Bella upon the air.

Junius Farraday lifted a tankard in The Broken Crown and took a deep draft of ale. Across the table from him, Mr. Shaughnessy did the same.

"I did not recognize you at first," Mr. Shaughnessy said, setting his tankard aside.

"I was a deal younger then," grinned Farraday.

"Yes, were not we all? You have spoken with Sir Cyril?"

"I have more than spoken with the old knight. I have rung a regular peal over that hoary old head. I said that he had best not plague the duke or he might himself be suspected of seeking his grace's life. And I informed him that I should lay it directly at his doorstep if the little duke should come to any knowledge of things best left forgotten and be harmed by it."

"And did he take you quite seriously?"

"I have not the faintest idea. But I took myself seriously, I promise you. Junius Farraday is not about to let The Diamond be harmed by any man and that's a fact."

"I depend upon it, Mr. Farraday. We all do. Mr. Sonnett explained to you, did he not, about the man lounging across the way from Derrinham House the other night? The one who ran off when he was challenged?"

"Yes, but I doubt it was the fellow we seek."

"Yes, so do I," sighed Shaughnessy, taking another

pull on his ale. "Much too blatant. Anyone sneaky enough to discover which horse his grace would ride, and then sabotage his gear that way, would not be likely to be so blatant as to linger about outside the house for his next attempt."

"No," concurred Junius Farraday. "I think it was someone in the house made that first attempt."

"Someone in the house? A member of the staff?"

"Um-hmmm. Thought at first one of the grooms or the stable boy, but they came up with you from Twiney Hill."

"Indeed. I cannot imagine any one of them attempting to do the duke harm."

"No, nor waiting until they reached London to do it. A deal easier to promote an accident in the country and no one the least bit suspicious. And likely, no one around to notice the evidence, like that pin and the cinch, before the villain had an opportunity to remove it."

Mr. Shaughnessy nodded. "I had not thought of that."

"I had," muttered Mr. Farraday. "I am thinking it is one of the new staff. But I'm damned can I figure out which one. I have been speaking with Mr. Piermont and checking out the letters of reference they all gave him. So far I ain't found one who has not come from where he or she says they have come. But I think it best that you keep a close eye upon the duke whenever he is at home, Mr. Shaughnessy. A very close eye. Things can happen to a man in his own home."

"Mr. Sonnett and I intend to do just that," declared Shaughnessy. "Indeed, Mr. Farraday, we intend to do just that."

The fairy lights twinkled along the walks and the music of Handel floated upon the air as Lord Nesbitt's party took their places in one of the supper boxes Friday evening at Vauxhall. Miss Davies, who had agreed to chaperone the entire group, was delighted to be in attendance. Lord Nesbitt and his friend Mr. Baylor were in high good spirits. Lord Barrington's cousin, Miss Octavia DeLacey, and her beau Mr. Cottsworth had put on their best faces and their finest clothes and everyone of the party intended, Bella could see, to make the most of the occasion.

"I am so pleased to make your acquaintance," offered Miss DeLacey. "Cousin James has spoken of you so very often. You have quite swept him off his feet, Lady Annabella."

Bella flushed at the words and did not know how to respond.

"As I recall, Bella did rather knock his feet out from under him," giggled Jane.

The memory of the incident at Hatchard's came immediately to Bella's mind and she laughed prettily, her dimple flashing enticingly in the lamplight.

"I did hear something to that effect," murmured Lord Nesbitt, gazing wonderingly at that dimple. "Miss DeLacey, will you have some punch? Miss May? Cottsworth, attend to the ladies and cease gazing off into nowhere as though you are under a spell."

"What? Oh! Pardon," muttered Mr. Cottsworth. "It is merely—is that not the oddest-looking gentleman you have ever seen? There, at the far edge of the Grove. Is it a child, do you think, in gentlemen's clothing?"

All eyes looked in the direction Mr. Cottsworth indicated.

"Well, I'll be," declared Mr. Baylor, his fine gray eyes crinkling with amusement. "I daresay we are being spied upon, Nesbitt. Is it someone you did not invite this evening?"

"He is staring directly at us," murmured Miss DeLacey. "Of all things! Is it someone you know, Lord Nesbitt?"

"Not I. Never saw the fellow before in all my days. A little fellow, too. I think you are correct, Cottsworth. It is a child. See how outsized his coat is. Why, the sleeves are rolled up and still one cannot see his hands, merely his fingers."

A gasp escaped both Miss Davies's and Jane's lips.

"Miss May? Miss Davies?" Lord Nesbitt's voice took on a tone of concern. "Is there something wrong?"

"It cannot possibly be," declared Miss Davies quite loudly. "We are mistaken, Jane. He quite resembles the footpad who thought to attack us outside Derrinham House that night, but he cannot possibly be."

"You were attacked?" asked all the gentlemen in one voice.

"You were not harmed?" asked Mr. Cottsworth.

"The footpad looked like that gentleman who is still staring at us?" asked Mr. Baylor.

"Your supper," interrupted a waiter, setting an array of chicken, beef, ham and pastries before them and offering them wine and more arrack punch. By the time the waiter had disappeared, the ill-dressed man had disappeared as well.

"I am quite certain it was not the same person," declared Miss Davies, turning her attention to her supper. To say the truth, she had rather enjoyed the sudden lunging of the gentlemen to attention. They would each of them have climbed over the box rail and given chase, she thought with a glow of amusement in her eyes, just to impress the young ladies. "No, not the same person at all, Jane," she continued. "And besides, we were not attacked. Whoever it was simply ran toward our coach and then ran away again. It was a veritable nonattack if ever there was one."

"Well, I am glad to hear that," proclaimed Miss DeLacey with feeling. "To think of footpads running loose in Great Stanhope Street! My goodness, where is a person to be safe?"

"Quite right, my dear," agreed Mr. Cottsworth, swallowing a bit of shaved ham. "Quite right. But you are always safe in my company, I assure you."

"Yes," grinned Lord Nesbitt, "so long as there is a proper chaperone beside you, Miss DeLacey."

"Well, I'll be d-deuced!" exclaimed Mr. Baylor, a most amused expression upon his open countenance. "I say, Nesbitt, we are about to have company."

"Company?"

"Indeed," he replied, gaining his feet. "Up, Nesbitt; up, Cottsworth; good evening, your grace," he finished all on one breath as the Duke of Derrinham strolled up to their box.

He was hatless and his curls shimmered in the lamplight. His eyes sparkled like the starlight in the night sky above and his smile set a spark alight in Bella's heart.

"Evening," he said with a nod. "Bella, Jane, Miss DeLacey, Miss Davies, gentlemen. Having a fine time, are you? They are about to ring for the Cascade. I expect you have all seen the Cascade, though, and are bored with it."

"Are you not bored with it, Duke?" asked Miss Davies with the most knowing smile upon her face.

"Well, I might be, but I have not seen it since Season before last, and everyone assures me it has undergone any number of changes. I rather thought I would take a look at it." It was at that very moment that the bell announcing the opening of the Cascade, a marvelous piece of magic that portrayed a miller's hut complete with waterfall and turning wheel, rang through the Gardens. "Will you join me?" he asked with a boyish smile.

"No, no, I believe I will stay and finish my supper," declined Miss Davies, "but perhaps the others—"

Jane was about to accept readily, but a kick under the

table from Miss Davies turned her acceptance into a negative shake of her head. Miss DeLacey, who felt Mr. Cottsworth take definite possession of her arm, declined as well. Mr. Baylor, with a wink at Miss Davies, said that he and Nesbitt were filled to the gills with looking at the blasted thing.

"I have never ever seen it," sighed Bella, gazing about the box and then at the duke. "But I expect it would be most impolite to abandon the rest of my party."

"Not at all," Miss Davies spoke up. "It is Vauxhall, not a formal dinner, my dear. Certainly his grace may escort you to the Cascade and when you have looked your fill, he will return you to us. Quite proper."

Jane stared at Miss Davies wide-eyed. Lord Nesbitt stared at Derrinham with a puzzled expression and Mr. Baylor barely suppressed the urge to chuckle. Miss DeLacey and Mr. Cottsworth merely appeared pleasantly disinterested as Bella exited the box on the duke's arm and they strolled off.

"What think you of Nesbitt?" the duke asked, his gaze fastened upon the scene before him. "Do you like him, Bella?"

"Why, I hardly know. This is the very first time I have ever gone anywhere in his company."

"Oh. He is quite handsome, though, don't you think?" asked the duke, his gaze never leaving the turning mill wheel and the tiny waterfall. "And he is honorable and upstanding and a devil of a horseman."

"Is he?"

"Yes. You do find Barrington interesting, I think. Betting at White's gives you ten-to-one odds of bringing Barrington up to scratch before the close of the Season. The odds were against you with Anders, though, until that nonsense with Arnold occurred. Then they rose highly in your favor because Anders is horse-mad and you were so magnificent."

"I was?" smiled Bella softly. "Magnificent?"

"Certainly. Of course, you have been magnificent upon horseback forever, Bella. Since you were seven, if I recall."

"But there are no wagers concerning myself and Lord Nesbitt?"

"There will be by tomorrow afternoon, my dear. Shall I come tell you the odds?"

"Yes."

"Really?" The Diamond turned from the Cascade and stared down at her.

It was the very first time that he had ever stared down at her in such an odd way and it made Bella shift her feet the tiniest bit. For all of her life those splendid blue eyes of his had spoken to her. They had murmured and grumped and laughed. But they had never once appeared as they appeared at this very moment. The spark that his boyish smile had lit as he stood outside the supper box sprang into flame at the quiet passion she now thought she saw in them and her cheeks grew hot.

"Your father would not deny you any of those gentlemen," Derrinham continued, turning again toward the Cascade. "They are all quite eligible. And Tottingham, too. And there are others, you know, who have not as yet gotten up the nerve to request your company at this or that entertainment. But they will before much longer, Bella. You may count upon it. You are in the midst of conquering any number of hearts. I am—I am most happy for you and proud of you, too. You have behaved just as you should. Exactly as I have always known you to behave. And you will never say that you are short and plump and plain as buttered beans again, will you? Because now you know that you are not and you have shown them all that you are not as well. You are what you have always been: a beautiful and a very special young woman."

He turned back to her then, and his hands grasped her arms and his head lowered until his lips met hers, softly, gently, like the whisper of silk on silk. "Be careful, my Bella," he whispered as their lips parted. "Be very careful. Your heart is a precious thing and you must not give it where there is not love."

And then, before she could make the least reply, he was taking her hand and leading her back through the crowd to the supper box where Lord Nesbitt and the rest of her party waited. He presented her to Lord Nesbitt with a flourish, bowed to the remainder of the group, and wandered off toward the Hermit's Walk without so much as another word.

"Did you like the Cascade?" asked Nesbitt, helping her to a seat. "I did not know that you had never seen the thing."

"No one invited me to Vauxhall last Season," Bella murmured. "I was not—well, you know that I was not— at all popular." Although she strove for a glimpse of The Diamond among the crowd, he was already lost to her, and so she gave herself a shake and directed her attention to her host.

"No," Lord Nesbitt was saying with a growing smile. "Not at all popular. As I recall, you were most unapproachable and very adept at spilling orgeat."

Bella laughed then. She had never thought she would do anything but cry over that dreadful, dreadful evening. She had thought only a few weeks ago that that was one of the many horrendous events she would never live down. But now, watching Lord Nesbitt's smile widen, she could not help but laugh. "Oh, my lord, I do remember it. My hand was shaking so very badly that the horrible stuff fairly leaped out of my glass."

"Yes, out of your glass and down the front of my coat

and waistcoat and breeches. It was everywhere," chuckled Lord Nesbitt. "I was deuced lucky nothing of import stuck to me on the way home, let me tell you. I must apologize, I think, for assuming you would do it to me again this Season. I was very wrong to think so. You are not the same young lady you were on that infamous evening."

"Am I not?" asked Bella, the thought of Diamond's eyes gazing down at her with such quiet passion, the thought of his lips pressed so gently, yet briefly, against her own beginning to overwhelm her only now that he had gone. "Lord Barrington and Mr. Anders and the others would say the same, I think. And yet his grace has only just finished telling me that I am just the same as I have always been. Do you not find that most curious?"

Ten

The Hermit's Walk was the shortest of the promenades in Vauxhall. Running parallel to the Grand Walk and bounded on the right by a wilderness and the left by a rural downs, it boasted at its upper end a most amazing transparency of a hermit sitting before a hut. Derrinham was not interested, however, in viewing the hermit. He was merely interested in finding a bit of privacy and the Hermit's Walk, at the moment, appeared quite deserted.

What the devil was Miss Davies about? he wondered now, scuffing along the gravel path, his hands shoved into the pockets of his breeches, the toes of his boots kicking up puffs of dust and his spurs jingling forlornly. What was she thinking to send Bella and me off unchaperoned? If she did not wish to accompany us to the Cascade, she should have forbidden Bella to go. "Quite proper," he muttered, giving the gravel a hard kick. "She knew damned well it was not proper, and now I have gone and kissed the girl in full view of a hundred people at the very least."

But it was not at all a long kiss, he attempted to console himself. Perhaps no one noticed. Or perhaps whoever did notice did not recognize us and so word will not get about. Yes, and perhaps the moon will come to earth tomorrow evening and we will all feast on green cheese, too!

The thought of what he was doing had not once entered his mind during the doing of it. That was the part that rankled most. He had truly been thinking only to discover if Bella had lost her heart to Barrington or Nesbitt or Anders when he had led her off to view the Cascade. He had wanted to know. He had needed to know. But the look in her eyes and the flush upon her cheeks and the way she had stared up at him had set all the unbrotherly thoughts about Bella that had distracted him in the past few weeks boiling to the front of his brain and for an instant he had wished to do nothing more than to sweep her up into his arms and kiss her soundly and proclaim that he loved her himself with all his heart and that she would belong to him and to no other.

"At least I did not do all of that," he sighed into the night. "But it is likely I have compromised the girl and if I have an ounce of honor, I must go tomorrow and speak to Lord Meade and offer for her hand."

"No, I will not," he told himself then. "I will wait and see if anything comes of it." That is a great deal more reasonable, he thought. Bella don't wish to be married to a man she thinks of as a brother. I will wait and see if anything comes of it, and if it looks to become *on dit* then I will do the honorable thing.

"But she will hate me forever," he groaned. "It may be the honorable thing to marry her, but Bella has only just begun to look around her with some confidence and she will wish to choose a gentleman for herself."

"She will be a fool if she does not choose you above them all," murmured a quiet voice, startling the duke back to a realization of where he was and causing him to turn toward a line of elms on his right.

"Who the devil are you?" he asked on a whisper, discerning in the shadows a gentleman sitting upon a stump. "And what right have you to be eavesdropping upon me?"

"I was not eavesdropping," declared the gentleman in

an odd little voice. "I was merely sitting here thinking and you came along mumbling to yourself."

"Do I know you? Your voice—"

"We have met, but we do not know each other," responded the gentleman, rising and making his way hesitantly toward the place where Derrinham stood. "You are the Duke of Derrinham and I stopped once to admire your horses in the Park."

The Diamond's eyes widened as the gentleman stepped into the pool of light in which he himself stood. "Miss Winstead? Great gawd, Miss Winstead—what in the name of all that's holy are you doing wandering about Vauxhall in gentlemen's clothing?"

Bella settled upon the blanket Lord Nesbitt had spread over the grass and looked up at the heavens, her eyes aglow as the sky lit with fireworks. "Oh, it is so very splendid!"

"Do not tell me," murmured Nesbitt. "Last Season no one treated you to the fireworks display either."

"Well, no, because I was not invited to Vauxhall, as I said."

"What dolts we men are," sighed Nesbitt. Miss May was correct, he thought. We all deserve to live out our lives in ennui and tedium because we cannot appreciate a truly fine gift when it is placed directly into our hands. If The Diamond had not come to town to tease this gentle flower into bud, we would none of us have come to know the true Lady Annabella yet.

"Castigating yourself, are you, Nesbitt?" whispered a voice in the gentleman's ear.

"Huh? What did you say, Baylor?"

"I asked, my friend, if you were sitting here taking yourself to task for having ignored the little Lady Bella all last Season."

"Exactly so. Do you not find her charming, Baylor?"

"Indeed. And with a unique style. You are not thinking of falling in love, are you?"

"Love?"

"Yes, because it will not do you a bit of good. There is someone else enamoured of her and if he allows himself to admit to it, he will have her, too."

"Barrington, you mean."

"No. I swear, Nesbitt, you are blind as a bat," whispered Baylor with a quick glance at Bella to be certain that her attention was still directed at the sky. "Did you think it coincidence that The Diamond appeared tonight? That he just stumbled upon our supper box?"

"No. I thought he came to check upon his niece."

"It ain't so, Nesbitt. The Diamond has lost his heart to the little Hedgehog, though quite possibly he does not know that to be the case himself as yet."

"Pardon me?" asked Bella, directing her attention to the two gentlemen conversing in whispers beside her. "I am afraid I was not at all paying attention."

"No, of course you were not," replied Nesbitt with a smile. "You were enjoying the fireworks as you should. And it was a pleasure to see you enjoying them, too."

Bella grinned. Only a year ago she had thought Lord Nesbitt a most fearsome beast, but now he seemed quite a nice gentleman as did his friend, Mr. Baylor.

Mr. Baylor, thought Bella, studying that gentleman for a moment. "Do you know, Mr. Baylor," she said on a chuckle, "that his grace has a horse named Baylor?"

"Yes," sighed that gentleman with a sad shake of his head. "He bought the beast at Tat's. And when he led it out, he said it sauntered just like me and named it Baylor on the spot."

"Oh, he is incorrigible!" exclaimed Bella.

"Worse than incorrigible," offered Miss May. "Do you know that horrid goose he has that runs free about the stables, Bella? The one who hisses and chases after all the men?"

"Indeed. Oh, Jane, no! I never thought!"

"What?" asked the rest of the party in one voice, all of them having been drawn to the conversation.

"Her name is Silence," giggled Bella.

"But that is what they call Lady Jersey," said Miss DeLacey.

"Yes, my dear," chuckled Mr. Cottsworth, giving her hand a squeeze, "but only behind her back. A goose, you say, Miss May? A bad-tempered, hissing goose?"

"Who chases men," Jane added demurely, only her eyes betraying the gleeful naughtiness of the appellation.

Anyone coming along the Hermit's Walk at that precise moment would have been most discomposed to see the Duke of Derrinham standing in the middle of the gravel path with his arms tightly around another gentleman and murmuring in that gentleman's ear as the fireworks died around them. Miss Winstead, though her brother's beaver had long since fallen from her head, had bound her long tresses into a tight knot and still looked the gentleman without it. But she was clinging to the duke in a most ungentlemanlike fashion as he bestowed another kiss upon the verimost top of her head and urged her quietly to cease her tears. "You ought to be happy, Emily," he whispered. "This is no time at all for tears."

"It is," sobbed Miss Winstead. "I should never have told you, because now you will—"

"Now I will what?" asked the duke.

"You will h-hate me."

"Hate you? Never. I could never hate you, my dear. It has come as an enormous shock to me, Emily, but it is none of it your doing. And if I cannot think of precisely the right thing to say, it is only because, while you have known for years and years, dearest, I have known for only the length of time it takes to watch the fireworks display at Vauxhall. Come, little one, do not cry anymore. Let me take you home."

"To Great Stanhope Street?" asked Emily, looking up at him hopefully, but then dreading his answer and looking down again.

The Duke of Derrinham did not know how to respond. "Is there no one awaits you at your own house, Emily? No one who would miss you and think you had been kidnapped or some such?"

"There are only Maggie and Bess, who come in once a week to help with the cleaning, and Mrs. Glendenning next door."

"The lady who chaperones you when it is convenient to her?"

"Yes."

"And no one else?"

Miss Winstead did think, then, to mention her brother Michael, but he was *not* at home and he would *not* miss her. She had not the least idea when Michael would ever come home again. He had lied to her about leaving his position at the jewelers' and about taking a new position and quite likely he had lied to her about when to expect him next. She had known for a long while that she was a burden to Michael and that having the care of her chafed him no end. That was most likely why he had lied—to break free of her without causing her pain. "N-no one," she replied therefore to the duke's question.

"Yes, then," The Diamond said, pushing her away from his chest and bestowing a most tender kiss upon the nose that had turned red from her crying. "You shall come home with me to Great Stanhope Street tonight and I will send one of my footmen to gather up all your things and bring them to Derrinham House tomorrow." With that, the duke snatched the beaver she had been wearing from the spot on the gravel to which it had rolled and placed it firmly upon her head. Then he took one of her hands into his own and led her back down the path toward the Grand Cross Walk and the entrance at the far side of the Gardens.

It did occur to Derrinham that it might look odd to some of the people milling about to see one gentleman leading another by the hand, but he did not care. He was not about to lose Miss Emily Winstead in the crowd. When at last they reached the gate, he tossed a crown to the boy who had kept watch over Arnold, then helped Miss Winstead to mount into the saddle and swung up behind her. Taking the reins into his hands, he turned all three of them toward home.

"What the devil was he doing?" Bella muttered when at last her abigail had tucked her neatly into bed and departed the chamber. "And who was it he carried before him on Arnold? Thank goodness none of the others saw. Jane would have been for chasing after him in the carriage to discover what was going on."

Well, it could not have been the villain who attempted to kill him, she told herself as she plucked unconsciously at the counterpane. Even Diamond would not take an enemy up before him on his horse and ride off into the night. But the gentleman did look very much like the odd little man who was spying upon us in the supper box. Perhaps he was merely some old friend who had no other way home. But the man could quite easily have hired a hack. And if he had not the money for it, Diamond could easily have given it to him. Bella sighed into the night and wiggled her toes beneath the blankets.

Really, it was not any of her business. The Diamond was her senior by eight years and a duke besides. He was quite capable of looking after his own affairs. Still, there had been something so very different about him this evening. "And he kissed me," Bella murmured. "Why did he kiss me?"

She took a very deep breath and for the longest time she listened to her pulse pounding in her ears. Almost, when he had smiled at her so boyishly and then led her off to view the Cascade, when he had halted in the midst of their conversation and looked down at her with that quiet passion in his eyes, almost she had thought he loved her. But that was nonsense. It had not been passion in his eyes, merely concern. He was concerned for her and wished her to find a gentleman to marry. A gentleman to love. Had he not discussed Lord Barrington with her and Mr. Anders and Lord Nesbitt? Had he not said that she might expect to receive invitations from even more gentlemen? And had he said one word about himself? Of course not. He was her friend, her almost-brother.

"And he does love me," Bella whispered, "but only in the purest and most honorable sense—as a young woman whom he has known and cared about his entire life."

She could not quite think why that particular thought brought a sensation of tears to her eyes or a shortness of breath. After all, Diamond had loved her precisely that way forever. Even when she had trailed behind him, demanding that he teach her all the things that he knew how to do—to ride like the wind and climb carelessly up into the branches of oaks, to whistle like the birds and pull hapless trout out of Twiney Creek—she had known that he loved her as purely and innocently as he loved his elder sister, Lady Diana. And if she had not been grateful for it, had not given it the least thought, had merely assumed in the way of all children that it was her due, still, she had always known it and she knew it now. "And I love Diamond as well," she told herself on just the merest hit of a sob. "And before I marry any gentleman, I shall make it clear to him that Diamond holds a very special place in my heart and shall always be welcome in our home."

Sonnett turned the most amazing shade of red and his eyes nearly bulged from their sockets.

"Breathe, Sonnett," ordered Derrinham, cocking an eyebrow at his butler as he stood before the poor man in the great hall with one hand upon Miss Winstead's shoulder. "You have not taken one breath since we entered the front door."

"I—I—" sputtered Sonnett, and then inhaled a great deal of air.

"There, now that's better, is it not? This is Miss Winstead, Sonnett. I thought we could put her in the rose chamber next to Janie, eh? It is made up, is it not? I thought it was when I passed by there the other day."

"Y-yes, of course. Miss—Miss Winstead?"

"Yes, Sonnett. Miss Winstead. And tomorrow, first thing, you will send one of the footmen to request Mr. Piermont's presence in my library as soon as possible. The elder Mr. Piermont. Mr. Arnold Piermont," said his grace significantly. "Jane and Miss Davies are home, no? We came the long way 'round to give them time to arrive before us."

"They arrived but a few moments ago, your grace, and are gone to their chambers."

"Good. Come with me, Emily, and I will introduce you to Jane and Miss Davies. One of Jane's nightgowns will fit you, I am certain, and she will be more than pleased to help you to your bed tonight." And with that the duke was leading Miss Winstead up the staircase all the way to the second floor.

Jane opened the door of the sitting room she shared with Miss Davies and gasped at the sight of the odd-looking gentleman who had been staring at them at Vauxhall. Only it was not a gentleman. "Why, you are a woman!" she exclaimed, looking Miss Winstead up and down.

"Indeed, she is," nodded Derrinham.

"Uncle Hill! This is the person who came running at us in the night from Mr. Palmer's stoop and then ran away. And she was staring at us at Vauxhall this evening, too, until we took note of her, and then she disappeared. Why—you are Miss Winstead!" Jane exclaimed upon closer inspection.

"You are known to each other already?" The duke looked from one to the other of them in surprise.

"Bella pointed her out to me in Bond Street," Jane explained, her eyes fastened suspiciously upon the young woman.

"Why on earth would Bella—well, never mind. Is Miss Davies presentable, Janie?"

"Indeed, your grace," called Miss Davies from the settee before the fire. "Do come in. I cannot think where Jane's manners have flown. Miss Winstead?" she added, rising to greet them.

"Yes," replied the duke, leading Emily into the chamber. "Miss Winstead, may I present my niece, Jane, and her companion, Miss Davies. Emily is going to be staying with us from now on."

"From now on, Uncle Hill?" Jane murmured.

"Yes, until the end of the Season. And after that— well—after that Mr. Piermont and I will decide what is to be done."

"D-done?" asked Emily, her great blue eyes staring up into the duke's own.

"Yes," smiled Derrinham. "I should think you would like to visit Twiney Hill. It is not the ducal seat, but it has been my main residence since I was a boy. I am much more fond of it than any of the others. You will like it, I think, Emily. Unless, of course, you should fix some gentleman's interest before then and go off and get married on me. I hope you will not. Not so soon, at any rate. But I expect it—"

He was rambling on and on as though the words could not keep from rolling off his tongue and Jane could not think what was causing it. Miss Winstead to make her home at Derrinham House? To attend whatever entertainments remained until the end of the Season? And then, to go with him to Twiney Hill for the summer? And now what was he saying? Jane pushed herself to leave off wondering at him and pay closer attention to his words.

"—a little filly. You will set the *ton* on its ear, the three of you. I vow you will."

Emily's hands in a gentleman's York tan gloves were fluttering witlessly just beneath her chin and the duke reached out and took them into his own. "I apologize, Emily. I am frightening you with all this blather. I do not know what has gotten into me. Yes, I do know." And transferring her hands from both of his into one, he began to take the pins from her hair, watching it fall in raven waves around her.

Miss Davies gasped at the familiarity of such an action and stepped forward. Jane reached out to stop her uncle in the midst of what could only be most embarrassing for the poor young woman and then they both felt the blood in their veins turn cold.

"You must only imagine it to be blond rather than such a rich, wonderful black," the duke drawled. "I did not know, Jane, quite how to present her to you, but—"

"Who—who is she?" Jane stammered.

The Duke of Derrinham stepped behind Emily and wrapped his arms about her, resting his chin on the top of her head.

It was uncanny. Jane and Miss Davies fairly gaped at the two faces one above the other. The same great sapphire eyes, the same stubborn chins, the same finely etched lips and perfect brows—the only difference that his features held a heavy masculine aura and hers a certain daintiness of femininity.

"Emily is my half-sister. I expect that is what Sir Cyril Blythe has been so eager to tell me all these years. He likely thought Papa's indiscretion would cause me a great deal of embarrassment but he was far out there. I have lost the most splendid elder sister in all the world, Janie, and you the most loving mama. But see now, in her place God has seen fit to send me a little sister and you an aunt."

"I think it is the best thing that could have happened," murmured Shaughnessy in the shadows of the front parlor where a small fire flickered on the hearth and one branch of candles added a dull gleam to the room. Only moments before he had seen an excited duke safely into his bed. Now he faced an extremely discomposed Sonnett, who had slouched into an armchair with a glass of his grace's burgundy in his hand.

"The best thing that could have happened? That she introduce herself to him and he take her into this house? And into his heart? He will take the wretch into his heart, you know."

"She is his half-sister, Sonnett."

"She is the offspring of an adulterous relationship between his grace's papa and the wife of a cit!"

"Quietly, Samuel, or someone will hear you."

Sonnett nodded and lowered his voice. "And it was likely her father who killed our little duke's papa and mama. I still think it was Winstead did the deed."

"Even so, it was not Miss Winstead did it. She was newly born and our Diamond merely five. And yet she likely suffers because of the past much as he continues to do."

Sonnett could discover no reply to that and so he took another sip of the burgundy and slipped down lower in the chair. "We ought to have been in this house that night," he murmured after a long silence. "We ought to have been here, Tim. None of it would have happened had we been attending to our duties."

"No, likely not," sighed Shaughnessy. "We were fools to take the bait as we did, all of us."

"And how do we know that Miss Winstead is to be trusted, Shaughnessy? How do we know that she is not the very person who desires his grace's death? To this day I do not believe that her father's hands are clean of Hallsworth blood. How are we to know what he told the girl? Perhaps he set her against the family."

"Mr. Winstead is dead, Samuel. Died near two years ago. This I had from the duke who had it from Miss Winstead. And Mrs. Winstead succumbed to a fever three years before that."

"That is not the least insurance against the girl if Winstead filled her head with thoughts of revenge."

"We shall speak to Farraday about it," Shaughnessy nodded, unable to gainsay Sonnett's suspicions. "We shall set him to watching her. And if the young lady should make the least move against his grace, Bow Street will have her. But if she does nothing to harm him, then we must abide by his grace's decision and we must treat her with respect."

Eleven

Bella sat upon the puce fainting couch in the morning room of her papa's Town house and gazed uneasily at the gentleman upon one knee before her. Her face fairly blazed with embarrassment. "Do rise, my lord. Come, sit here beside me."

"But I have not come near to finishing. There is a great deal more. I practiced the thing for hours on end last evening."

"You did?"

"Yes, because I did not wish to make a muck of it. I do not know why it is, Lady Annabella, but I find I am fiercely in love with you. I think of you night and day and I cannot bear to be apart from you. You are everything desirable in a woman." Lord Barrington's fine hazel eyes flashed up at her hopefully and he ran his tongue nervously over his lips. "I have—I have never done this before," he stuttered. "I hope you will overlook any little mistakes I may make."

"Is there more to your speech?" asked Bella, her own embarrassment fading in sympathy for his obvious anxiety.

"A good deal more," gulped Lord Barrington. "I am to say how beautiful I find you, and how my heart aches to hold you close and kiss those most alluring lips of yours."

Bella cocked an eyebrow. "My alluring lips?"

"Uh-huh. And I wanted to remember to say what delight I find in your company, and how I adore the way your eyes sparkle and flash whenever you are verbally engaged."

"Verbally engaged?"

"Yes, you know. When you are arguing with me or giving The Diamond a setdown or when you are ordering us about."

"I do never argue with you or give his grace setdowns or order either one of you about."

"Yes, you do. All the time. Well—perhaps I ought not to have used those words exactly."

"No, you ought not," replied Bella with a bit of a smile. "Because it makes me seem a veritable shrew, you see."

"Never! I assure you, you are not that nor could you ever be. You are everything wonderful and kind and thoughtful."

"Is that supposed to be in there?" asked Bella. "Or did you just make that up on the spur of the moment because of what I said about seeming a shrew?"

"I—just tossed it in," admitted Barrington, quietly. "But it is all true. I cannot think how I could have been so blind as not to have seen the true wonder of you all last Season."

"Yes?"

"I thought—I was waiting for you to interrupt me again."

"Oh. Well, but I was not going to interrupt you. I very much liked that part—about your having been blind all last Season."

"Well, I was," continued Barrington determinedly. "But now the scales have fallen from my eyes and I see you as the charming and exquisite young lady that you are. And I love you, Lady Annabella, with all my heart."

"You do?"

"Yes, I do, and I wish—I hope—that you will make me the happiest of men."

Bella sat gazing down at him expectantly.

"Well?" he asked.

"Well, what? Oh! That is the end of it!"

"Yes. Will you make me the happiest of men, Lady Annabella? Will you marry me?"

Bella's great brown eyes looked upward toward the ceiling and then down at Lord Barrington. "I cannot think what to say," she murmured, taking his hands into her own and tugging him up from the floor to sit beside her upon the fainting couch.

"Say yes."

"I am very cognizant, my lord, of the honor that you do me."

"Yes, well, I don't want you to be cognizant, Bella. I want you to be mine."

"You called me Bella."

"Yes, I should love always to call you Bella just the way The Diamond does. But I must not be so familiar, you know, unless we are to become engaged."

"And I would call you—"

"James."

"James is very nice," smiled Bella. "I shall like to call you James."

Lord Barrington stared across at her, wide-eyed. "Does that mean that you will?" he asked, holding tightly to her hands. "Does that mean that you will marry me, Bella?"

"It means that I shall give the idea my most serious consideration, James," Bella informed him with a tiny frown. "But it does not mean that it is, as Diamond is accustomed to call things, a *fait accompli*. You will not mind to wait for a time before I give you a more definite answer, will you, James?"

"N-no," replied Lord Barrington, tripping over his

tongue, his heart racing at the sound of his Christian name not once but twice upon her lips. "I shall wait forever, my darling Bella."

"Well, you will not be required to wait quite that long. I hope I am more decisive than that. It is merely that I wish to give my heart only where there is love," she said, The Diamond's words of the evening before abruptly coming to mind. "And you must do the same, James."

"I intend to do the same," nodded Lord Barrington. And quite of a sudden, the young lady beside him was gazing into his eyes with the most curious expression upon her upturned face. And he found the temptation irresistible. His arms went around her and pulled her closer, and his head lowered, and his lips met hers with a most resounding enthusiasm.

"You want me to do what?" asked The Diamond, staring down at Bella with the most quizzical look upon his face, the glass of champagne in his hand tilting precariously.

"To kiss me."

"Bella, we are in the midst of a *soirée.*"

"Well, I do not want you to do it in front of everyone."

"I should think not."

"No, we should wander out into the rose garden. It is a very small rose garden and the middle of the night besides, so I doubt if anyone else will even think to go out there."

Bella was most astounded to see the quizzical look wiped from The Diamond's countenance by a sudden cloudburst of worry.

"I was so excited last evening after discovering about Emily that I forgot," he muttered, running his fingers through his hair distractedly and spilling champagne from his glass as well. "Damn! Excuse me, Bella. I did not intend to use such language. It has not got on your gown, has it?"

"No. Discovering what about Emily? Emily who?"

"I shall explain it all to you, Bella, but not here and not now. I only say, it was that which put the episode out of my head."

"What episode?" asked Bella, thinking how odd it was to see Diamond's ears slowly turning red. Why on earth were they turning red? Goodness, she had never seen anything quite like it.

"Bella," the duke hissed, "cease staring at my ears."

"But they are turning red, Diamond."

"I do not care if they are turning purple. Do not stare at them so. You are drawing any number of gazes in our direction. I must ask you something, Bella. And it is important that you answer truthfully."

"All right," nodded Bella, wondering what on earth had gotten into the gentleman. "It is not as though I am in the habit of lying to you."

"No, no, I did not mean to insult you, Bella. It is merely about—about last evening at the Cascade when I—when I—"

"Kissed me," Bella provided.

"Yes, that. Has anyone mentioned it to you? I did not stop to think after Emily—but I did give it a deal of thought before that. Have we become grist for the mill, you and I? Is it that kiss you wish to speak to me about in the garden?"

"Yes, that is precisely what I wish to speak with you about," Bella nodded. "The kiss."

Setting his partially empty glass upon the sideboard and setting Bella's there as well, the Duke of Derrinham offered his arm and made a path for the two of them through three saloons overflowing with people and out onto the balcony at the rear of the long drawing room from which a set of marble steps led down into the rose garden.

The evening was fair with the merest breath of mist in the air and that felt marvelous to Bella after the sad crush inside the house itself. She sighed as her slippers touched the cobbled path that led off through the flowers.

"There is a bench a little way down the path, Bella. Will you sit there with me for a moment or two?"

Bella nodded and allowed him to lead her to the place. When first they had met in the red saloon this evening, Diamond had been as merry as a grig. But now a pall had come over him and since it apparently had been her words that had brought on his gloom, Bella set herself the task of driving the gloom away. "You look splendid this evening," she murmured as he divested himself of his coat and laid it upon the stone bench to protect her gown as she sat. "And you were so very merry. What was it made you smile so and laugh?"

"Nothing. It was nothing. Tell me true, Bella, about last evening. Has someone mentioned to you about my kissing you so in the midst of the throng? I should not have done it. I cannot think why I did."

"You cannot?"

"No. It was most improper of me. I had hoped that no one had taken note of it, but if it has become a topic of conversation then we must do something about it immediately."

Bella stared up at the duke, who stood with one foot propped upon the bench beside her. Truly, he was the most handsome gentleman of her acquaintance. She had thought so for as long as she had been old enough to consider such things and she thought so now, too. "What must we do?" she asked quietly. "I do not wish to see you frown so, Diamond. What do you think we must do?"

"Marry," murmured Derrinham.

"M-marry?"

"Yes. I had hoped my thoughtlessness had not compromised you, my dear. But if it has, I must do the honorable thing by you. I will speak to your father the first thing in the morning. Perhaps it will not be so very bad, Bella."

Bella rose straight up from the bench, but he pushed her back down with one large hand. "I know," he sighed. "It was not at all what you planned, but it cannot be helped. Unless—unless there is some gentleman wishes to marry you regardless of my having so thoughtlessly damaged your reputation."

"For your information, your grace," declared Bella, "my reputation has not been damaged in the least. If anyone at all saw that—that—kiss—they most likely thought it a brotherly peck and made nothing of it. You are worried for naught."

"I am? But then why did you—what was all that talk inside about my kissing you?"

"I merely wished for you to kiss me again," muttered Bella, her temper beginning to boil. Honestly, to think that the mere thought of marriage to her should sink him into gloom. Not that she wished him to want to marry her. That was ridiculous. He was nothing more to her than a friend—a very good friend—an almost-brother—oh, bosh, she had known him all her life and there was nothing the least bit romantic about him. For the life of her she could not think why she had even thought to ask him for a second kiss. Yes, she could. She knew precisely why she wished for him to kiss her again.

"Kiss you again?" One of The Diamond's eyebrows cocked dangerously. "You cannot mean it, Bella. Why?"

"Because this afternoon Lord Barrington proposed marriage to me and—"

"He did? Did you tell him yes, Bella?"

"I told him that I wished to think about it for a time."

The duke nodded. "That's likely best. You have not known each other so very long. But he is a fine catch, Bella."

"I am pleased that you think so, your grace."

"No, really, Bella. I am only thinking of your happiness."

"Of course. So you will kiss me again, will you not? Right now? Because Lord Barrington kissed me, you see, after he proposed and I could not quite think—that is—I have never been kissed by any gentleman before but papa and—and you." Bella cursed herself silently, took a deep breath and stared up into the duke's questioning eyes. "What it is, Diamond, is that I wish to compare your kiss with Lord Barrington's. His did not seem at all like the kiss you gave me last evening. But perhaps my memory is at fault. I wish to know."

Her eyes were like deep pools of melted chocolate in the glow of the single light that stood beside the bench. And her chin, tilted so stubbornly up at him, was quite as delightful as he had ever imagined a chin could be. And her lips were plump and sweet and would taste of champagne if once he placed his own upon them. And she was requesting him to do just that.

The Duke of Derrinham gave himself a great mental shake. What was he thinking? This was Bella! Bella! "All right, you little baggage," he grumbled, lowering his foot from the bench and pulling her up into his arms. "I shall refresh your memory for you." And in an instant his lips were upon hers and he was tasting of the champagne that lingered there. And what he had intended as an impatient brotherly peck that would prove a dead bore compared to the kiss that Barrington must have bestowed upon the girl became instead a silken probing of the inviting softness of her. His tongue whispered across those incredible lips, parting them, touching the white, hard teeth that had snapped abruptly closed in surprise, urging them soundlessly to part and allow him entrance. His arms tightened around her. His hands wandered up and down her back. His fingers lingered upon her neck and fluttered behind her ears and tangled themselves at last in her hair.

The Diamond knew, deep in the midst of that kiss, that he loved Bella. There was not the least doubt in his mind. There was no foolishness about its being brotherly love or the fondness of a neighbor for a childhood friend. He thought for a moment that his heart would burst from the knowledge and he sought at once to end the kiss, his hands coming to grasp her arms and shove her away from him. "There," he growled. "I expect now you have something to judge Barrington by. If he did not kiss you quite so soundly, it is only because he loves you and fears to frighten you. I, on the other hand, know perfectly well how fearless you truly are. Now we must go back, Bella. You will be missed shortly and your mama will come looking for you."

With a few deft movements the duke repaired the damage his fingers had done to Bella's hair. Luckily it was not long and piled and knotted upon her head, but only a cluster of loose curls which could be easily righted. He retrieved his coat and shrugged into it as Bella straightened her gown. Offering her his arm, he led her back toward the steps to the balcony.

"You did—you did not tell me what it was made you so very merry this evening," Bella fairly gasped on an exhaled breath. Honestly, she could not think of one thing to say that made the least sense. His kiss had fairly scrambled her wits. And now she was more uncertain than ever about everything. Why had he kissed her so? Goodness gracious, it had certainly been an education! She had never once guessed that a man might kiss a woman in such a way. She had found the whisper of a kiss The Diamond had bestowed upon her at the Cascade most intriguing and most invigorating to her senses, but this kiss—this had been thoroughly outrageous. Lord Barrington's chaste salute, though more what she had romantically expected a lover's kiss to be, seemed so very tame beside The Diamond's efforts.

"I have discovered that I have a half-sister, Bella," the duke informed her.

"You have what?"

"You asked what put me in such high stirrups this evening. It was learning that Miss Emily Winstead is my half-sister. You remember Miss Winstead, Bella. We met her in Hyde Park."

"Yes, of course I remember."

"Do you not think it wonderful? To suddenly have a sister?"

"Well—well—perhaps."

"Yes, perhaps," sighed the duke, leading her into the first of the saloons.

"Oh, Diamond, no! I did not mean to stifle your happiness again. Of course it is wonderful. And now," added Bella, the thought just occurring to her, "there will be not the least need for you to meet with Sir Cyril Blythe on Wednesday, will there? Because you already know what he intended to tell you."

"Most certainly Emily is part of what he intends to tell me, but she cannot possibly be all of it, Bella. I thought at first she was, but there must be more. Diana and Will were forever calling Blythe perverse and dangerous—especially to me. But what danger can there be in discovering that one has a half-sister? A great many of the gentlemen in London have half-sisters and half-brothers marching about the streets whether they know it or not but I cannot think they are in danger because of it. No, something else keeps Sir Cyril's eyes upon me whenever I am come to town. And I shall keep our appointment and discover the whole of it. And neither you nor Jane are to have any part in it," he added with a most intimidating glare. "Do you hear me, Bella? If I should see even a shadow that looks like one of you lurking within twenty blocks of Pickering Place, I shall beat you both up one side of London and down the other!"

Miss Emily Winstead, in a most sedate dinner dress of dove gray with a puce riband at the neckline and hem and matching puce slippers, had with the help of Jane's abigail at last unpacked and distributed all of her clothing brought from Curzon Street earlier that day. After a tidy little dinner in her chamber, she had gained the courage to wander down into the library of Derrinham House where she curled in a most unladylike position into a mammoth armchair with her legs tucked under her and paged languidly through a number of the duke's well-worn volumes of poetry. Once he had discovered her whereabouts, Sonnett had seen to it that a fire blazed upon the library grate to ward off the evening's chill and at fifteen minutes of ten, he sent the first footman up to the chamber with tea and pastries.

"There is a young woman visiting," he informed James as he held open the door to the first floor corridor. "She arrived last evening and will remain until the end of the Season. You are to treat her with the proper decorum." It was all Sonnett could bring himself to say on the matter. It was good enough. If his grace wished to take in one of his father's by-blows—especially this particular by-blow—he could not gainsay him, but by gawd, he would not elevate the chit to any higher level in the eyes of his staff than that of guest. Noting that the library door stood open and so James would not require his assistance further, Sonnett made his way back to the staff's parlor, grumbling quietly at the pure pigeon-brained whim that had made the duke take the girl in.

James sauntered into the chamber and gazed about him, perplexed. And then he saw the top of her head from over the back of the chair and sighed quietly in relief. He had thought for a moment that Sonnett had sent him to the wrong chamber and that he was going to end in searching all over the first floor for the young woman. "Tea, miss," he announced, stepping forward to place the tray upon a mahogany table beside the chair. "Mr. Sonnett thought perhaps you might enjoy some of Pierre's apple whimsies with your bohea. Emily!" he gasped, suddenly recognizing her. "What the devil are you doing here?"

"Michael?" Miss Winstead's face colored up on the instant. "Michael, is that you? Whatever are you doing here? And why are you dressed like a footman?"

"Because I *am* a footman. What are *you* doing here is the question. You cannot be here, Emily. You must be gone at once."

"N-no, I must not, Michael," stuttered Emily, un-curling herself and rising from the chair. "You do not understand. His grace has invited me here and asked that I stay in this house for the remainder of the Season. Oh, Michael, he is everything Mama said he would be. He is the handsomest and kindest and most—"

"Nonsense," growled Michael Winstead, grabbing his sister's arm and tugging her close before him. "He is the Duke of Derrinham, Emily. His father took Mama from Papa and got her with child and then spurned her. His father drove Mama to madness and then to atone for it ruined Papa as well. His father stood laughing upon the cobbles when almost all we owned was sold at auction and we were forced out into the street. If Sir Cyril Blythe had not stepped in and given Papa the deed to the house in Curzon Street and found him another position, I would likely be a carter, Emily, and you selling flowers in Covent Garden."

"I do not care a fig," replied Miss Winstead, her little nose turning upward in disdain. "That was a long time ago and this duke is not that duke. This is Mama's little duke who grew into the most splendid of gentlemen in all of her stories. He is my brother, Michael, just as you are. And I have told him so."

"Emily, how could you!" Michael Winstead wished to do nothing more than to give his sister the thorough shaking she deserved, but he could not. He could not because she was staring up at him with those guileless blue eyes and her lower lip was twitching just the tiniest bit which it always did when she was certain she had done everything just as she should and did not understand why her mama or her papa or her brother had become disturbed over it.

"Emily, you cannot stay here in this house. You do not understand at all."

"What? What do I not understand?"

"You do not understand that I promised—that I must—"

"I know what I do not understand," interrupted Emily so boldly that Michael's hands dropped from her arms in surprise. "What I do not understand is why you have taken a position as a footman here in Derrinham House when you already have a perfectly good position at Rundell and Bridges. I spoke to Mr. Willis only yesterday and they all think you are ill, Michael, and they are expecting you to return to your work at any time. The elder Mr. Rundell has even thought to send you his own physician if you are not better soon."

"Emily, you did not tell them I had taken another position?"

"Well, I ought to have done so, for that is what you

told me. Though you did *not* tell me you intended to become a footman to the little duke."

"But you did not tell them—"

"No, Michael. I told Mr. Willis a great bouncer on your behalf and I am certain I shall never be able to look that gentleman in the eye again."

Mr. Winstead's heart, which for a moment had risen right straight up into his throat, jarred back into its rightful place again. But it ached. It ached something fierce. "Did the duke really say that you are to remain with him for the Season, Emily?"

"Indeed he did."

"Devil," sighed Mr. Winstead, rubbing the back of his neck with one hand and knocking his footman's curly white wig askew. "I should have thought he would avoid you like the plague. But that is neither here nor there," he muttered to himself, beginning to pace. "I gave Father my word. On his deathbed I swore to him that I would see it done. Derrinham's father was a devil, and the apple cannot fall so very far from the tree as it seems. It is some dastardly plot on his part to foil me. Or to ruin Emily. Or both. It must be. It must be."

Miss Emily Winstead gazed with fearful eyes upon her pacing, muttering brother. Visions of her mama pacing and muttering just so when her illness overwhelmed her came rushing back. Emily's hands twisted together at the memory and tears began to sting behind her eyes.

Twelve

"I cannot conceive why it is, Mama, that his grace must be so very odd about everything," Bella sighed, as she sent her mama's abigail to bed and set about brushing out her mother's hair herself.

"Odd?" Lady Meade's splendid hazel eyes gazed questioningly back at her daughter from the looking glass before which she sat.

"Yes, odd. I cannot think of any other word for it. Have you never noticed before, Mama, how very odd he is?"

It did occur to Lady Meade to inform her daughter that their neighbor had been odd likely from the very day of his birth, and that he, beyond any other gentlemen, had grounds for it. But she had vowed never to speak of the duke's tragedy and, knowing that mention of the thing would bring any number of questions she could not answer from her daughter, thought better of it. "His grace does not always do or say what one would expect him to do or say," she replied instead. "But he has always been a splendid friend to you, Bella, and a considerate neighbor to your papa and me. Has he done something to put you out of patience with him?"

"Yes. No."

"I see," murmured Lady Meade. "He has done something quite whimsical, I expect."

"Exactly," nodded Bella, relieved to have such a word

provided for it. "And I do not know what to think. We went down into the Meltons' garden for a breath of air, Mama, and Diamond kissed me, and—"

"His grace kissed you?" interrupted Lady Meade, frowning into the looking glass. "How dare he to do such a thing!"

"I requested him to kiss me, Mama."

"You did what?" cried Lady Meade, turning from her reflection to stare up, horrified, straight into her daughter's eyes.

"I merely wished to see why—how—if—" The look upon her mama's face as that lady turned from the looking glass and confronted her eye to eye brought Bella to a stuttering halt.

"How dare you, Bella, ask a gentleman to kiss you?"

"But it was only Diamond, Mama."

"His grace is still a gentleman, and a duke besides, and you were beyond brazen to speak to him of kissing at all, much less to invite him to kiss you!"

"But Lord Barrington kissed me, you see, and—"

"Lord Barrington quite properly applied to your papa for permission to seek your hand in marriage, Bella. And you did not tell him no, I think."

"No, Mama, I did not."

"Well, he, then, might be allowed to kiss you, hoping to further his suit. He may be expected to kiss you, Bella. Once. Upon the cheek. A gentleman may be permitted that when he has just undergone the strain of making a proper declaration. Yes, and a young lady may not be faulted for allowing him such liberty when she has just undergone the shock of a proposal. But no proper young lady goes about requesting a gentleman to kiss her. It is brazen and forward and beyond anything improper. And most certainly his grace knew better than to comply. I cannot think what has got into him. He has always been the highest stickler. Well, for a Corinthian, I mean. It is quite likely that inhabiting that dreadful house preys upon his mind and nibbles at his reason in some way. I shall speak with your papa about it the very first thing in the morning."

This conversation was not going at all as Bella wished, and worse, now she had gotten Diamond into a world of trouble with her mama and papa. "Oh please, Mama, you must not speak of it to Papa," she said, urging that lady to turn back toward the looking glass so that she might finish brushing out her hair. "I am quite certain that Diamond did not at all wish to kiss me. In fact, I know he did not. But I begged him to do it because I wanted to know—I wished to discover—"

Heavens! That is exactly the wrong thing to say, thought Bella, cutting her words off quickly. After Mama's reaction to Diamond's having kissed me at Lord and Lady Melton's, how can I possibly say that he kissed me without the least warning in the middle of Vauxhall?

"You wished to discover what, Bella?" scowled her mama.

I wished to discover why Diamond's whisper of a kiss at Vauxhall set my heart to pounding and my breath to rasping and turned my mind to pure mush but Lord Barrington's kiss did nothing but make me blush, thought Bella. And I wished to know if it would happen again. But I cannot possibly say that to Mama now.

"Bella?" Lady Meade tilted one finely drawn eyebrow at her in the mirror. "What was it you wished to learn by kissing his grace in the Meltons' garden?"

"Only what it would be like to be kissed by a gentleman who was not Lord Barrington," lied Bella in a rush of words. "To have something to compare Lord Barrington's kiss to, you see."

"Oh. Yes, I do see," nodded Lady Meade, surprising Bella no end. "And how did his grace's kiss compare to Lord Barrington's?"

Bella thought to tell another bouncer and to extol the virtues of Lord Barrington's kiss over The Diamond's. She even parted her lips to do so. But she could not. Her mama was studying her so very intently in the looking glass and—and—

"Oh, Mama, they were nothing alike. I thought I should burst into flame when Diamond kissed me. My stomach began to ache and my toes positively curled up inside my slippers and I did never, never, want him to stop!"

"Bella!"

"I cannot help it, Mama. That is how I felt. And when Lord Barrington kissed me, I only felt embarrassed."

"Oh, Bella," sighed Lady Meade, rising and taking her daughter into her arms. "I feared it would happen. And it all began so innocently, too. His grace came to London intending to put you at your ease and make it easier for you to meet eligible gentlemen. And it worked very well. But now you have gone and fallen in love with *him*. And that will not do at all."

"But perhaps—perhaps The Diamond loves me, too, Mama."

"He has always been extremely fond of you, my dearest. But you must not assume his kissing you to be anything more than compliance with your wishes. What you felt when he kissed you is not necessarily the same thing that his grace felt."

That was true, Bella thought as she kissed her mama good night and wandered off to her own chambers. Now that she thought about it, Diamond had not said one romantic thing to her in that garden. In fact, he had discussed the possibility of being forced to offer for her hand and the very thought of marriage to her had apparently sunk him into a deep gloom.

* * *

The Duke of Derrinham poured himself a second glass of brandy from the decanter upon his nightstand and scowled at Shaughnessy. "If you are finished piddling about, Shaughnessy," he grumbled, "go to bed. And do not think to sleep upon that blasted cot you have stowed away in my dressing room, either."

"My, but we are in exceeding good humor this evening," murmured Shaughnessy. "We must have had an amazingly good time at Lord Melton's *soirée*."

"Yes, we did," muttered the duke. "An amazingly good time. Cannot remember when I have enjoyed such nonsense more. Now shove off, Shaughnessy."

"I will shove off, as you so quaintly put it, your grace, in a moment or two. Just as soon as I have stowed your diamond studs safely away. Is it your back bothering you again that has put that scowl upon your face and that brandy in your hand?"

"No. It is nothing to do with my back. It is—"

"What, your grace?"

"Nothing. Go away."

Shaughnessy, having dealt with a petulant duke any number of times in the past, took up a stance beside the bed and with his hands upon his hips studied the gentleman beneath the counterpane with a deal of patience and curiosity. "You do know, your grace, that I am to be counted upon in any crisis," he said quietly.

"There is no crisis, Shaughnessy."

"Nevertheless, something troubles you. When you were a lad you were never loath to confide in myself or Mr. Sonnett."

"No, no, I was not, was I? But this is a good deal different than having sent a cricket ball through the window of the long drawing room at Twiney Hill."

"Has it to do with Miss Winstead, your grace?"

"No, it has not. Emily could never make me unhappy. I thank God that she found the courage to present herself to me. She is like a gift from heaven, especially after losing Diana. You do not like Emily do you, Shaughnessy?"

"I do not know the young woman, your grace."

"No, so I should think that for that reason alone both you and Sonnett would give her the benefit of the doubt."

"We do, your grace. I assure you."

"Well, you had best, because I am not about to turn her out of this house. What were my mother and father like, Shaughnessy? Why do I not remember the least thing about them?"

"You are drinking a second glass of brandy and scowling like an angry bear because you cannot remember your mama and papa? We have discussed them any number of times over the years, your grace. Mr. Sonnett and I and even Lady Diana have told you all sorts of tales about them."

"Yes, I know. And that is not the reason I am upset. I just happened to think about them now. I was five years old when they died, Shaughnessy. There ought to be something about them that I remember—the smell of my mother's perfume or the sound of my father's voice or some particular phrase one or the other of them was accustomed to repeat. But there is nothing. There are only the tales that you and Sonnett and Diana have spun for me and what I see of them in their portraits and nothing else. And that is most odd, don't you think?"

"No," replied Shaughnessy. "Not odd at all. Can you not give me so much as a hint of what it is disturbs you? I promise you that I shall be most discreet. And I may be of some assistance, your grace. I have lived a good deal longer than you and have considerable experience to draw upon."

"Have you any experience with love?"

Shaughnessy's emerald eyes began to gleam. "Do you think that you are falling in love, your grace?"

"I have already fallen in love and apparently there was no thought at all connected with it."

"But that is wonderful news! You ought to be rejoicing, not scowling and downing brandy."

"Not even if the lady I love is the same lady that I have come to London to help find a husband?"

"Lady Annabella?" gasped Shaughnessy.

"Just so."

"But, your grace, she thinks of you as a brother. And you have been attempting since the day we arrived in London to increase her standing among the Town beaux."

"Merely among the Corinthians, Shaughnessy. I have no influence over any of the others. But I have increased her standing so well among the Corinthians that this afternoon Lord Barrington proposed to the chit. And word at the clubs is that Nesbitt, Anders and Tottingham are leaning in a like direction."

"Did she accept Lord Barrington's proposal, your grace?"

"No, but she did not turn him down flat, either. She told him that she should like to wait upon her answer until she knew him better. What am I to do, Shaughnessy? From your vast experience over the years, have you any suggestions?"

"Declare yourself to her at once."

"She will laugh."

"No. Why should she?"

"Because I am the one, Shaughnessy, who recommended Barrington and the others. I said that any of them would be most acceptable to her father and good catches as well. Gad, I could cut out my tongue!"

"Too late," Shaughnessy pointed out, sinking down onto the ladder-backed chair on the other side of the nightstand. "A case of closing the stable doors after the horses are run out, your grace. May as well leave your tongue alone now."

"Brandy?" offered the duke, producing a second glass from the drawer in his night stand.

"Most improper," sighed Shaughnessy. "I ought not, your grace."

"I did mention that I might marry her," mumbled the duke after a long, glum silence.

"You did?"

"Yes, because I kissed her last evening at Vauxhall."

"You did what?"

"Kissed her. In the middle of Vauxhall. While we were watching the Cascade."

"Amidst all those people?"

"Apparently no one noticed, Shaughnessy. Bella assured me that her reputation was quite intact and that anyone at all who might have noticed would have thought it nothing but a brotherly peck. But I cannot think, from the way she assured me that such a sacrifice as marriage would not be necessary, that she found the idea of marrying me at all attractive."

"What did you say exactly, if you do not mind my asking?"

"No, don' mind a'tall," the duke responded, growing a bit tipsy but pouring himself a third glass of brandy anyway. "You an' Sonnett have looked after me from the day I was born an' I trust you beyond anything. Le' me see. I said—I said—oh, yes—I said that I did not mean to've kissed her an' I was sorry that I had. An' I said if it had become grist for the mill that I would do the honorable thing by her an' request her hand in marriage. I told her, Shaughnessy, that I did not think it would be too very bad to be married to her."

"Oh, glory, is it any wonder that you are drinking yourself into oblivion? What a thing to say to the woman you love!"

"Yes, but, I did not think then, Shaughnessy, that I

truly loved her. I thought, per'aps 'twas all in my imagination, y'know. But then—"

"Then what?"

"Then I kissed her again an' discovered it wasn't—in my imagination."

"You kissed her again? Where?"

"On the lips, Shaughnessy."

"No, no, where? Where were you, your grace, when you kissed her again? Not in the midst of another throng?"

" 'Course not," muttered the duke and hiccoughed. " 'Course not. Never make that mistake again. We were alone in Lord Melton's rose garden. Asked me to kiss her. Said she wished t'compare it with Barrington's kiss. Little baggage. Compare m'kisses to a halfling's like Barrington. Showed her, I did."

"Showed her what, your grace?"

"Showed her what a real kiss was all about."

"Oh, you did not, your grace!"

"Indeed I did. Think I frightened the wits out of her, Shaughnessy."

Mr. Shaughnessy nodded thoughtfully, and gazed longingly at the brandy he could not accept. The duke sighed and drained his glass in one gulp.

"Sleep on it," murmured Shaughnessy, rising and whisking the brandy decanter from Derrinham's grasp even as he reached out to pour himself another glassful. "Nothing to do but sleep on it. Answer will come to us."

"I was about to drink that, Shaughnessy."

"I know, but you have had quite enough of it for one night, your grace. You are already foxed."

"Not foxed enough."

"Sleep on it," mumbled Shaughnessy again, nodding and wandering out of the chamber with the decanter in his hand.

Derrinham waited forever for him to wander back in

again, but he did not. "Devil it," grumbled the duke. "Gone off t'bed with m'brandy tucked underneath his arm. Cheeky bastard!" But then he hiccoughed again and grinned and allowed himself to sink down into the feather ticking and rest his head upon the pillow. He could always count upon Shaughnessy and Sonnett to make him grin in the end, no matter how impossible a situation seemed or how grouchy he got over something.

He attempted to think of a time when those two gentlemen had not stood steadfastly beside him, but he could not. Truly, it was the oddest thing. He could remember how Shaughnessy and Sonnett had looked and smelled and sounded when he was no more than a tad. And he could remember Bella from the time she was a babe wailing away in her crib. He could even remember Diana and that funny little hat she had worn with the cherries upon it. The one that Bella's had so reminded him of. And he could remember Lady and Lord Meade before either of them had taken to considering themselves old. But he could not for the life of him call to mind the least thing about his father or mother. If there had been no portraits of them about, and Sonnett had not at one time or another stood him before them and explained that these two people were his parents, he would have had no idea of them at all. But how could that be? He had been all of five when they died. How could he not remember them in the lcast?

The watchman called the hour of three just as Junius Farraday slipped soundlessly into Derrinham House through the kitchen door. *It is most helpful to have a butler on one's side,* he thought. *Mr. Sonnett gave his word the kitchen door would be open and damned if it ain't. Makes everything a deal easier.*

The kitchen fires had been banked and their coals

glowed hauntingly, little red circles of heat holding steady amongst the white ash and the black cinders. Upon a countertop near the bottom of the servants' staircase, a lone candle burned, beckoning Farraday in that direction. Above him, a second candle kept silent vigil at the first floor landing. And above that, at the second floor landing, he knew there would be another. Best get on with it, then, he told himself and moved silently, candle in hand, to explore the chambers of the ground floor one by one. He nodded to himself as he padded lightly across the floorboards and the carpeting, entering and exploring one chamber after another, the sound of the watchman's voice lingering in his mind.

This is the true witching hour in London, he thought. At least, 'tis the true witching hour for those of us who have lived through the years of The Society of Lost Souls.

The very thought of that infamous club sent shivers up Farraday's spine. They had come close to setting the entire city into a panic, those highborn hellraisers. Thievery and rape, murder and mayhem, and no one able to lay it at their doors. No one able to prove a thing against them. Each one of them vouched for by the others. All of them with three or four friends to say they had spent this evening together in such and such a place. And no one able to say them nay. And no one *willing* to gainsay them, either, with the Derrinham power and fortune known to be involved, he thought.

They had been worse by far than the present day Hellfire Club. Worse than any club of devils ever imagined. And here he was, sneaking into the house of the very devil who had bestowed upon them the protection and support of his nobility. Rumor, in fact, said even more, said that the devil had conceived of the notion of the club all on his own. That he had even gone about recruiting the members. Of course, as Mr. Sonnett and Mr.

Shaughnessy had been careful to point out to him, that particular Duke of Derrinham had begun to repent his ways and besides, he was long since dead. But still, a man can feel the evil, thought Farraday as he completed his search of the ground floor and made his way carefully back to the kitchen and the servants' staircase. 'Tis as though all the man's sins have seeped into the very walls, staining them black forever.

His fingers trembled as he reached the first floor landing and took that candle into his hand; he was truly amazed at himself. Junius Farraday had never been so afraid as to send his fingers quivering in all his life. "Stupid," he whispered into the shadows as he warily opened the door and stepped into the first floor corridor. Thick carpeting hushed his footsteps as he made his way down the passage, stopping at each chamber, slipping cautiously into it and checking the shadows for the least sign of a figure concealed in the darkness. He knew exactly what figure he sought to find, too. Miss Winstead, with a knife or a pistol in her hand, waiting on the duke to come walking in his sleep. Did she know, Farraday wondered, that he walked so, and that his footsteps inevitably led him to the servants' staircase—to those infamous steps near the third floor?

Most likely she did not know. Most likely she would think to attack him in his own chambers, or in the library if he should go down to fetch a volume in the night. Farraday's mind searched back over all he knew about Miss Emily Winstead—all that Mr. Sonnett and Mr. Shaughnessy together had been able to tell him. His grace's half-sister and raised by the man whom everyone, including himself, had suspected of murdering the seventh duke and his duchess. But they could not prove the crime against Mr. Winstead then, and they could not prove it to this very day.

Still, he had reasons, thought Farraday. Good reasons.

And like as not, this Miss Winstead was set upon revenge
for all the harm that The Diamond's papa has done her
family. "But The Diamond is not the one who did the
harm," sighed Farraday to himself, "and he knows nothing of all that cold-blooded villainy. *Nothing.*" The word
hung in Junius Farraday's mind. To this very day the lad
knew nothing of his father's evil. He remembered nothing
of all that had happened in this ugly establishment. And
thank the Good Lord that he does not, thought Farraday.
Thank the Good Lord that he does not. As he prepared
to mount to the second floor, Junius Farraday allowed
his memory to carry him back twenty-one years to the
early hours of the morning on the fifteenth of May in
1793.

Once more, he felt the pale, shivering, silent child bury
one cold, wet, tiny hand in his own and tug him fiercely
from the Charley's box straight up Great Stanhope Street
and through the front door of this very house. Once more
in his mind, the two of them climbed the main staircase
in the midst of an enormous and unsettling silence. No
one was about. No one at all. He remembered thinking
that the servants were most likely all asleep and that quite
likely this little chap's mama and papa were sleeping as
well. He remembered questioning the intelligence of allowing this infant to tow him deeper into the place as
he pulled the boy abruptly to a halt in the second floor
corridor.

What the deuce am I doing? Yes, that's what he'd
thought at that very moment. What the deuce am I doing?
I will be taken for a burglar and hauled off to Newgate
and no one will listen for a moment to this little one
when he says that he brought me here. But the child had
clung to him with both hands and pulled with all his
might until Farraday, resigned, had moved forward again.

Never saying a word, the boy had led him down the
second floor hall to the servants' staircase at the far end.

And on that staircase, midway to the servants' quarters on the third floor, in the flickering light of the branch of candles that Farraday had grabbed up from the front hall, lay the lifeless bodies of a man and a woman in what seemed an incredibly large and ever-expanding pool of blood. *Blood.* On the walls, on the stairs—even on the ceiling. *Blood everywhere!*

And that was the first time that I looked closely at the little duke, he reminded himself, and he was covered in blood as well. Not merely his hands were slick with it, but it was in his hair, on his face and all over his night-clothes. Even his bare feet were stained red with it.

"Well, but he is not about to be covered in blood like that again," Farraday sighed to himself. "Especially not in his own blood. It is not about to happen on Junius Farraday's watch. No one will discover The Diamond's body all cold and clammy and lying upon that damned staircase like I found his mama and papa. Never, so long as there is breath in my body."

Thirteen

Jane and Bella and Emily, under the guardianship of Miss Davies, strolled along the paths of Green Park on Monday afternoon, their brightly colored parasols open and twirling because they thought it wonderful fun to set the reds and golds and greens spinning behind them in the bright sunlight. They were discussing any number of interesting topics including the arrival in London of the Duchess of Oldenburg, the Tsar's sister, and the rumor that there was a distinct possibility that General Wellesley was about to be made a duke, when Emily's voice faltered and she came to a standstill in the middle of the path.

"Miss Winstead—Emily, what is wrong?" asked Miss Davies with some concern. "You look as though you have seen a ghost."

"N-no, not a ghost," stuttered Emily. "It is Sir Cyril."

"Sir Cyril?" asked Jane and Bella in one voice. "Where?"

"There, standing in the doorway of the little farm cottage, speaking with Mrs. Searle."

"That," asked Miss Davies with the cock of an eyebrow, "is the infamous Sir Cyril Blythe? Why, he is nothing more than a rickety old man. This is the extremely dangerous person, Jane, that your papa warned you against?"

"Dangerous?" asked Emily. "I had no idea that he was actually dangerous."

"Then why have you grown so very pale at the sight of him?" asked Bella.

"Because I do not like him. And I do not wish him to see me. No doubt he has visited in Curzon Street by this time, expecting to find my brother Michael and myself. And since he discovered neither of us there, and now I am strolling about with the two of you, whom he knows I should never have had the opportunity to come to know, he will likely ask me any number of questions. And I will not be able to answer a one of them."

"Then you need not answer," declared Bella righteously. "He has not the least authority over you, Emily. He is not your guardian or any such thing."

"N-no."

"I had not thought," murmured Jane. "Is your brother Michael—is he—related—to us in some way as well?"

"Oh, no," replied Emily, reddening. "Michael is not—I am the only one who—Michael is a *true* Winstead. Oh, gracious, Sir Cyril *has* seen me and he is coming this way."

Bella found the look of panic upon Emily's countenance most disconcerting. Certainly Sir Cyril Blythe was not at all a pleasant man, but what on earth did Miss Emily Winstead fear he could do to her on a bright, sunny afternoon in the middle of Green Park? With a most audacious smile, Bella returned the gentleman's greeting as he approached and introduced him with notable aplomb to Miss Davies. "And of course," she added with the lift of an eyebrow, "you will remember Miss May and you are already acquainted with Miss Winstead."

"Yes, indeed," droned Sir Cyril, looking quite dapper in a russet morning coat and buff pantaloons, despite the overt signs of dissipation that clung to him like a second skin. "Good afternoon, my pretty ones. This beautiful day is brightened even more by your presence in it. I do regret, Miss May and Lady Annabella, that our tea on Thursday was so rudely interrupted. I was quite enjoying your company. I have not had such young and beautiful ladies pay me a call in a very long time."

"Your tea?" asked Miss Davies, astonished, her gaze darting from one young lady to the other. "You paid Sir Cyril a call on Thursday and had tea with him?"

"Indeed," nodded Bella with a lift of her chin, determined to face Sir Cyril down with elegance. "Lord Barrington and Miss May and myself and his grace all paid a visit at Pickering Place, and Sir Cyril was so gracious as to invite us to remain for a time and taste of his hospitality."

"At gunpoint," added Jane bluntly, catching and sharing in Bella's daring attitude.

Emily gasped and Miss Lydia Davies scowled.

"It all came to nothing, Lydie, and I did not wish to worry you with it," Jane stated with a toss of her head. "We were not harmed, after all."

"No, no, never intended to do them harm," laughed Sir Cyril in a most hideous tone. "A prank merely, for his grace's benefit. His papa and I were accustomed to play such pranks upon each other from time to time. Emily, I did not discover you in Curzon Street yesterday nor this morning," he said, changing the subject. "And Miss Glendenning could not tell me where you had gone. She had not, in fact, so much as realized that you were not safely at home. We do worry about you, my dear. We have all told you again and again that it is not safe to go traipsing about London without a chaperone. Even Michael has attempted to make you realize the truth of that, has he not? But here, you are perfectly well chaperoned and so I shall cease to scold you. However did you come, Emily, to make the acquaintance of these particular young ladies?"

"We made each other's acquaintance through— through—"Bella began uncertainly.

"Miss DeLacey," breathed Emily softly.

"Yes, Miss Octavia DeLacey," lied Jane quite capably.

"Who attended Miss Youngquist's School for Young Ladies with me, and has had me to visit at her house," provided Emily.

"Exactly," Jane said with a nod. "Miss Winstead has come to keep me company for a time," she continued, tucking her arm supportively through Emily's. "We have become enormous friends."

Bella came close to gasping at the look of hatred that flashed for a moment in Sir Cyril's muddy brown eyes. But it was gone on the instant and the man continued to smile at them.

"How novel for you, Emily," he murmured. "You have taken a step up in the world, have you not, to become a welcomed guest in the home of a duke? I can imagine what your papa would say to such a thing if he were alive."

Miss Emily Winstead stared at the man with wide blue eyes but made not the least reply, though Bella noticed that she began to nibble at her lower lip.

"I stopped by Rundell and Bridges, by the way, to be certain that Michael had received my message, and they informed me that the dear boy was ill. Odd that he should be ill and yet not be at home in his bed. And very odd that you should be traipsing about Town with your new friends when your brother is in need of you. It is all most confusing and distressing, my dear." Sir Cyril's smile had altered into a most knowing sneer. "Come, Emily," he fairly hissed, "you and Michael have been keeping secrets from me, have you not?"

"N-no," managed Emily very softly.

"No?"

"Are you Miss Winstead's guardian, sir, that you question her actions so?" asked Bella in a most exasperated tone. "If you are not, then I cannot see that she owes you any explanation for visiting Miss May at Derrinham House. And how she may be held accountable for what her brother does when he is a grown man and may do as he pleases is quite beyond me."

Most unaccountably, Sir Cyril bestowed a wide, yellow-toothed smile upon Bella. "A point well made, my lady," he chuckled. "And very nicely said, too. Not a bit of The Hesitant Hedgehog left in you, I see. Derrinham's influence, no doubt."

Bella blushed at the mention of that hated appellation and cursed herself silently for doing so.

"Oh yes, my lady," Sir Cyril said with a horrible wink, "I do manage to keep abreast of things, though I am generally thought to be outside of Society these days. And I was most entertained to hear of rumors of a bit of dalliance between The Diamond and The Hedgehog. What a fine fable that would make, I thought when I heard of it. The Diamond and The Hedgehog."

"How so a fable?" asked Bella, her tone bordering on belligerence and her eyes growing stormy.

"I shall tell you the gist of it, shall I?" responded Sir Cyril, focusing his gaze upon Bella alone. "It goes like so. A most exquisite Diamond glitters and glows in the sunlight and the very dazzle of him attracts the attention of an old fox. Now the old fox is quite rich and very wily and also very vain, and he longs to break The Diamond into fine little pieces with which to adorn himself. So he lures The Diamond into his den where he allows the beautiful jewel to remain, oblivious to the fate that awaits him while he, the fox, goes out to gather a pack of foxes about him and the best of all jewel cutters as well."

Emily gasped the tiniest bit, but Bella and the others did not notice, so intently were they listening.

"Though The Diamond is exquisite, he possesses no means at all to protect himself from the fox. He possesses neither the means nor the intelligence to run away, nor can he fight the wily creature because he has not the least concept of the way in which the fox will attack him. His only defense, in fact, is his very denseness and immutability, and that is no defense at all against a creature ingenious enough to include others in his plan and to find himself the perfect jewel cutter."

Emily gasped again and raised one gloved hand to cover her lips, but Bella, Jane and Miss Davies merely stood glaring at the gentleman and listened in silence as he continued.

"And then one day, quite by accident, a young Hedgehog discovers The Diamond in the fox's den. Now she is a very smart little Hedgehog and knows all about foxes, especially this particular vain and wily fox. And discovering that she has fallen in love with The Diamond's glitter and glow, she urges The Diamond to leave the fox's sight and hide in the shadows of another, far different den. But when she at last sees that he will not, she seeks to protect The Diamond from the fox and to keep him whole by wrapping herself into a ball around him. 'My spikes,' she says, 'will protect you, Diamond. They will prick and sting that dreadful fox and discourage him from snatching you up and cutting you into pieces.' "

"And when the fox comes," offered Bella with a freezing scowl, "he attempts to snatch The Diamond from The Hedgehog and her spines prick and poke at his muzzle until he runs yelping like a frightened puppy, off into the night with the other foxes and the jewel cutter running and yelping right after him. And The Diamond and The Hedgehog live happily ever after."

"No, my dear," smiled Sir Cyril. "That would be nice, but no. When the fox returns and discovers The Hedgehog, he simply invites the jewel cutter and his fellow foxes to remain with him. And while they spend the days and nights feasting and drinking and laughing, the Hedgehog grows very hungry and very thirsty and at last must decide either to abandon The Diamond to save her own life or to die curled around him. And the fox will have The Diamond in the end either way, my dear. Because even if she is not intelligent enough to abandon him and thus save her own life by surrendering him to the fox, why, everyone knows it is a deal easier to remove a dead Hedgehog from a Diamond than a live one."

"I should have liked very much to have knocked his yellow old teeth down his nasty, wrinkled throat," declared Bella, flopping down onto one of the upholstered armchairs in the Floral Parlor of Derrinham House. "The man is an ogre and a villain and a toad!"

"Yes," agreed Jane, tucking her feet beneath her as she sat upon the sofa. "And a perfectly conceited beetlehead, as well. I have a good mind to tell Uncle Hill all about that insulting little fable of his. Uncle Hill will call him out for thinking to insult you and to threaten you as well, and that will be the end of Sir Cyril Blythe, you may believe me. We shall see, once there is a pistol ball through his evil heart, if he still believes The Diamond cannot defend himself. I cannot believe that you actually *know* that man!" exclaimed Jane, glaring at Emily. "And that you have invited him into your home!"

"I did never once invite him into my home," replied Emily. "He just comes. He walks right in and makes himself comfortable without one word from me. He has always done, for as long as I can remember."

"Well, then I pity you," sighed Jane, "for I would not have that man in my home for all the money in the world."

"Who?" asked the duke as he turned into the parlor. "Ah, three Buds of Spring in the Floral Parlor—how appropriate. Pardon me, three buds and a blossom. Miss Davies, I did not see you there. You are practically hidden behind that wretched rhododendron. I do wish someone would forget to water that monstrosity for a month or two. Who will you not have in your home for all the money in the world, Jane?"

"Oh, it is of no import, Uncle Hill. Merely someone whose conversation raised my hackles. Bella is to spend the night with me. In fact, she is to spend the entire week because her mama and papa must go to Bath to look in upon her Aunt Adeline. Dear Miss Davies volunteered to chaperone Bella for a se'nnight the moment she heard and Lady Meade could find no fault with it."

"I *am* a dear, am I not?" grinned Miss Davies, peeking around the rhododendron at The Diamond. "Not one young lady, not two young ladies, but three and each of them as pretty as a picture. I shall need a whip soon to beat off the beaux. I wonder, your grace, if I might have a private word with you before dinner?"

"Certainly, Miss Davies. Whenever you like."

"Now?"

With a cock of an eyebrow and a bow, the duke escorted Miss Davies to his office, where he set a chair for her beside his table and took another for himself. "Now, what may I do for you, Miss Davies?" he asked, settling into the chair and crossing one knee over the other. "You have been a veritable saint, you know, through this whole thing. From the very first, when you agreed to bring Janie from Vienna and then to remain at home and pretend to be ill so that I might escort her about, I knew you intended to be an absolute trouper."

"I intended to do all that I could to be of service to you, your grace," smiled Miss Davies. "I have always had a fondness for you, but you know that."

"Yes. You never once hit me over the head with a skillet—or anything else, for that matter. And when I turned up uninvited upon May's doorstep from time to time, usually in a most disheveled state as I recall, I do believe you kept several butlers from turning me away simply by the lift of an eyebrow as you passed through the hall."

"I assure you, I did."

"So I thought. Now, what may I do for you, ma'am?"

Lydia Davies had long been a most sophisticated woman. The daughter of an impoverished viscount, she had been forced to make her own way in the world but had lost none of the gentility of her upbringing in the process. And since Lord and Lady May had treated her as a member of their family and included her in their own dinners and entertainments, Miss Davies had proceeded to add a great deal of European polish to that gentility. It was that sophistication which now served to put her quite at her ease with a gentleman who gazed bemusedly at her through the most gorgeous sapphire eyes upon the face of the earth—eyes that would have set any other governess or lady's companion to stammering and stuttering and at last have driven her into flight.

"I think you know that I have always held a particular place in my heart for you, your grace," she began, smiling back at him in a most beguiling way. "In fact, if I were twenty years younger, I should throw my cap over the windmill for you."

Derrinham laughed. "Is this to be a declaration of your intentions then, Miss Davies? I must warn you that I am not at all a good catch. I am a grouch with a bad back and a most unforgiving attitude."

"Balderdash! You are a decent man who has lived through trying times. And even as we speak, you ought to be looking about you for a wife."

"This *is* a declaration of your intentions!" teased the duke.

"No, merely a probing of yours."

"A probing of my intentions?"

"Yes. First, I wish to be advised of your intentions toward Miss Emily Winstead. Do you mean to acknowledge her in some way? I ask, because if that is so, you must be very careful how you go about the doing of it. You cannot, you know, simply walk into the midst of the *ton* and announce that she is your half-sister. That is tantamount to publicly labeling the girl a bastard and they will never accept her."

"I expect you are correct on that account," sighed Derrinham, attempting to make himself more comfortable in his chair. "Though I should like to give Emily an opportunity to enjoy what is left of this Season and if she does not make a match, to take her with me to Twiney Hill for the summer and then return for the Little Season. Emily is quite fetching and perhaps she will find herself a husband, don't you think?"

"I think it quite likely," nodded Miss Davies.

"Of course, I shall need to privately explain to any gentleman who offers for her exactly how we two are related."

"Of course."

"The senior Mr. Piermont and I have discussed it. I should like Emily to share the Hallsworth name if she cares to do so. Perhaps she can make use of the bar sinister. Emily Winstead-Hallsworth? Well, whatever she decides, as long as Mr. Piermont assures us it is legal."

"And will you provide her a dowry, your grace?"

"Yes, of course. And if she does not care to marry, I shall see that she has an independence. That would be quite proper, don't you think, Miss Davies? I will keep it secret, of course, so as not to provide the *ton* with grist for the mill. But life is never easy for a woman alone. Well, you know that."

"Indeed I do. Though I was most fortunate to obtain a position with Lord and Lady May."

"Yes, well, I will see to it that Emily will not need to obtain a position with anyone. And there is any amount of money I can bequeath her in my will and Twiney Hill is not entailed. Perhaps I can leave her Twiney Hill as well."

"There is a good deal of time before you need think of wills and entails, your grace. Perhaps you will marry and have children, and then your will must, perhaps, be altered. But the dowry and the independence are capital ideas and I am certain Miss Winstead will be thrilled with either. At the moment, however, Emily is more in need of fashionable gowns and folderols so that she may accompany Jane and me and Bella into Society."

"Indeed! You must see that Emily is rigged out in the very best and then we will introduce her around. No one will quibble if our party should appear with one extra young lady, do you think? No, they will not," he answered his own question, "because the hostesses are always so pleased that I have deigned to make an appearance, they will accept Emily without a thought. There are some advantages to being a duke, I assure you, Miss Davies."

"Indeed. And perhaps you might introduce Miss Winstead as a long-lost relative. Yes, that's the ticket. A distant relative who has but recently come to your attention. No one will cavil at that. And Jane and Bella and I shall set about to refurbish her wardrobe first thing tomorrow. Which brings me directly to my second order of business—Lady Annabella."

The Diamond's eyebrow cocked and from his waistcoat pocket he fished a quizzing glass and stared at Miss Davies through it, which set that lady to laughing.

"No, really, Duke. I am aware it is none of my business but I could not help but notice—"

"Notice what, Miss Davies?"

"That you have formed a *tendre* for the girl."

"Me? In love with Bella?"

"Yes, and do not attempt to deny it. I have thought so since first you requested Jane's and my presence in London. And I knew for certain at Vauxhall. You are beyond smitten with her, your grace. You have completely lost your heart and you really ought to tell her so."

The duke dropped his quizzing glass and stared at Miss Davies in astonishment.

"I know I am being outrageous to interfere, but if you do not tell her, you may lose her, your grace. Lord Barrington is infatuated with her—and several other gentlemen are as well."

The Duke of Derrinham stood up and paced toward the fireplace. He ran his fingers through his curls and balled his hands into fists and stuffed those fists into his pockets. Then he kicked at the hearth with the toe of his boot and spun about and paced back to Miss Davies. Coming to a halt before her, he stared down into her eyes. "I should like to tell Bella that I am in love with her," he mumbled, "but the more I think on it, the more I think I should not."

"Goodness gracious, why not?"

"Well, as to that, I have devised for myself any number of excuses. But the truth of it is, Miss Davies, that the more I think about declaring myself to Bella, the more aware of myself and my failings I become. And the more aware of myself I become, the more certain I am that something dreadful is wrong with me."

It was Miss Davies's turn to stare in astonishment. "Wrong with you? But how do you mean, your grace? You are not ill?"

"I am. At least, I think I am. I think I am ill in my mind."

"Never," declared Miss Davies emphatically, the look upon the duke's face sending a great pang of sympathy through her.

"Yes, that is what I tell myself, but I cannot move past the fact that there is something most peculiar about me. I have thought so since I was a child and I have grown to be more peculiar as a man. And it would be most unkind and selfish, too, for me to attempt to engage Bella's heart when it is quite possible that if I am not mad already, I am at least tottering on the very verge of madness."

The voices in the chamber below continued to float up the chimney, but Michael Winstead had ceased to listen. Without the least thought to creasing his livery, he sank down into one of the chairs in the sewing room and pushed his high white wig to the back of his head. Damnation! Rather than despising her and plotting for her downfall, Derrinham truly intended to give Emily a Season? Fit her out in fashion and introduce her into Society? Share his name with her and provide her an independence or a dowry? And think to put her into his will, of all things?

If he did not know for a fact that the duke had not the least idea that James the first footman was truly Emily's brother Michael—if he did not know for a fact that the duke did not at all suspect that he was being eavesdropped upon—why, he would think the whole conversation going forward in the room below some dastardly plot to draw him off. But he was certain on both counts. The Duke of Derrinham imagined James the first footman to be no one other than James the first footman and only Mrs. Neville, the housekeeper, knew he had come to this room to fetch the broken mantel clock to her so that she might send it to the clockmaker's to be fixed.

What the devil was he going to do? Winstead wondered forlornly. He had promised his father to avenge the horrors done his family by the seventh Duke of Derrinham. He had sworn on the old man's deathbed to kill this eighth Duke of Derrinham, this spawn of the devil, this heir to the legacy of The Society of Lost Souls. But ever since he had taken the position of first footman to get close enough to the duke to do the bloody deed, every time he steeled himself to take that irreversible step, The Diamond said something or did something that proved him to be most undeserving of such a fate, most unlike the demon duke who had sired him, and more like the little duke in the fairy tales Michael's mama had loved to tell Emily.

Emily. The very thought of her sent Winstead deep into the doldrums. If, at last, he did manage to convince himself again that this Derrinham was deserving of the fate he had planned for him; if, at last, he could convince himself again that revenge would be sweet; if, at the last, he actually did the deed; how was he ever going to face Emily again? He had not thought of that before. Of course he had not. Because up until this Friday past it had not been of the least import. Up until this Friday past, the duke had only been a shining figure in his sister's dreams. But now he was a living, breathing soul who had invited Emily to share in his life and who had been as good and kind to her as she had dreamed in all her dreams. Oh, damnation! thought Winstead. How can I kill the man when he has finally become a real person to Emily and she finds such joy in him?

What was it The Diamond had said moments ago— that he feared he was on the verge of madness? "Odd how madness seems to be the very height of fashion in some circles these days," Winstead muttered. "The duke's father drove Mama mad. Something is driving the duke mad. And I am driving myself mad. 'Zounds, what a gay time we are all having now! It is more fun than two hares and a hound in a hollow log."

Fourteen

Bella could not get to sleep. With an exasperated sigh, she turned up the wick of the lamp upon the table beside her bed. "It is merely because I am away from home," she muttered to herself. "I shall read a bit and that will make me drowsy and in no time at all—drat!" she muttered, remembering that she had not brought one single volume with her. Well, she knew very well where the library was in Derrinham House. She would just take her lamp, slip down to the first floor, find herself a book and come quietly back to bed.

In a robe of red satin and her red-and-blue knit bedroom slippers, Bella padded her way down the hall and then, very carefully, down the staircase. It always frightened her a bit to be traipsing about in her floor-length night rail with an oil lamp in one hand—especially when she need descend a staircase. One misstep, she thought, and I shall be toast and Derrinham House a roaring blaze. Now, why must I think of that? Honestly!

Bella held the lamp high in one hand as she searched for a title that promised to be interesting. There were any number of stale, old treatises and ancient scribblings. There were volumes of philosophy and religion. And an entire section of works on agriculture. Bella's lamp stirred eerie shadows within the chamber as she raised it higher, then lowered it, then moved it to the left and right, searching. "Oh, my goodness," she murmured aloud, her eyes catching, of a sudden, the sparkle of gold leaf in the lamp-light. "What have we here?"

The volume was enormous. Bella knelt down upon the carpeting and set the lamp beside her so that she might use both hands to tug the book from the bottom shelf. I shall never be able to carry this upstairs to my bedchamber, she thought, easing the heavy volume to the floor. I will just have a quick look at it to satisfy my curiosity and then return it to the shelf and find something that is not quite such heavy reading.

Bella grinned at her play on words, then looked closely at the volume before her. *The Book of Secrets.* The very thought of what might be contained therein set Bella's heart to thumping. Whose secrets? And if they were secrets, why put them in a book and label them as such? Checking to see that the lamp was at a distance not to be knocked over, Bella opened the volume and began to read.

They struck like lightning, again and again, pummeling him mercilessly from out of the darkness. And he struck back, his arms up, his fists punching decisively in a rapid staccato like the born fighter he was. But they were too fast; they danced too quickly; they were too ethereal. By the time the full force of his blows reached them, they were gone. When he realized the futility of his efforts, he cried out angrily and gasping; he dropped his hands and turned and ran. But they ran with him, behind him, beside him, even ahead of him. Like a plague they covered him over, blinding him, deafening him, stealing his very breath away.

It was a nightmare, of course. Hillary Holland Hallsworth told himself it was a nightmare over and over again, but his self did not choose to listen. Instead, he was forced to continue struggling against the visions, attempting to dislodge the sight and sound and smell of them from his very being. But he could not do it alone. Diana, he thought. Sonnett, Shaughnessy. And continuing to do battle, he fled in search of the three people he was certain he could trust. The only three people whom he knew would help him. Nightmare or reality, Diana and Sonnett and Shaughnessy were to be depended upon. That was truth. That was certain. That was his hope.

Bella gasped as a dark shadow towered over her. She had been so absorbed in the volume that she had not heard anyone coming down the staircase or padding along the corridor or shuffling into the library. She looked up quickly and in the glow of the lamplight gasped again. "Diamond, whatever is wrong?"

His beautiful countenance had taken on the most tortured look and he appeared to be struggling for breath and though he stood directly above her, he seemed not to see her at all.

"Diamond, answer me. What is wrong?" Bella abandoned the volume, reached for the lamp and rose to her feet. "Diamond?" she said with a bit less anxiety, the odd look in his eyes giving her the first hint that though he stood before her, harassed, in his nightshirt and nightcap and nothing more, he was not at all awake. "Diamond, it is Bella. Do you hear me?"

The duke mumbled, but his words were most incoherent.

He is asleep, Bella thought. He is walking about in his sleep. And having reached that conclusion, Bella carried her lamp to the library table, set it down, then returned and took one of the duke's large, strong hands into her own. Murmuring the most inconsequential phrases, she drew him along beside her to a red leather armchair and urged him into it.

"Diamond?" she whispered.

"Huh? What?"

"Diamond? Can you hear me?"

"Diana, help me! I can find no one to help me!"

There was a plaintive note in the duke's voice that Bella had never heard there before, and the sound of his dead sister's name upon his lips set her heart to aching for him.

"Diamond, it is Bella, my dear. Do wake up. You are having the most dreadful dream."

"B-Bella?"

"Yes, Diamond, it is Bella. Your Bella. Do wake up now. You are perfectly safe. There is no one here to hurt you. I promise."

"Bella?" The duke leaned far back in the chair and his eyes closed and then opened, blinking encouragingly up at her. "Bella? What the devil are you doing here? No, where the devil am I, is what I mean to say," he muttered with a shake of his head as he began to register his dimly lit surroundings. "No, where the devil are we? That is more like it. Where the devil are we, Bella? Oh, by gawd, I am in my nightshirt, ain't I? I have been doing it again!"

"You have been walking in your sleep. Is that what you mean, Diamond? Have you done this before?"

"Innumerable times," grumbled the duke, snatching his nightcap from off his curls and running his fingers through his hair. "Lord, Bella, I do apologize. You ought not be treated to the sight of me like this. Close your eyes and I will absent myself immediately."

Bella could not help but laugh. "Do you think I have never seen you in your nightshirt before, your grace? Well, I have."

"Never."

"Oh, yes indeed. You were twelve and an insufferable prig."

"Never. I was never an insufferable prig."

"You were. I came to you a tiny child seeking your

aid and all you did was to climb down the trellis in your nightshirt, seize me by the hand, and drag me home across the fields, spouting platitudes all the way. And if that is not an insufferable prig, I should like to know what is."

"But you were escaping your keepers at five o'clock in the morning, Bella," chuckled the duke, remembering. "And you tossed a rock through my window. Smashed it. Nearly hit me in the head."

"Oh, I did not nearly hit you in the head," grinned Bella, settling down upon the arm of his chair. "You do tell the greatest clankers."

"How did you get that rock as far as my window, Bella? I always wondered. You were no bigger than a flea."

"With the slingshot you made for me the day before."

"Damn!" exclaimed the duke. "Well, I shall be more careful what I make for you from now on. We are in the library," he added, peering up at the shelves.

Bella nodded. "Will you tell me your dream? Sometimes it helps to speak about your dreams, especially bad ones."

Derrinham shook his head. "I do not remember it. I never do. It always dodges just to the side of my mind and I cannot quite reach it when I am awake. What's that?" he added, spying the volume lying flat upon the carpeting.

"The book I have chosen to put me to sleep," laughed Bella. "But it is so large I cannot possibly carry it up the staircase with a lamp in one hand and holding to my skirts with the other."

"It is large," murmured the duke, staring at the thing. "And it looks ancient."

"Well, I do not know how ancient it is, but it is all writ by hand. It is a book of secrets, Diamond."

"Secrets?" Derrinham cocked an eyebrow in disbelief. "What sort of secrets?"

"All sorts. You will not believe it when you see." Bella, excited by thoughts of sharing the book with him, took his hand and tugged him to his feet. "It says, for instance, that William the Conqueror was frightened of piglets."

"Piglets?"

"Yes, and that if you mix three portions of powdered foxglove to one portion of pulverized elm leaves in a pint of apple cider—"

"You will have the most wretched apple cider you ever tasted," finished the duke, kneeling down with her upon the floor before the volume.

"No," giggled Bella. "You will have a cure for stuttering."

"Indeed. It is difficult to stutter for long after you have poisoned yourself. It *is* handwritten," murmured the duke, moving the lamp closer to the pages. "Look here, Bella. This one mentions the Duke of Derrinham. 'In the year of the granting of the letters patent to William Moreland Hallsworth, first Duke of Derrinham, it was discovered at that nobleman's castle in the West Riding the secret of turning lead to gold.' "

"The secret of turning lead to gold? What is it?"

"Ugh, you do not wish to know."

"I do," declared Bella, pressing up against him to get a better view of the page. "Oh, Diamond, that is the most disgusting thing!"

"Yes, and wouldn't you know that someone would attribute it to one of my ancestors?"

Junius Farraday was convinced that he could not last a moment longer, curled up as he was upon a step of the iron staircase that led to the little walk that circled before the highest of the bookshelves in the duke's library. He had been in the midst of his nightly inspection of the house when a young lady had come wandering down the hall with lamp in hand, and he had scrambled quickly for a place to hide. Whether or not the young lady was the infamous Miss Emily Winstead made no difference. No one but Mr. Sonnett and Mr. Shaughnessy were to know of Farraday's presence upon the premises in the late hours of the evening and the early hours of the morning.

He had been amazed to discover that the young lady was neither the infamous Miss Winstead nor the duke's niece, but a new young lady entirely. Well, he would make a point of asking Mr. Sonnett who she was at the very next opportunity. But he had hoped she would hurry and choose a volume, because he had a great many more rooms to inspect before he would be at all comfortable about the duke's safety this night.

And then the duke had come wandering in and Junius Farraday had been at first appalled by the duke's appearance and then tenderly moved by the most innocent affection he had witnessed between the two. This, he had found himself thinking, is just the young woman to stand beside the gentleman in his hour of need. Just the young woman indeed. And when the two at last departed, the duke carrying both the enormous volume and the lamp, Junius Farraday was most inclined to stand up and wish them well.

He did not do so, of course. He held his position until the very last of the lamplight faded from sight. He was just about to stand up and make his way back down the stairs when he heard a swishing of cloth and a quiet footstep upon the floor below him. He glanced down through the space between the steps and watched, amazed, as a shadowy figure appeared from behind the draperies at the far end of the chamber and glided silently forward. It stopped beside the fireplace and in a moment a candle sputtered into light upon the mantel, and then a second and then a third, and then Miss Emily Winstead, in a robe of pale lavender, her long black tresses trailing freely across her shoulders and down her back, was easily discernible as she stood twisting his grace's forgotten nightcap in her hands and staring toward the doorway through which the duke and Bella had but recently exited. It was all Junius Farraday could do not to leap down upon her and arrest her there and then. But he dared not. He had not the least evidence against her.

The Diamond had carried both book and lamp into Bella's bedchamber, placing the one upon the bedside table and the other upon the bed itself. He had gazed down into those extraordinarily trusting chocolate-brown eyes and bid her a proper and most polite good night and then he had trundled off to his own chambers, his nightshirt flapping against his shins and his bare feet freezing.

He did not allow himself to think of anything until he was safely between his own sheets, but then his mind soared to the most awkward and unacceptable heights. His nightmares forgotten, visions of Bella flitted and flirted before him. Bella. His own precious Bella. Only she among all the young ladies he knew would have laughed at being alone with him in the library in their night gear—and he without even a robe. "Any other girl would have run screaming from the room the first I entered," he murmured. "And I would not blame her, either. I must have looked a perfect lunatic in nightshirt and cap, walking about in my sleep. Most likely I was muttering to myself, too. I am always muttering to myself when I am awake."

But Bella had not run screaming from the room. Not Bella. Because Bella had seen at once that he needed her and had come directly to his aid. Not that he remembered her doing so, because he did not. He remembered nothing before awaking in the red leather chair with Bella gazing hopefully down at him.

What am I going to do? he thought then, running his fingers through his hair and only at that moment remembering that he had abandoned his nightcap in the library. Bah! A pox upon it! Who needed a nightcap, anyway? He only wore it to give Shaughnessy and Sonnett ease. They were always frightened that he would catch a chill and come down with an inflammation of the lungs and wither away. As if he could wither away. As if he were some delicate flower and not The Nonpareil, the Nonesuch, The Diamond.

The Diamond—he was The Diamond—the hard and glittering jewel of the *haute ton.* He did not fear withering away from some stupid chill, nor would he allow himself to fear withering away from some mysterious madness. No, nor would he allow the visions that haunted him to stand between himself and the woman he loved. He would not! He would discover what was the cause of these uneasy spirits that surrounded him and he would deal with that cause and then—and then—he would deal with Bella!

Bella sat in bed, stroking the enormous volume upon her lap but not once glancing down at its enticing pages. Her curiosity had lessened considerably. The thought that The Diamond needed her had taken precedence over her interest in a mere volume. He needs me even though he does not say it, she mused. And I will stand beside him. We will discover what haunts him. We will discover it together and we will face it together.

Sir Cyril knows what it is, she thought suddenly, his nasty fable rising to the forefront of her mind. Oh, what a devil he is! The reason he said The Diamond had no defense against the fox was because he knows what causes Diamond's dreadful dreams and he plans to destroy Diamond with that knowledge! Blast him! I will cut down that vile little man in his tracks. I vow I will. If that dastard thinks me a mere bumbling hedgehog, he is sorely mistaken. I will show him that I am a veritable Brunhilda of a hedgehog when it comes to the man I love. I will do whatever is required of me to save Diamond. *Whatever* is required!

"You may come down now," murmured Miss Winstead, without taking her gaze from the empty corridor beyond the library door. "They are gone and I doubt they will return."

Junius Farraday, startled, unfolded himself and made his way down the winding iron steps.

"You must have been most uncomfortable up there, all curled up as you were," said Emily, turning to glance up at the man with a confused look in her great blue eyes. "You would have done much better to step behind the draperies as I did when you entered."

"Yes," nodded Farraday, "you could well be right, miss. Would have been a sight more cozy. You were already here then when I came in?"

Miss Winstead nodded. "I am Miss Emily Winstead and you are a Runner, are you not?"

"Yes, Miss."

"I thought as much by your red vest. Michael says the Bow Street Runners are a great blessing to the citizens of London."

"He does, Miss?"

"Indeed. But Mrs. Glendenning says that you are nothing but a throng of evil little snitches."

Junius Farraday stared down at the young woman,

speechless. Mr. Sonnett and Mr. Shaughnessy both had spoken to him of the evil Miss Winstead, but neither of them had thought to mention how fragile she appeared in a lavender robe with her hair curling in long strands down her back and against her porcelain-like cheeks. Nor had they bothered to mention the heart-stopping innocence of her magnificent blue eyes.

"You must tell me why you are here," Emily continued, still twisting the duke's nightcap in her hands. "It is not—The Duke of Derrinham has not done anything—You are not come to take his grace off to Bow Street?"

"No, Miss," managed Farraday, wondering how anyone could think that such a flower of perfection as Miss Emily Winstead could be a murderess.

"Well, I am most thankful for that," breathed Emily, "because I have just found him, you know, and I intend to spend a deal of time with him before I must let him go. And if you were planning to carry him off to Bow Street, I must have thought of some way to prevent you from doing so."

Junius Farraday ran a finger around the inside of his collar. He shifted his weight uneasily from one foot to the other. He nibbled at his lower lip, then sighed. Never in his life had he felt so totally flummoxed as he did now in the light of those truly adorable eyes set in that extremely beguiling face. "What it is, Miss," he replied, astonished to hear the words falling from his lips, "is that his grace's life has been threatened, and I am here to keep an eye open so that no one will attack him in the night. But no one is to know of it," he added, astonished that he should betray himself—and to the very person he had thought to catch in the act.

"I did not know," gasped Emily, the tassel of the poor, mangled nightcap rising to brush against her lips. "Oh, it cannot be! And just when I have come to know him! Oh, Mr.—Mr.—"

"Farraday, Miss. Junius Farraday."

"Oh, Mr. Farraday, you must protect him. You cannot allow anyone to—to—harm the duke!"

"And so I shall, protect him, that is," stated Farraday with a confident nod. "But you must not tell anyone that I am here in the night, Miss. It is possible, you see, that the one who intends his grace harm is a member of this household."

"I shall not breathe a word," whispered Emily. "Not a word. How very brave you are, Mr. Farraday, to think to confront a murderer all on your own. I am come to find a book," she added as she moved toward the shelves, completely altering the topic and sending Junius Farraday's already dizzy mind into another whirl. "I have never seen so very many books in one house, have you?"

"N-no, Miss."

"No, I should think not. It is quite wonderful, but it does make it so very difficult to decide what one wishes to read." Emily wandered along the shelves, tugging first one volume out and then another and another, replacing each as she decided against them. "I do wish I had discovered the *Book of Secrets* before Lady Annabella," she offered with a bright smile. "That I think will be an interesting thing to read, do not you?"

"Yes, Miss," nodded Farraday, keeping at least three feet between them but compelled to wander down the line of shelves after her nonetheless.

"Oh, here is an entire section of poetry. Do you like poetry, Mr. Farraday?"

"Yes, Miss."

"So do I. Very much. Why, here is *The Task* by Mr. Cowper. Goodness, it looks as though it has been read by thousands and thousands of people. Well, I shall read it as well, despite its worn condition. I must bid you good night now, Mr. Farraday," she added, tucking the volume under her arm and taking one of the candles to light her way up the staircase. "Shall I extinguish the remainder of the candles for you? You came with but one, I think. And here I have gone and lighted every one I noticed."

"I will extinguish them, Miss," Farraday replied.

"Thank you, Mr. Farraday. And you must not fret. I shall be most careful not to betray your presence to anyone. Truly, you must be the most remarkable gentleman."

And with that, Miss Emily Winstead swept from the room, leaving behind her a Bow Street Runner whose entire insides had become little more than a mass of quivering jelly.

Sir Cyril Blythe leaned back in the comfort of his brocaded wing chair before the hearth and took a sip of brandy. It amazed him that Lady Annabella should still occupy his mind. Insufferable little hedgehog, he thought with a sneer. Interfering female. In some ways, she reminded him of the Duchess of Derrinham and Lady May. The duchess had been just such an audacious, meddling woman and her daughter the same. But they paid mightily for it, he reminded himself. They both paid mightily for it, as will Meade's chit if she interferes once too often. Just let her stick her nose into my plans for Derrinham and she will be equally as dead as they when I am finished with her. Equally as dead!

Blythe swore and took another sip of the brandy. Could he depend upon The Diamond to keep their Wednesday appointment? He rather thought so. But then, perhaps he could not. Perhaps the insipid little hedgehog would convince him not to appear. And that would be maddening. He had waited near twenty-one years to complete his revenge upon the Duchess of Derrinham and his patience was at an end. He would have Hillary Holland Hallsworth. He would have him—mind and body and soul. And he would have him this very week. So what if the wretched duchess had managed in her wheedling way to convince Holland to abandon the Society? So what if she had, through foul lies and wanton kisses, convinced Holland to betray the agreement and bestow the guardianship of the boy to a bank, a butler, and a valet? It was nothing, nothing! All she had done was to make him angrier. And her son would suffer all the more for it.

He would introduce Derrinham to the very pits of hell. And he would sip contentedly at the exquisite agony that would be The Diamond's when he learned the truth from which his harpy of a mama and his shrew of a sister and those two old clowns, Sonnett and Shaughnessy, had thought to shield him. And at the last, at the last, he would rejoice in the sweet taste of victory when The Diamond finally shattered and The Society of Lost Souls was reborn among his glistening shards.

Fifteen

Michael Winstead greeted the dawn with the most sinking feeling in the depths of his soul. Rapidly donning his livery, he made his way as soundlessly as possible down to the second floor and scratched upon his sister's door. "Emily," he murmured when at last she opened it to him, "I am sorry to wake you so very early, but I must speak with you about something."

Emily yawned and rubbed at her eyes with a childlike innocence. "I cannot think why it must be now, Michael. It cannot be seven o'clock so soon. I am always awake by seven."

"Yes, you are," agreed Winstead, placing an arm about his sister's shoulders and leading her back into the room, closing the door behind him. "It is much before seven, my dear. A footman's day, I find, begins at an even earlier hour than a jewel cutter's."

"A jewel cutter's!" Emily's big blue eyes were quite suddenly staring at him in undisguised astonishment. "Michael, you are a jewel cutter!"

"Yes, Emily. I have been a jewel cutter for years now. You know that." Winstead could not imagine what had put that look upon her face, but he chose to ignore it and to escort her to the tiny sopha in her sitting room. "There now," he murmured, taking a seat beside her as she tucked her feet up under the skirt of her robe. "Are you warm enough, Emily? Shall I fetch you a cover from the bed?"

"No. You are—you are not Sir Cyril's jewel cutter, are you, Michael?" she asked with a most plaintive sigh. "I could not bear it if you were. I had not thought when he said the thing."

"When did you speak with Sir Cyril, Emily?"

"Yesterday. In Green Park. Oh, and I have almost forgot completely. He has asked you to meet with him in Pickering Place on Wednesday. That is tomorrow, Michael. But he did not say what time. He ought to have told me what time."

"It does not matter. I cannot meet him. I am required to be here all day. Why did you ask if I were *his* jewel cutter, Emily?"

"Well, because—Oh, Michael, he and Lady Annabella discussed the most frightening tale. It was about a diamond and a hedgehog and a fox. And the evil fox had a jewel cutter. And the jewel cutter was going to cut The Diamond up."

"Cut the diamond up? A diamond and a hedgehog and a jewel cutter?"

"And an evil fox," nodded Emily.

"Well, I'll be devilled. Can you remember exactly how the tale went, Emily? Will you tell it to me?"

With a very serious nod, Miss Emily Winstead related the fable. The fact that her brother listened to her every word without once interrupting her made her concentrate very hard to get the thing correct. It must be important, she thought. Michael would tell me to cease directly if he did not think it important.

When she had at last come to the end and the hedgehog had died—because Emily could not imagine that the hedgehog, whomever it represented, would abandon The Diamond—she stared searchingly up at her brother whose face had taken on a most stricken look. "What is it, Michael? I know it is about our Diamond, but I cannot think who can be the hedgehog. And you are not the jewel cutter. Oh, you cannot be! You would never help that evil fox to destroy our Diamond. You would not, would you?"

"He is not *our* Diamond," muttered Michael Winstead, rubbing angrily at his chin. "I wish you would understand that, Emily."

"Well, but he is my brother."

"Your half-brother, yes. But he is nothing to me. You may call him your Diamond if you like, but please do not include me in the relationship. You went to walk in Green Park with Lady Annabella and The Diamond's niece?"

"Yes, and Miss Davies. And today we are to go shopping and I am to have a new gown! Miss Davies says I must because the duke will take me to Almack's on Wednesday night."

"To Almack's?" Mr. Winstead's eyebrows rose so high as to meet the verimost front of his wig. "Emily, you cannot go to Almack's. They will not let you in."

"Miss Davies says that the duke will see they do. It will not be a gown made especially for me, because that will take much too long. But Miss Davies says there are any number of pretty gowns that have been returned to the shops for one reason or another and that I shall have my pick of them. But for the very next time we attend, I am to have a gown of my own made by one of the finest modistes. What was it you wished to speak with me about, Michael, when you woke me?"

"It was—I was—Emily, if something were to happen to the duke, something grave, I mean—"

"Oh, there is not the least chance of that," interrupted Miss Winstead, her eyes growing suddenly bright. "Did you know that he had been threatened, Michael? I did not know you knew. But the very nicest Runner is looking out for him. He comes into the house after everyone is abed and actually walks all about on each floor to be certain that the duke is safe. His name is Mr. Farraday. Mr. Junius Farraday. Oh!" gasped Emily, "I was not to tell anyone about him! But he could not possibly have meant you, Michael. He meant not to tell anyone else, because he did not wish the person who threatens the duke to hear of him. But you are my brother. You would never threaten my little duke's life."

Michael Winstead stood up directly his sister informed him that he could not be the person for whom the Runner searched and began to pace the tiny sitting room. He harrumphed. He rubbed at the back of his neck until it turned bright red. He stuffed his hands into his pockets and cursed roundly but very quietly so that his sister could not make out what he said. Then he came to a halt before her and stared down at her with the most puzzling expression upon his face. "Emily," he said. "When Mama told you tales of the little duke, did she never say anything of the little duke's papa?"

"Oh, yes. He was a great villain who delighted in causing pain and sorrow."

"So I thought," nodded Winstead. "Tell me, Emily. Why was the little duke not evil like his papa but the hero of Mama's stories? Did she ever explain?"

"Why, Michael Winstead," said Emily, "I thought you did not care one blink about Mama's stories."

"I did not," confessed Winstead. "I always attempted to avoid hearing them. But I care about them now, Em."

"Why?"

"Because I am working for that same little duke now, Emily, and I wish to know more about him so that I—so that I—may be of more assistance to him—especially now that you say he is like to be murdered."

"I did never say he was like to be murdered. I said he was threatened. He is not at all like to be murdered,

Michael, because Mr. Junius Farraday is here to protect him. Mr. Junius Farraday is likely the greatest and bravest and most important Runner in the history of Bow Street," she added with the most overwhelming adulation. "And the little duke was not villainous because the little duke's mama fought and fought to make his papa come to his senses and he finally decided to become a good person. But he died and the little duke had to become the good person in his papa's stead."

It was all too much for Winstead to digest. If he had been discomposed and indecisive about murdering Derrinham after his last conversation with Emily, and more so after overhearing Derrinham's plans for his sister, now he was totally befuddled. The villainous duke had decided to become a good person; the fox had a jewel cutter; the hedgehog died to save the diamond; Emily was to attend the dancing at Almack's; and there was a Bow Street Runner making free of the premises after everyone had retired. Zounds, how his head was spinning!

Jane was amazed to discover Miss Davies bringing her a cup of hot chocolate rather than the little maid whose job it was. She sat up in the bed, yawned and thanked Lydie very nicely as that lady drew apart the draperies and let in the morning sunlight. "But why are you here? Peggy is not ill? I could well have done without my chocolate. There was no need for you to—"

"I offered to bring it, Jane. There is something we must discuss seriously and in private. It is about your uncle."

"What?" asked Jane, her eyes growing wide. "Has something happened to Uncle Hill?"

"As a matter of fact, yes. Something quite serious," offered Miss Davies, settling down in the little chair at the foot of the bed. "I have thought about him all night and I have decided that we must go to his aid in this instance. If we do not, his grace's one opportunity for true happiness will be thrown out the window with the wash water."

"Whatever do you mean, Lydie?"

"I mean that your Uncle Hill is in love, my dear, but is providing himself with excuse after excuse for not speaking up to the young woman. I could barely believe it when he told me yesterday that he feared he was running mad and that was why he could not say a word to her."

"Running mad? Uncle Hill?"

"It was merely an excuse, Jane. He does not speak up because he is afraid she will laugh at him or turn him away without a word—who knows what it is that gentlemen think?—but none of that is at all likely to be the case."

Jane set her cup down upon the bedside table and began to untie the ribbons of her ruffled nightcap. "Who is it, Lydie, that he loves?" she asked with a smile. "I cannot guess who it might be. He has been so busy attempting to push Bella forward that he has barely had time to spend with any other—Oh, my goodness! Lydie? Uncle Hill has formed a *tendre* for Bella?"

"Head over heels for the girl," nodded Miss Davies. "She is driving him to distraction."

"Good heavens, Lord Barrington has already proposed marriage to her. She told me so only last night. And Mr. Anders and Mr. Tottingham are merely waiting until her papa returns from Bath, I think, and if she does not know that Uncle Hill loves her—"

"Just so," nodded Miss Davies. "We must draw Bella out upon the subject of your uncle. If she loves him in return, then we must provide one of them with the courage to speak of love to the other. They will lose each other else. Perhaps this afternoon would be best. After we return from Bond Street."

Bella stared down at the sheet of vellum in horror. The flowery black lines that criss-crossed the page had faded badly, but were still legible if one studied them closely enough. She had declined to accompany Miss Davies and Jane and Emily to Bond Street and instead had enjoyed a leisurely breakfast and then settled down upon the sopha in the pretty morning room to continue reading the *Book of Secrets*. It was not until she had reached the end that she had noticed the vellum inside the back cover. Bella stared at the words. She read them over and over again. She scowled.

Her first thought was to take the thing immediately to The Diamond. But The Diamond had already gone out. To Tattersall's, he had informed her with a smile as he had departed the breakfast room shortly after her arrival there. Her second thought was more considered. She would call for Mr. Sonnett. Mr. Sonnett had been butler in this establishment and at Twiney Hill since before The Diamond's birth. He would know if the handwritten lines were to be believed. Taking a deep breath, Bella rose from the sopha and crossed the room to tug upon the bellpull. In a matter of moments the first footman was at the morning room door.

"I should like to speak with Mr. Sonnett," Bella informed him. "Will you tell him I should like him to come to me as soon as possible, please, James? It is most important."

"Yes, my lady," Michael Winstead nodded, gazing curiously at the sheet of vellum in her hand, and then he was gone.

Sonnett stared at the lines, gazed up at the impatiently pacing Bella, then stared down again. After a long moment, he strolled determinedly to the bellpull. When the first footman again appeared, he sent the man off in search of Shaughnessy.

"Can it be true?" asked Bella quietly as the two waited for Shaughnessy to appear.

Sonnett nodded. "Sir Cyril poses a greater threat to his grace than any of us ever realized, my lady. I might have known her grace would not go quietly to her grave. Though how, in the midst of such mayhem, she managed to scribble these few lines and place them here, I cannot imagine."

Shaughnessy entered the room and upon reading the lines, a most pain-filled look overwhelmed him. "In this volume?" he asked, closing the book to stare almost broken-hearted at the cover. "What sound thinking went into it then. How brave was our duchess to think so clearly at such a time. It was Lady Diana's favorite book. They shared bits of it over and over between them from the time Lady Diana was in leading strings."

"Indeed," agreed Sonnett with a despairing shake of his head. "And the duchess could not know that Lady Diana would cease to peruse it forever after that horrific evening because it reminded her so of her mama."

"I wish to know the entire story," declared Bella, coming to a halt before the two upper servants with her hands upon her hips, one small foot tapping impatiently upon the carpeting. "And I wish to know it at once. It was his grace's mama wrote those lines? You are certain?"

"Yes, my lady," replied Shaughnessy. "If the words do not identify her, the handwriting and the truth of the circumstance she addresses do. You cannot, my lady, show this to the duke. It will break his heart."

"But I must," declared Bella. "If it is true, I must show it to him and as soon as possible. He thinks to meet with Sir Cyril Blythe tomorrow."

"It will do more than break his heart," Sonnett murmured, ignoring Bella's words as though they had not been spoken. "It may well bring the entire thing back to him, Timothy, and he could well lose his mind again."

"Lose his mind?" murmured Bella, gazing from one to the other of the men. "Lose his mind *again?*"

It was Shaughnessy who saw the disbelief begin to mingle with fear in Bella's eyes, and Shaughnessy who took her by the arm and led her back to the sopha and sat her gently down upon it. "I have known you since you were a stirring in your papa's soul, my lady," he murmured, sitting beside her and holding her hands in his own. "And I have always known you to be pluck to the backbone. Why, you followed his grace up into every tree and down into every gully."

"And across every meadow," added Sonnett quietly, sitting down upon the other side of her.

"Yes, indeed," nodded Shaughnessy. "You are not to be upset, Lady Annabella. Not now, after all this time. Samuel did not mean to imply that his grace is now or has ever been a lunatic."

"No, no," mumbled Sonnett. "Never intended to imply that."

"What did you mean to imply?" asked Bella. "You did say, Mr. Sonnett, that his grace could well lose his mind *again.*"

"Yes, I did. I did say that. It is because when his mama and papa died, my lady, he became so distraught as to cease speaking to everyone. Not a word did he say for almost a year. And he screamed at night and could not be comforted. And he threw things and pounded upon things and broke things for not the least reason. The only times he smiled and acted properly were the times when your mama and papa invited him to Meadowlark to come and see you. He seemed to find comfort in the very sight of you flailing away in your crib or nestling comfortably in your mama's arms. And then at last, because he became so fond of watching you, he seemed to find forgetfulness and peace."

"But he was merely five when—when—and I was not born until he was eight. That is three whole years," breathed Bella, aching to the very soul for him. "Three whole years that he was—as you said."

"A long time," agreed Shaughnessy. "A very long time. But long forgotten as well. He remembers nothing of it."

"Nothing?"

"Not a thing," Sonnett assured her. "Not that dreadful night, not the three years following, nothing. He does not even remember his mama and papa. Not really. The mama and papa he recalls, Lady Diana and Mr. Shaughnessy and I provided him from their portraits and our imaginations, because we could not possibly tell him how they truly were."

"How were they?" Bella asked. "What were they like and what happened to them?" Her hands trembled and Shaughnessy caught them up and held them in a most comforting grasp. "That note—that note implies that the duke and duchess were murdered."

"Yes, murdered," nodded Sonnett. "Cut to ribbons upon the servants' staircase to the third floor and the little duke witness to it all."

"Samuel, use some delicacy," urged Shaughnessy.

"Well, but there is no delicate way to say that," mumbled Sonnett rather shamefacedly.

"He was witness to it? Diamond was witness to the murder of his parents?" gasped Bella as Mr. Sonnett's words shuddered through her.

"Yes," sighed Shaughnessy. "At least we have always thought it to be so because he ran off into the night, covered in their blood, to fetch the Watch and then he— he ceased to speak, as I said. He could not accept such blood and violence, we thought, and we gave thanks, Sonnett and I, when at last he lost the memory of it."

"We always thought, and Lady Diana with us, that Sir Cyril's intention was to revenge himself upon the father by telling the son the tale of his parents' demise in the hope of bringing back the lad's memory and causing him to—to suffer exquisitely. It would be just the sort of evil thing he would delight in. He hated the duke's father in the end, you know. Well, of course you know, now that you have read that note," groaned Sonnett. "What fools we were!"

Bella found it very hard to listen to them any farther. Each new revelation wrenched at her heart. Her Diamond, the very gentleman she had loved for all her life— to have watched his mama and papa die such violent deaths, to have recoiled so completely from the horror as to— "And he knows!" she exclaimed in horror, withdrawing her hands from Shaughnessy's and putting them to her cheeks. "Oh, my dearest God, Diamond knows who the murderers were and if he remembers and does not go mad with the memory, he will tell and they can none of them risk his telling!"

The woman who put a hand upon his sleeve at Hyde Park Corner as he exited Tat's seemed vaguely familiar and Derrinham peered down at her questioningly. "May I help you, madam?" he asked, wondering why he could not put a name to her.

"You are the Duke of Derrinham, are you not?"

"Indeed."

"I am Mrs. Glendenning. Perhaps Emily has mentioned me?"

"You are her neighbor in Curzon Street?"

"Yes." The woman took hold of the sleeve she had

touched. "I must speak to you, your grace, about Miss Winstead."

She was an elderly lady with rouged cheeks and the smell of powder and paint clinging to her. The duke could not quite think why she was clutching at his sleeve so and turning him into the tiny alley that ran between Tat's and Tiecher's, but it was obvious she was flustered and her words came haltingly as she led him deeper into the alley. "I have known Emily from the day she was born and—her mama was mad, you know. Quite, quite mad."

It sounded like someone thumping a melon. Derrinham's hat fell to the cobbles. Before he could follow it down, two pairs of large hands grabbed his arms. A coach rumbled up to the alley entrance and in the wink of an eye the unconscious duke was shoved inside and two ruffians and Mrs. Glendenning climbed hurriedly in after him.

Barrington stood and stared as the coach pulled away. What the devil has happened to him? he asked himself dazedly. Was The Diamond standing across the way a moment ago or was he not? Confused, Barrington hurried across the street and peered into the alley to see if perhaps his grace was strolling through to the other end. He saw no one. And then he saw the hat the duke had been wearing lying upon the cobbles. He picked the beaver up. "My God, there is blood on it," he hissed. And in a moment he was running full tilt in search of a hackney.

Michael Winstead glanced at the note in his hand as the Duke of Derrinham's second-best Town coach traversed the streets of the city, John Coachman in search of Number 18, Darlington Square. The note, Mr. Sonnett had told him, was intended for the eyes of a Mr. Junius Farraday and he was to deliver it directly into that gentleman's hands and then was to bring that gentleman back to Great Stanhope Street directly.

Mr. Junius Farraday, Winstead thought. Emily's Runner. What the devil does Mr. Sonnett want with him? Nothing has changed, has it? He has not—no one has discovered that I was the one attempted to—no, of course not! Why would Mr. Sonnett send me off to bring the man back if he knew I were the person had attempted to murder the duke?

Winstead stared at the screw of paper in his hand. It would be easy enough simply to untwist the thing and read it. It rankled that he should be forced to do so, because in his heart, Michael Winstead was an honorable gentleman though he lived in reduced circumstances and was forced by necessity to make his livelihood through trade. And a man of honor did not read notes intended for others. But if the confounded thing were about himself and this a trap to turn him over to Farraday—Michael Winstead shamefacedly opened the note and read it. With a frown and a sigh, he twisted it back into its original form and leaned back against the squabs.

Mr. Sonnett wishes Mr. Farraday's escort to Number 10, Pickering Place? Now, why the devil is that? he wondered, tapping the screw of paper against his knee just as the coach pulled up before a row of houses upon a tiny square not far from Whitehall and within viewing distance of St. James's Park. "That'll be the place," John Coachman called down through the trap. "The one with the sign in the front window."

Winstead stepped down from the coach. The sign in the window announced that there were rooms to let. He pulled the knocker and waited patiently until an elderly woman swung the door open and eyed him in amazement, then peered around him at the coach that sported Derrinham's crest. "Never thought to see the day a footman in full regalia should come a-prancing up to my own door," she said with a tentative smile. "Who is it ye be a-lookin' for?"

"Mr. Junius Farraday?"

"Aye, Mr. Farraday be one of my boarders. Step in. Step in. I shall send Maizie up for him."

Sixteen

Junius Farraday folded the sheet of vellum most carefully and placed it into his pocket. "I shall locate the old ba—the old demon—and take him off to Bow Street where I shall present both himself and this writing to Sir John," he announced in an icy voice. "I expect he is either in Pickering Place or at that gambling hell of his."

"Shaughnessy and I are going with you, Mr. Farraday," announced Sonnett, abandoning the stance he had taken beside Bella in the antechamber where they had anxiously awaited Farraday and stepping out into the great hall to fetch his hat and cane. "You cannot tell but you will be glad of an extra hand or two."

"You cannot!" exclaimed Bella, grasping Mr. Shaughnessy's sleeve to keep him from following Sonnett. "What if that wretched man should shoot at you or bring out a sword or—or—You cannot go with Mr. Farraday. If either of you were to suffer an injury, his grace would be devastated. You have watched over Diamond since he was a mere infant and he loves you both with all his heart. He could never bear to see you injured or—"

"Dead," provided Farraday with a scowl. "Her ladyship is correct. You will both remain here."

"No, I am afraid not. Samuel and myself shall accompany you," responded Shaughnessy, prying his sleeve from Bella's grasp. "We have a debt to pay, Samuel and

I, and at last there is a step we may take in the repayment of it."

"No," pleaded Bella, the great fear in her tone causing Shaughnessy to pause after but one step and bringing Sonnett back to the open doorway, his hat already upon his head.

"You do not understand, my lady," murmured Sonnett quietly, going to hold her hands as Shaughnessy went to fetch his own hat. "Tim and I owe this to his grace's mama and to the lad. It is our duty to see Sir Cyril and all of them caught and brought to justice. It is our fault that no alarm was raised that night, that no one came to their aid. Had we remained in our quarters instead of allowing ourselves to be cajoled into joining Mr. Twimbly for a farewell drink at The Cock and Crow, we would have been here to defend them."

"Or to be murdered along with the duke and duchess," Bella replied. "Please be sensible, Mr. Sonnett. Both you and Mr. Shaughnessy are a good deal older now and—"

"We allowed Sir Cyril's butler to lure us away. We left the house empty of servants and the duke and duchess and the lad completely unprotected," sighed Shaughnessy, returning dressed for the outdoors. "Those servants hired for the Season had all been dismissed and departed that very afternoon. We knew it to be so. The household was bound for Surrey early the next morning. Lady Diana had already gone off, a week before, to a house party. She was to meet us at The Speckled Pike Inn the following day."

"Even the nursery maid had gone, and Mrs. Whitfield, the nanny, gone. Though she had merely taken the time to bid her brother farewell and expected to return to us by six in the morning," groaned Sonnett. "It was selfish and thoughtless of us to so much as consider Twimbly's invitation. We ought to have remained to keep watch over the boy." His pain at the memory was evident in the old butler's every word and movement. "But the lad slept. They all slept. And we intended merely to have one glass of ale to bid Twimbly goodbye."

"And we ended in drinking ourselves into a stupor," mumbled Shaughnessy. "We meant to have but one glass and yet ended in sleeping like babes with our heads upon the table until early light. Never could think how we came to drink so much."

"Likely did have but one glass," offered Farraday thoughtfully. "If this Twimbly fellow was one of them, he likely laced the ale with some sort of sleeping potion."

"Regardless," declared Sonnett soberly, "we are coming with you, Farraday. Twimbly will be at Pickering Place even if Blythe is not. And we have a debt to pay that is long overdue."

"Aye," nodded Farraday, frowning. "I can see as how you are forced to accompany me. But you must do as I say when we arrive. Do not fear, my lady," he added, giving Bella's hand a pat. "I shall look out for them and bring them safely home."

Lord Barrington fairly leaped from the hackney and tossed the driver a guinea, then rushed for the door without once looking back to see the look of amazement upon the driver's face. He prized the knocker of Derrinham House with an urgency he had never felt before. He was, indeed, so upset by the bloodstained hat that he held in his hand and the image of Derrinham being turned toward the alley by an old woman that he barely noticed the young woman who opened the door to him. He made, in fact, to rush right past her until she caught at his arm.

"Lord Barrington, whatever has happened?" asked an already nonplussed Bella. "Why are you in such a hurry that you do not even see who has opened the door to you?"

"Bella! Bella? What are you doing answering the door—and in Derrinham House? You ought not to be here, ought you? Or are you visiting Miss May? Where is Miss May? I must speak with her at once. I cannot wait upon the proprieties."

"Jane is not at home."

"Not at home? Then why are you—never mind. Perhaps I ought to speak to his grace's butler first, anyway. Yes, perhaps that would be the kindest thing to do and then he will help me to tell Miss May when she returns without upsetting her out of hand. Or the Runner! Is he somewhere about or not, Bella? Do you know if there is a Runner about the house? Never mind, the butler will know where to reach him. Devil it, perhaps I ought to have gone directly to Bow Street. I was not at all thinking straight. Yes, I ought to have gone to Bow Street."

Bella, her nerves already ajangle, stared at the hat his lordship held in dawning horror. "James, that is Diamond's hat."

"Yes, yes, so I thought. You are positive?"

"Unless there is another gentleman in London keeps Diamond's favorite trout fly pinned to his hatband."

"Trout fly? Oh, is that what that is? Thought it was an odd sort of decoration to have. Where is the butler, Bella?"

"He is—not here. Why have you Diamond's hat in your hand? What has happened? James, tell me!"

For the first time Lord Barrington took a good, long look at Bella. Her face was flushed, her eyes dark with worry, her hands twisting and untwisting of their own accord.

"My dearest girl," he murmured, putting an arm about her shoulders, escorting her into the tiny antechamber near the front door, and encouraging her to sit upon one of the chairs there. "I have frightened you."

"No, I was already frightened before you came. You

have only served to frighten me further. How did you come by Diamond's hat, James? And what is that stain upon it? Oh, my dearest Lord," gasped Bella, taking the hat into her own hands, her fingers touching the inside of the oddly dented brim, "it is blood!"

Lord Barrington attempted to reassure her by explaining what it was he had seen happen. "And it is not near as much blood as might be expected if they had actually cudgeled him to death, Bella. Nor was there any other blood in the alley. Merely knocked him unconscious, I think, and carried him off somewhere." This explanation, however, far from reassuring her, only served to make Bella's flush fade to a dull white.

"We must go at once," breathed Bella when at last she could find her breath.

"To Bow Street? I will go, Bella. You need not."

"No, no, not to Bow Street. To Pickering Place, James. Mr. Sonnett and Mr. Shaughnessy and the Runner have gone to Pickering Place to confront Sir Cyril and his butler and that is very likely where these villains have taken Diamond."

"You think the duke was abducted by Sir Cyril?"

"Indeed. I shall get my hat and we shall go immediately. There is no telling what may happen if Sir Cyril has already gathered his ruffians about him to attack Diamond. It may well be that Mr. Sonnett and Mr. Shaughnessy and the Runner are also in grave danger and cannot escape themselves."

"Sir Cyril?" queried Barrington, trailing after Bella as she walked to the closet below the stairs to fetch her hat and pelisse. "But I have not said one word to you about Sir Cyril. It was a woman approached The Diamond, not Sir Cyril Blythe."

"Yes, but—" Bella's words faded as the door knocker sounded once again and then the front door was pushed inward amidst a bevy of feminine voices.

* * *

Jane could not believe her ears as she listened first to Bella's account of finding the scrap of vellum and what was written upon it and then heard Lord Barrington's tale of her uncle's abduction. Miss Davies grew absolutely livid and was moved to use the most scathing expletives. Emily remained silent, but fear turned the blue of her eyes to a much deeper shade and her face turned pale with apprehension.

"Well, most certainly you must go to Bow Street immediately, your lordship," declared Miss Davies. "And, Bella, you must not think of going anywhere at all," she added, taking note of the little hat with the cherries upon the brim that had been jammed hurriedly atop Lady Annabella's shining curls. "Thank heaven we returned in time to stop you from going to Pickering Place."

"Oh no, you have not," declared Bella. "I will go to Pickering Place and at once."

"Think, Bella," urged Miss Davies, taking her by the arm and giving her a tiny shake. "What is it that you think you can do? Once Lord Barrington reaches Bow Street, Sir John Fielding will send his Runners to Pickering Place immediately. He will not delay a moment, my dear. It is the Duke of Derrinham, after all. And certainly his men will know much better than any of us how to rescue his grace and the others."

"And how can we be at all certain that this strange woman had the least thing to do with Sir Cyril?" asked Jane, sinking down upon the windowseat. "You did not see Sir Cyril anywhere about, did you, my lord?"

"No, not a sign of him," replied Barrington, sinking down beside her. "Though after hearing Bella's story, I think the old man may well have been inside that coach."

"Can it be true?" asked Emily, her hands trembling.

"Can what be true?" asked Bella with a scowl.

"What you said about her grace's message, Bella—the one she left in the—in the—"

"Book of Secrets," provided Jane.

"Yes," Emily nodded. "In the *Book of Secrets.* She said that Sir Cyril and the others had come to kill her husband? But why? Did she write why?"

"Because he had withdrawn from The Society of Lost Souls," muttered Bella, pacing the length of the chamber angrily. "Because he had withdrawn and because he knew all of their secrets and therefore he could not be allowed to live."

"The Society of Lost Souls," whispered Emily, close to tears. "And Sir Cyril one of them! Michael! Oh, Michael!" she exclaimed as James, the first footman, appeared in the entrance to the antechamber where the little group had gathered to discuss the matter. "Michael, Papa lied to us! And all this time Sir Cyril has been lying to us as well! Sir Cyril was one of them—and likely Papa, too. One of The Society of Lost Souls!"

And with that, Miss Emily Winstead ran to James, the first footman and, throwing her arms around his neck, buried her face in his shoulder and began to cry, causing Lord Barrington and the three ladies to stare at them both in astonishment.

Michael Winstead stood frozen only a moment and then his arms came around his sister and he held her, gently rubbing her back and whispering words of encouragement into her ear. "It is all right, Emily," he murmured. "Do not cry, dearest."

"It is not all right!" exclaimed Emily wetly, snuffling against his livery. "It is not all right at all, because the little duke has been attacked and carried off and Bella has discovered a message that says Sir Cyril was one of the men who killed the little duke's mama and papa. It was her grace herself who wrote the note the very night she died, Michael. She would not have lied. She would not have lied about who it was that threatened her and her husband and her little boy. Oh, Michael, Sir Cyril is a murderer and perhaps Papa was as well!"

Michael Winstead could find no words to say. With his sister sobbing in his arms and Lord Barrington and three ladies staring at him with varying shades of disbelief and suspicion upon their faces—and a very grim and sudden suspicion of his own that his sister might well be correct about their papa—he was speechless. He drew Emily farther into his arms and rested his cheek against the soft taffeta of her bonnet and closed his eyes. He had to think. He had to think clearly and quickly and without bias. How had the tale gone all those years ago? He had been eight years old. He ought to remember. The Runners had come to the house in Curzon Street and questioned his papa over and over again.

Where had he been that night? With Sir Cyril Blythe, a dear friend, celebrating the birth of his new daughter, Emily.

Had they gone to a pub? No, they had gone to Sir Cyril's establishment in St. James's Square.

Had anyone seen them there together? Oh, any number of gentlemen. Any number of gentlemen willing to swear to it.

"Papa was with Sir Cyril Blythe in his establishment in St. James's Square. Any number of gentlemen saw them there together," mumbled Winstead to himself. "But Sir Cyril was here murdering the duke and duchess. Was Papa here then as well?"

Though Barrington wished to hear more of what this footman, who evidently was not a footman, had to say, he agreed with Bella that it was more important for him to procure a hack from the duke's stables and relate what he had seen of the abduction and what he knew of Sir Cyril to the men at Bow Street.

"You will say as well, James, that Mr. Farraday and

Mr. Sonnett and Mr. Shaughnessy have all gone to Pickering Place and have not as yet returned. They have been
gone the most of an hour," Bella instructed him, her
hands holding tightly to his. "We must find The Diamond, James. We must! And we must pray that the others
are in no danger."

Michael Winstead was then escorted by the ladies upstairs to the long drawing room where he sat upon the
very edge of an overstuffed chair, his elbows resting upon
his thighs and his hands dangling inconsequentially between his knees.

He doffed his footman's wig and his dark hair curled
damply across his broad brow. Across from him, Lady
Annabella, Jane and Miss Davies shared the brightly
striped sopha and immediately beside him, upon a footstool, sat Emily. Occasionally during his discourse, Winstead shifted his position and reached out to take his
sister's hand or stroke her cheek tenderly with one gloved
finger. "His grace would be dead even now if he had
not awakened upon those stairs and looked at me with
such astonishment. I could not bring myself to thrust the
knife home with him looking at me like that. There was
barely enough light for us to make each other out, and
yet his eyes shone at me with such incredible intensity.
And such incredible innocence," he added on a sigh as
Emily gasped at the revelation of his perfidy.

"But you have not made an attempt upon him sincc?"
asked Miss Davies with a demeanor as determinedly un-
ruffled as a becalmed sea. "You know nothing whatever
of what happened this morning near Tattersall's?"

"Nothing. Since that vile night when I almost killed
him upon the stairs, I have had nothing but second
thoughts and third thoughts and fourth thoughts. Zounds,
once Emily revealed herself to him and he proved to be
so kind to her, I could not reconcile myself at all to the
doing of it. How could I kill a gentleman who wished

only to welcome my sister into his family and make her life comfortable and bring her joy? I believed my father when he said he was unrevenged upon The Diamond's father and I was convinced that The Diamond was as evil as his sire. I promised my father upon his deathbed to carry out his revenge upon his grace. Yes, and Sir Cyril pretended to be my friend and urged me on in my hatred of the duke every chance he got, though I am certain he had not the least idea of the vow I made Papa. The fiend! The miscreant! What is it Blythe thinks to gain from me? What does he intend for me to do to the duke? How could I have been so misguided and so very stupid?"

"Her grace wrote that Sir Cyril and The Society of Lost Souls had come unhindered into this house to kill her and her husband," said Bella. "She gave no other name but that of Sir Cyril. Perhaps your father knew nothing of it, sir."

"Perhaps not," murmured Mr. Winstead. "But it was Sir Cyril who stood witness for my father when the Runners came looking for him. Any number of people assumed that my father had done the deed because of the evil the duke had done us in the past and because of—Mama. Sir Cyril was not suspect. My papa was suspect. Why would Sir Cyril lie for my father if they were not in the thing together?"

"We will never know," mused Miss Davies. "There is no one now can tell us the truth of it but Sir Cyril and I would not trust a word that devil said."

"And Diamond," whispered Bella. "Diamond knows. Diamond saw everything. And now he is abducted."

It struck him from out of the mist like a bolt of lightning. Struck him so solidly that he gasped aloud and cried it out. "You are Bessie!" he shouted. "You are called Bessie!"

"Shhh, your grace, do not upset yourself," murmured Mrs. Glendenning, pressing a fresh cloth soaked in lavender water against the side of his head. "You have been hit upon the head with a rather stout cudgel and you will make yourself very ill if you become overly excited."

"Hit upon the—" Derrinham tried to sit up, winced in pain, and lay down again against the pillows.

"So, you remember Bessie, do you?" rasped a most familiar voice. "And what do you remember about her?" Sir Cyril Blythe's smiling face came suddenly into focus above the duke. "Tell me, Diamond. I may call you Diamond, may I not?"

"No. Only Bella."

"Ah, Bella. The Hesitant Hedgehog. Such a charming girl."

"She is ch-charming," mumbled Derrinham, pain stabbing him swiftly behind the eyes.

"Indeed. Is that not what I said? Charming. But tell me what you remember about Bessie, your grace. We are all waiting quite impatiently to hear."

"All?" Derrinham fought to sit up again, fought to ignore the pain and gaze about him. He was on a sopha in a most ornate parlor which he did not at all recognize. Sprinkled about in several chairs and leaning against the mantel and gathered before one of the tables was a confusing assortment of gentlemen.

"Unfortunately," sighed Sir Cyril, "Mr. Winstead could not attend. I was unable to contact him in time. It was a spur-of-the moment thing, you see. I truly did plan to hold this little gathering on Wednesday afternoon, but then I thought that perhaps your little hedgehog might attempt to dissuade you in some way from attending. Come, Derrinham, satisfy our curiosity. What is it you remember about Bessie?"

"That—that—she held me and whispered things in my ear when I was quite small. Were you my nurse?" he asked, squinting in pain at the woman.

"Oh, no, not your nurse," chuckled Blythe, drawing a chair up before the duke and lowering himself into it. "You truly have forgotten everything. I never thought it possible. Oh, you might well have forgotten our faces, but to forget all! Think harder, Derrinham. We are all here to help you remember, my dear."

A gentleman of near fifty, in gray kerseymere pantaloons and a broadcloth coat of drab brown, swung a ladder-backed chair around and straddled it beside Blythe. "You remember me, do ye not, lad? Stare hard. Think. I was one of your papa's closest associates."

"I do not—Why would I know you? My father would not have introduced his associates to a boy of five."

"No, no, we were not introduced, my lad, but we met, you and I. We did meet."

From the corner of the room, one of the other gentlemen giggled in the most peculiar manner.

It was like a nightmare. His head ached; his eyes ached; his back ached; and the duke had the most uneasy feeling that he was surrounded by lunatics.

Lord Barrington returned with the news that Sir John Fielding had immediately set four Runners in search of the Duke of Derrinham and four more to seek for Sir Cyril Blythe at all the establishments known to be in his possession, beginning with the mansion in Pickering Place whence Mr. Farraday and Mr. Sonnett and Mr. Shaughnessy had not yet returned.

"Except that we *have* returned," announced Mr. Sonnett soberly, entering the long drawing room with the tea tray. "Good afternoon, your lordship."

"Good afternoon, Sonnett. You are safe then."

"Indeed. But worried beyond measure. Sir Cyril was not at Pickering Place nor anywhere else he might be expected to be and so we came home."

"You had no luck at all?"

"Some luck," admitted Sonnett. "Mr. Farraday has taken Mr. Twimbly to Bow Street in the hope that he may be persuaded to admit his part in—in—that night—and to say where Sir Cyril has gone. We did not know at the time that his grace had been abducted. Had I known that, I should have thrashed Twimbly within an inch of his life. I should have taken a horsewhip to him until he confessed where the villains had taken our lad."

"Yes," frowned Bella, "and I would gladly have helped you to do it, too."

"Likewise," nodded Barrington, taking a seat midway between Jane and Bella and staring across at the mysterious footman who held Miss Emily Winstead in his arms.

"He is Emily's half-brother," Jane said softly. "Mr. Michael Winstead. It was he put the hat pin in Arnold's blanket."

"What?" Lord Barrington's eyebrows rose clear up to his hairline and that set Jane to smiling.

"That is not to be held against him now, my lord," she continued. "It is a very long story, but Mr. Winstead has come to his senses and is most willing to help us locate Uncle Hill and bring Sir Cyril to justice. Only he cannot think where they may be, either."

"Did you notice nothing at all about the woman?" Bella asked querulously. "There must have been something distinguishing about her, James. Can you not think of a single thing?"

"Well, there was her hat, Bella, but I cannot think how a hat could possibly lead us to—"

"What about her hat?"

"It was—grotesque. Immense. Lavender silk with

bluebirds upon it and things that looked like wilted lilies."

"Mrs. Glendenning!" gasped Michael and Emily together.

Seventeen

Gradually but with horrendous force, the visions that had haunted The Diamond since childhood began to take on solid form. The great sapphires of his eyes lit with a violent blaze. Now he recognized the cries that for two decades had haunted his nights. They were his mother's wails, his father's curses. And the odd smell and the slick, wet, sticky feeling that had for years overcome his senses in the darkness of sleep—blood. It was blood. His parents' blood.

Derrinham stared from one to another to another of the gentlemen in the parlor. The blue of his eyes darkened. His breath gathered in his lungs until he thought he might explode, but he could not bring himself to breathe out or in. These were the faces he had attempted for so long to bring into focus. These were the spirits who attacked him night after night until at last, in the silence of Derrinham House this Season, they had sent him running blindly through deserted corridors and compelled him to huddle against cold staircase walls. All of them. He remembered all of them and one other—one other face that did not grin and snicker at him in this wretched chamber he could not escape—Winstead, he thought. The missing villain's name will undoubtedly have been Winstead.

"Murderers!" the duke hissed, the air at long last expelling itself from his lungs. "Foul, damnable murderers!" And then the Duke of Derrinham gasped for breath, slapped Bessie Glendenning's hands away from him, and unsteadily gained his feet.

"Yes, indeed," nodded Sir Cyril, a triumphant smile upon his face as he stepped up before the duke. "Now you are beginning to remember. I knew you would, Derrinham. I knew if only I could get you to sit down with myself and these gentlemen and Michael—though Michael has missed it, you see—that you would begin to remember. But you are shaking like a willow in a high wind, lad. Now, why are you doing that?"

"Thinks we mean to kill him as we did his mama and papa," laughed one of the gentlemen. "Frightened beyond breathing."

"And why not?" offered another, sipping at a glass of sherry. "I should be frightened if I were him. What a remarkable sight, is it not, The Diamond shivering like a schoolroom miss?"

"Yes, but will he shatter?" murmured a third in a russet coat, standing with one booted foot propped upon Mrs. Glendenning's low maple table. "He is not of the least use to us, Blythe, in this state. He is a threat, rather."

"Enough," growled Sir Cyril at the gentlemen, and taking The Diamond's arm he urged him to the far side of the room, away from the others. "You are remembering but one night, and there is so much more. So very much more to be remembered. Your papa, for one. My dearest friend, Holland. Can you even begin to remember what a fine gentleman your papa was, Hillary? I may call you Hillary, may I not? I was accustomed to call you so when you were small and your papa would set to harassing you. You ran into my arms any number of times to escape your papa's vagaries. You know you did. You must merely let the memories come, Hillary. Merely allow them to come."

And they did come. Derrinham sank down upon a

ladder-backed chair and then doubled over as the memories rushed into his mind, filling him with horror and disbelief and despair. How could he have forgotten? How could he have forgotten the monster who had sired him, the devil who had filled the first years of his childhood with dread and fear? But he remembered now. He remembered. And he groaned with the very real pain of it.

"Those two old fools who raised you, Hillary," whispered Blythe's voice close beside him, "they would not tell you the truth of it, would they? No, nor your sister Diana, neither. But you remember now how it was. Such a charming family. A shrew of a mama who would not protect you, who made your papa even angrier, forced him to beleaguer you even more. And a demon of a papa and a sister who deserted you from the day you were born. She could not be bothered with you then, could she, Hillary? Diana could not be bothered to protect you. She only protected herself. She ran off and left you behind at every opportunity. Do you know why she did so? To protect herself, Hill. To protect herself. She abandoned you to hell so that she might discover heaven."

The Diamond straightened in the chair and gazed at the man who knelt whispering beside him. The duke's hands shook; his eyes grew cloudy. He nodded dazedly. "Left me," he mumbled. "Diana left me alone with them."

"Right you are. Left you alone that very night. She knew what was coming. She knew, but she did not love you enough even to take you away with her."

"No."

"And Sonnett and Shaughnessy, they abandoned you as well."

"Yes."

"And when we came to speak with your papa that night, when we came to confront him in his own den, when the screaming and the crying and the horror began, who was it picked you up and carried you to the nursery? Who was it held you and protected you and kept you safe?"

"B-Bessie."

"Indeed. Bessie. Not your sister or your mama or either of those two old fools, eh?"

"Bessie," mumbled the duke, rubbing at his eyes with the backs of his trembling hands. "Bessie."

"I'll be damned," grunted one of the gentlemen, "if the old devil ain't doing it. Just look over there, Henry. Our Diamond's going to shatter any moment now. We will have the power and the fortune of the Derrinham title and the pure evil genius of a Derrinham behind us once again. I will lay you odds upon it. Give Blythe five more minutes and our little duke will be a quiverin' bit of jelly to be molded into whatever we wish."

"And what we wish is to have his papa brought back to us in all his sinister glory, eh?"

"Be even better than his papa, this one. Don't have a wife to challenge him and cajole him and seduce him into changing his ways. The Diamond will be a devil we can be proud of and he will last forever. This Derrinham will not betray us once Blythe strips him to the marrow and builds him up again into the gentleman we require him to be."

Bella's patience was being sorely tested. Mr. Farraday had returned and Bella sat quietly with the others as he explained that Sir Cyril's butler, Twimbly, had not answered one question that Sir John had put to him and could not be made to answer any, either, because there was not the least bit of evidence against him. It could not be proved that he had drugged Mr. Sonnett and Mr. Shaughnessy, and the mere fact that he had been with them gave him witnesses who placed him far from Derrinham House the night of the murders.

"And he is not mentioned in the duchess's note, either. Only Sir Cyril is mentioned by name, so we had to set him free. But I was that stunned," Mr. Farraday added, running his fingers through his hair as he settled himself upon the red-and-gold settee beside Emily, "to hear that the duke had been abducted. Thank goodness you saw it and reported it directly, my lord. It could be no one but Blythe behind the thing. That is what I think and what Sir John thinks as well. And we will find Blythe. You may depend upon it."

"We think we know where he may be," Mr. Winstead offered. "Lord Barrington was just about to set out again for Bow Street with the information."

"What information?" asked Mr. Farraday.

"The woman his lordship saw with his grace," murmured Emily, swiping at tear-filled eyes with a tiny lace handkerchief. "Michael and I think it must have been Mrs. Glendenning. She is our neighbor in Curzon Street and known to Sir Cyril. And she has a hat with birds and dead lilies upon it just like the one the woman whom his lordship saw was wearing. Michael and I think that perhaps they have taken the duke there—to her house."

"Number 16, Curzon Street," added Winstead, nodding. "But I doubt you will be able to walk up to the front door and demand the duke back. They will not be so careless as that."

"No, no, they will be guarding him heavily, most likely," nodded Farraday. "I shall go immediately to Sir John and we will devise a plan."

"To go to Bow Street again will take another hour," sighed Bella in frustration.

"Can we not do the thing ourselves?" asked Barrington. "I am handy with my fives when need be and Winstead will be glad to help, won't you, Winstead?"

Michael Winstead nodded. "It is the very least I can do."

"Shaughnessy and I will join with you as well," declared Mr. Sonnett. "That should make enough of us to give them pause."

"Aye," nodded Farraday. "We might do it. But we must have a plan of approach and we must all know what is expected of us when at last we gain entrance."

Each of the gentlemen had something to contribute to the plan as they began to decide how they would go about rescuing The Diamond. Even Miss Davies and Jane and Emily offered suggestions and commented upon what they thought might work and what definitely would not. The whole lot of them droned on and on and on until Bella's patience was worn to a frazzle. How can they? she thought in frustration. How can they all sit about, discussing and planning and nodding and murmuring and doing nothing while Diamond may well be fighting for his very life!

A pox upon them all! thought Bella, rising abruptly and swirling from the room in a swish of apricot skirts. They are all talk and not the least action. Diamond will be dead before they decide how to go about saving him. Well, I am not in the least afraid to go and confront those beasts and I know perfectly well how to reach Number 16, Curzon Street, too!

And that was all she needed to think and all she needed to know. With a deal of impatient wrath, Bella jammed her hat upon her curls and hurried out of the house by way of the kitchen door. She paused in the stable, pacing, for barely four minutes, while one of the grooms hitched up a gig for her and then she climbed into the tiny vehicle and urged the horse forward, taking him out into the street and turning him in the direction of Mrs. Glendenning's residence.

Bella did not care in the least that she might well be

driving straight into terrible danger. She gave not one fig that Sir Cyril and any number of other men might well be in that house along with Mrs. Glendenning and The Diamond. She paused not one moment to consider that she might well be dead before the evening was out. No. Her blood was boiling in her veins. No matter what those in the long drawing room thought, this was not a time for consideration, not a time for discretion; this was a time for action and action was exactly what she planned to take!

With a scowl upon her face and the hat with the cherries on its brim perched at a most unlikely angle upon her curls, Bella tugged the horse to a halt before Number 16. She took a precious bit of time to tie the horse to the post and then stamped hurriedly up to the front door, turned the knob and pushed. Surprisingly, it opened. That brought her to a halt at once for she had thoroughly expected it to be barred from within. It was the first thing that gave her pause. Was it some sort of trap, perhaps? No, she thought after a moment. They are merely so very confident that we shall never discover them that they have not taken the slightest of precautions.

From the top of the staircase the sound of a number of gentlemen's voices in spirited conversation filtered down to her; lifting her skirts, Bella mounted the stairs, paused to get her bearings, and then turned down the corridor in the direction from which the voices arose. She was upon them before she knew. There were six of them and Sir Cyril and an elderly woman with graying hair who she thought must be Mrs. Glendenning.

"Well, well, well," cackled Blythe hoarsely as Bella spun around the doorframe and into the room. "It is the little Hedgehog come to save her Diamond. But you are too late, my dear. Much, much too late. Your Diamond no longer requires saving."

Bella raised the duelling pistol she had taken from the

duke's library as she had exited that establishment and pointed it directly at Sir Cyril's heart. "If The Diamond is dead," she whispered as a roomful of astounded faces stared at her, "then you, sir, are dead as well."

And then she saw him sitting upon an ugly puce sopha, a glass of brandy in his hand, staring most oddly up at her.

"What the devil is going on, Cyril?" The Diamond drawled. "Do you mean to say that you abducted me so awkwardly that even Bella knew where to find me? Bad show, that. Do put that thing down, infant. You will most likely shoot yourself and there is not the least need for it."

"Diamond?" The pistol wavered in Bella's hand as the duke stood and strolled toward her.

"Give me that thing, Bella," he ordered, taking the barrel of it into his hand as he reached her, twisting it from her grasp and tossing it to Blythe. And then he pulled Bella into his arms and pressed his lips roughly against hers. It was an awful, spiteful kiss and Bella struggled to free herself from it, but he held her to him until at last he must take a breath. "A veritable tigress," he laughed then. "What do you fear, Bella? That Barrington will not want you when I have finished with you? Most likely he will not. But there, I shall take you regardless of what that stiff-rumped rascal thinks to do once I have had my way. I have wanted you for years, baggage. How sad that I forgot I am a Derrinham and may take what I want without anyone's permission. You will excuse us, will you not, gentlemen?" he added with a broad wink over his shoulder. "Or must I share the chit? No, I think not. Not this one. My papa would not have shared this one until he had had his fill of her, would he?"

* * *

"Bella, cease flailing at me," Derrinham hissed once he had locked the bedroom door behind them. "I am not about to ravish you, infant. What do you think I am, a scoundrel? Take that clock from the mantel, throw it against the wall with all your might and scream as loudly as you can."

Bella stared at him, her mouth open.

"Do it, Bella," he murmured. "I wish them to think that I am attempting to deflower you and that you are resisting me with a passion. They are murderers, infant, all of them. They murdered my mother and father and they will murder us if they do not believe that I have gone 'round the bend and have come to despise all those whom I once loved and to hate all innocence and godliness. They think they have stripped me bare with their lies and remade me into the image of my father. They think they have made me come to view them as my compatriots instead of the bastards they truly are, Bella, and we must treat them to a show in order to keep them thinking exactly that."

Bella reached for the clock and threw it against the wall with all her might, screeching.

Derrinham stamped across the floor, seized her around the waist and cut her off in midscreech by placing his hand over her mouth. "Now," he whispered in her ear, "I am going to drag you to the bed and you must kick and fight me all the way. I know they are listening from below, Bella, and they will expect the sounds of a struggle, including the sounds our feet will make."

And the sounds of a struggle were exactly what the parlor full of gentlemen and Bessie Glendenning heard. And then a series of cries and gruff mutterings, more objects crashing against walls, another mad scrambling of Hessians and half-boots upon the hardwood floor, and then the squealing of the old ropes beneath the feather mattress as two bodies fell solidly upon it and tossed and rolled about, then a loud scream, the sound of a heavy slap, whimpering, and at last silence.

"Now what?" Bella whispered, her lips pressed against The Diamond's ear.

"In a bit I will lead you, crying and disheveled, down the stairs and announce that I am taking you home with me," he replied. "And I will drag you out the front door while you pull back and plead and cry. You can do that, Bella, can you not?"

"Yes indeed. I brought your gig, Diamond."

"Good. At least I shall not need to drag you all the way home along the flagway then. That would raise a number of eyebrows along the way. I thank you, dear one, for coming but you ought not have done. I cannot bear to think of the harm that might have befallen you. Take your hat off, Bella, and tear your dress a bit. No, infant, tear it at the bodice. Yes, that will do."

"Do not you think, Diamond, that your hair ought to be messed up as well?" Bella asked, disrupting his curls with a vengeance. "And your cravat undone? And your vest unbuttoned?"

"Yes," nodded the duke. "And there ought to be scratches upon my face, Bella."

"No, I could not!"

"Do it, infant. There and there."

He dragged her down the stairs a quarter hour later, his hand bruisingly tight around her wrist. And he was laughing, and his eyes held the most chilling look. If Bella had not known for a fact that she had not been ravished she would have been certain she had. He looked thoroughly demented. Piratical. Good heavens, of course! Bella thought abruptly. He is playing pirate! All he need do is squint his right eye and he will be the very same Long John Silver he was used to be when we were children playing by the pond. The scoundrel! I will bet he is enjoying every moment of this abduction. Well, perhaps not every moment, she reminded herself, for he had been knocked unconscious and forced to remember the most dreadful things, and made to face his ghosts. But he is enjoying this part of it, she thought with a secret smile. How very whimsical of him to discover a source of joy even in such adversity as this. He is odd, just as I have always said, she told herself. He is notoriously grumpy and whimsical and odd and I am so in love with him that I could fly straight to the moon.

"Mine for as long as I wish," Derrinham chuckled so evilly that the sound would have sent shivers up Bella's spine if she did not know that he was playing a part. "Let Meade try to find her. He will not dare to search for her at Derrinham House! Hold, sweetings," he growled as Bella attempted to free herself from his bruising grip upon her arm. "Remember you are damaged goods, my dear. Not one of your sanctimonious little beaux will want you even if you should escape me—which you will not. And you will remember to do as I bid from this moment forward, too, or I shall rent you out for a whore in Blythe's little bordello."

Bella whimpered in fear on cue, and attempted to grow pale.

"And does your papa send the Runners after you or come himself, I will have his guts for garters, baggage. I swear it. Tomorrow, gentlemen," he added with a flourishing bow. "I shall await you outside Almack's at the hour of three."

"And then The Society of Lost Souls will begin again," grinned one of the gentlemen as the duke turned and dragged Bella out into the hall.

"We shall begin again," Sir Cyril nodded, tugging Mrs. Glendenning up into his arms and bestowing a smacking kiss upon one rouged, wrinkled cheek. "We shall begin again with the most audacious thundering of power. All of London will hear of it from every terrified innocent who descends those sanctimonious steps into our waiting hands!"

"She is his mistress?" asked Bella, astounded, as The Diamond turned the gig into Great Stanhope Street.

"Exactly what she told me and not a bit shy about it, either. Was an actress until the old knight took her up. Not as fine an actress as you, however, Bella. They believed every bit of it."

"How do you know?"

"Because they would not have allowed us to walk out of that house alive, infant, if they had not believed you. They would have known I had deceived them and never trusted me to live. Because I know now, Bella. I remember everything—and who did everything, too. And I can send the lot of them to the gallows."

The door of Derrinham House swung open wide at the gig's approach and a groom came running to the horse's head as Shaughnessy and Sonnett came bounding down the steps to help Bella and his grace to the cobbles. As though they feared that someone followed, the two old gentlemen hurried the duke and Bella back to the residence where any number of people waited and watched just inside the great hall.

"I rather think everyone noticed that you had slipped away, Bella," murmured the duke in her ear as they climbed the steps. "My hall is packed with people—Barrington among them. You said it was Barrington saw me taken away?"

"Yes, and came to tell us immediately."

"Good man, Barrington. But then, I have told you as much already, have I not? Evening, Barrington, Farraday, ladies. We are both quite safe, you see, despite our recent adventure. Sonnett, Bella tells me that you and Shaughnessy have had an adventure of your own this afternoon.

I should like to hear about it—all of it—my mother's note included."

"Note, your grace?" asked Sonnett, closing the door behind them and following the entire party up the staircase.

"Yes, Sonnett," replied the duke with a cock of an eyebrow as he gazed back over his shoulder. "Bella told me, you see, that she had discovered my mother's note, so do not pretend to me that it does not exist."

"It is at Bow Street, your grace."

"No matter. You will remember what she wrote, Sonnett. It was not that long ago you read it, eh? I remember now her writing of it. She set me upon her lap and pretended to be crying over me to cover the fact that she wrote. Then she tucked the vellum beneath my jumper and told me to hide it for Diana. And I did. When all was chaos in the house and the pack of them fighting with my parents upon the staircase, I saw Diana's favorite book under the table in the nursery and I screamed and cried and broke away from that wretched Bessie and crawled under the table. She left me there long enough for me to stuff the vellum in the book."

Bella's heart came near to breaking for the child she saw in her imagination. The man he had grown to be tucked his arm through hers and led her down the corridor and into the front parlor where a fire blazed upon the hearth.

"And then I forgot all about it," he said, turning to look directly at Sonnett. "Forgot the book and everything else until Sir Cyril was kind enough to remind me of it all this afternoon."

"You know," breathed Sonnett and Shaughnessy as one.

"Not everything—or at least I do not quite understand everything. There are bits and pieces the two of you must explain to me, I think. That pack of liars attempted to persuade me that you and Shaughnessy and Diana knew what they intended and, being concerned only with yourselves, abandoned me."

"No!" exclaimed Shaughnessy as the rest of the party sat around the fire and listened in astonishment.

"We had no knowledge of what they intended, your grace," murmured Sonnett, his heart still heavy with guilt.

"Well, but I remembered you were gone, you know, though I have no idea where you had gone to. But I knew the moment Blythe said the word 'abandoned,' that he was lying. He and his cohorts wanted me to despise you, you see, and to despise the whole world, I think. They want my father back, Sonnett. They want my father back the way he was before my mother finally touched his heart and convinced him to turn upon those monsters, Shaughnessy. They want me to be him the way he was or they want me dead. They will get neither."

Eighteen

Dinner was a haphazard affair at Derrinham House that evening. The group gathered around the table included a Runner, a butler, a valet and a footman as well as the duke and Lord Barrington and the ladies. Derrinham related the tale of Bella's short but effective career upon the stage with a certain relish that brought a momentary scowl to Barrington's face. But the scowl cleared when Jane pressed his hand in her own beneath the table and smiled widely into his true hazel eyes.

"I cannot give you all of their names, Farraday," said the duke as the sweetmeats were brought to the table, "but they will all gather outside Almack's tomorrow night. The Society of Lost Souls, you see, intends to rise again precisely at three a.m. before the eyes of the Assembly Room patrons by instilling terror into innocent hearts."

"I and my fellows will be there to stop them," nodded Farraday with a deal of self-assurance, his eyes sparkling across the table at Emily, who smiled adoringly back at him.

A Runner? thought Derrinham, neither sparkle nor smile escaping him. My new sister and a Bow Street Runner? I shall have to watch and see how that develops.

"Did—do you remember—anything about my father?" asked Winstead hesitantly as the ladies and gentlemen adjourned en masse to the withdrawing room. "I mean, was he—did he ?"

"Have a hand in the murders? No," Derrinham replied, placing a hand upon Winstead's shoulder. "Every face I remember from that night appeared before me in Curzon Street and your father, of course, being dead, was not among them."

It was a lie. Bella knew it was a lie because The Diamond tugged distractedly at his left earlobe as he said it and he had always tugged distractedly at his left earlobe when he lied from the time Bella was old enough to notice.

Emily gazed about her in awe. Almack's. She was standing up to dance in Almack's with a true lord! Lord Nesbitt, he was called. And to one side of her stood Jane and to the other, Bella. It was like a fairy tale come true.

"If you do not speak up you may well lose her," murmured Miss Davies, noting that the duke's eyes followed Bella's every step upon the dance floor even as he took a seat beside her.

"I have only to get through this night and see Blythe and his devilish brood incarcerated, and I shall be free to speak my mind to Bella," he replied softly.

"But will you, your grace?"

"Emily shines like a bright new sun, does she not?" he asked, changing the subject immediately.

"Indeed, but how did you procure her vouchers so swiftly?"

"Mentioned her to Sally Jersey as we were leaving St. Paul's Sunday. Said that Emily was a distant relation and that I had brought her up to join Jane and get a taste of London. Also mentioned, quite by accident, of course, that she had a dowry of twenty thousand pounds."

"Oh, you did not!"

"Yes, I did, and you would be proud to see how subtly it slipped out from between my lips, too. The vouchers arrived on Tuesday morning. I thought the patronesses would inspect her a bit more closely, to tell the truth."

"Not when she has a dowry of twenty thousand and is related to you, your grace!"

"No, I suppose not. Bella has not confided in you her decision regarding Barrington, has she?"

"No, your grace. Once she learned of your abduction yesterday, all else quite fled her thoughts."

Everyone and everything but The Diamond had fled Bella's thoughts yesterday. But now, in the midst of a country dance, she could not help but dwell upon the likelihood of marriage to her dance partner. Lord Barrington would be kind to her, she was certain. And her mama and papa would quite approve of the match. Diamond was correct about that—Diamond. Her heart raced at the very thought of him. And after yesterday, after all of the dread and fear and excitement of yesterday, she knew that she belonged to The Diamond. Even if he never came to love her, her heart would always be his. That was why, as the dance ended, she took Barrington's arm and led him to a spot at the side of the floor.

"James, I must speak with you. I am certain that this is not at all the right time or the right place—but I must tell you."

The smile that had lit Lord Barrington's face faded. "What is it, Bella? What have I done?"

"Nothing! You have done nothing! You are a fine gentleman and I am privileged to know you, James. But I cannot marry you and I must tell you so. There is someone else possesses my heart and I cannot give it elsewhere. It would be most unfair of me to marry you or anyone else. And there are so very many fine young ladies who would be pleased to love you and to marry you."

"Who?" Lord Barrington whispered hoarsely.

"Why, Jane, for one. She is always smiling upon you."

"No, I mean who is it possesses your heart?"

Bella studied the gentleman before her and wondered if she ought to say. And then she took a very deep breath and gazed up into his hazel eyes and whispered, "Diamond."

"Oh, damnation," mumbled Barrington. "I ought to have known, oughtn't I? If it had been anyone else—anyone else—I might have gone on hoping that you would come to change your mind. But The Diamond! Bella, what if he does not return your love?"

"I have thought of that, but it does not matter. My heart will always be his. I find I am not free to give it to another. You would be miserable, James, married to a woman whose heart did not truly belong to you. You know you would."

"Yes," nodded Barrington. "But will you allow me to continue to be your friend, Bella? Will you do that, at least?"

"Oh, my goodness, of course I shall. I shall depend upon it."

The Duke of Derrinham's heart lurched when he saw Bella lead Barrington aside and it sank to the very bottom of his dancing slippers as he watched them in conversation. Is she accepting his proposal? he wondered. Oh, God, don't let it be that. Do not let me have lost her before I have ever attempted to win her.

His heart ached, his head ached, his back began to ache and he felt not at all like dancing, so he sat the entire night beside Miss Davies and not even Emily's excitement could make him smile a smile that reached to his lovely sapphire eyes.

By shortly after two a.m., Junius Farraday had taken up a position against the east wall of the assembly rooms.

In the shadows he and three other Runners appeared to be little more than loungers engaged in conversation, though all four of them watched alertly for the approach of the members of The Society. And one by one, they spotted them. A gentleman in a tall beaver stepped down from a hackney and leaned against the lamppost at the bottom of Almack's steps. Another in shoes with silver buckles strolled up the street and paused beneath Almack's awning to be joined in minutes by a third who engaged him in conversation. Two men rode up to the curb and dismounted, tying their horses between two waiting carriages and, shortly before the appointed hour, Sir Cyril Blythe himself appeared in a landau driven by a liveried servant, with Mrs. Glendenning at his side.

When Mr. Willis opened the door to allow his grace's party to be the first to exit the place at three, the street appeared quiet and not the least dangerous. Bella and Jane, Emily and Miss Davies made their way carefully down the steps, the duke and Lord Barrington directly behind them. From the end of the street Derrinham's Town coach pulled out to fetch them and directly behind came Lady Bedford's coach and then Mr. Tottingham's stanhope and from the other end of the street several more carriages swept into view. And behind the duke's party, a throng of London's elite swarmed out into the night, the buzz of their voices like a swarm of contented honeybees.

Abruptly a rock smashed the glass surrounding the streetlamp's flame. A pistol roared and then another as horses reared and plunged in their traces. The buzz of the honeybees became screaming and shouting. Those people near the top of the steps scrambled madly back toward the door. Those already upon the flagway began to flee in panic, stepping upon each other, knocking each other to the ground, fighting to stay clear of gunshots, flailing hooves, and carriages out of control.

A strong hand seized Bella's arm and flung her into the duke's coach; Jane and Emily and Miss Davies were shoved unceremoniously in behind her. Then The Diamond turned and, pointing at a man who had grabbed one of the fleeing young ladies by the wrist and was tugging her, screaming, into his arms, sent Lord Barrington after the fiend while he himself grabbed another man by the elbow, knocked a blade from his fist and thrust him into Junius Farraday's arms. Bella heard a voice roar out above the commotion, "Runners! There are Runners! Another Derrinham seeks to betray us!" She peered immediately from the coach window to see Sir Cyril Blythe leap from his landau, a duelling pistol gleaming in his hand, and rush in the duke's direction.

"Diamond!" Bella shouted, pulling free of Jane's grasp, pushing Emily away, and slapping Miss Davies's hands aside as she fought to exit the coach. "Diamond! Sir Cyril! He has a pistol!"

The Diamond spun around at the sound of her voice and immediately a pair of men pounced upon him from behind. He spun back again, landing one a facer and the second a heavy punch in the stomach. And suddenly all the terror of the night came to center at the place where the duke stood. Runners, villains and even some of Almack's gentlemen converged upon that spot. Cudgels rose and fell. Knuckles crunched against solid bone. Knives rose from boots and dropped from sleeves and came flying out of pockets, glittering sinisterly in the wildly flaring lamplight.

For a moment Bella, running with skirts raised, lost all sight of the duke and Sir Cyril both. And then she saw The Diamond dancing on his toes among the growing mob, fists pummeling first one, then another, then another. She had never seen anything like this gentleman pugilist. She literally stopped in her tracks and stared to see the quickness and the power of him. But there were so many, so many, and one could barely tell the Runners from the villains. And then she was running again. She had seen Sir Cyril, pressing in among the mob. Not fighting. Barely noticeable. Pressing in closer and closer. In less than a minute he would be directly behind The Diamond, the pistol in his hand pressed directly into The Diamond's back.

Bella threw herself amidst the men, spinning against one and another of them, bouncing into this one and kicking at that one until at last, breathless and bleeding from a stray punch by one of the Runners, she threw herself between Diamond and Sir Cyril just as the pistol exploded.

"I cannot believe that you did that," The Diamond was growling, his arms wrapped about her, the night quiet at last as the coach trundled over the cobbles toward Great Stanhope Street. "Are you lunatic, infant? To put yourself before the business end of a duelling pistol? You might have been killed!"

Bella could not believe it. Was she actually lying across a banquette with her head resting upon Diamond's lap? Were his arms truly around her, holding her as though she would disappear should he ease his grip. "I—I am not dead?" managed Bella, her eyes opening wide in the coach light.

"No, you are not dead, Bella. You fainted. And who would not have fainted to watch a pistol explode right beneath their nose?"

Indeed she was lying with her head upon Diamond's lap and he was scowling down at her and grumbling just like his old self, but his hands, his hands were caressing her gently now, and now brushing the curls from her brow, and now his fingers were tickling at her ears.

"Are you certain I am not dead?" she asked with a

puzzled pout, thinking back on what had happened, at least what she thought had happened. "Did not that dreadful wretch shoot me? Why am I not dead, Diamond?"

Bella thought she heard someone who sounded quite like Emily murmur, "You must tell her what happened. She does not in the least remember. I am sure I should not."

And then The Diamond was speaking again, his voice hoarse with emotion. "The pistol misfired, Bella, and came near to blowing off Blythe's own hand. That is the only reason you did not die. Thank God, you did not die. God must have been smiling down from His heaven upon you. That is all I can think. Of all the fool things to do," he added, the rough hoarseness of emotion lingering beneath the gruff tone he once again sported. "If ever you do such a lunatic thing again I will take you across my knee and—No, no, I will not do that. I would never do that, no matter how much I think you deserve it. But if you had died, Bella—if you had died."

The Duke of Derrinham searched his mind for something else to say to the lovely young lady upon whose cheek his finger was now drawing silent kisses. But he could not wipe his terror for her from his mind. He had not known she was behind him until he had spun around at the explosion of the duelling pistol. Blythe had begun to scream. Flames had spread up his arm as the lace at his cuffs had ignited from the sparks of the misfire, and Bella, Bella had fainted directly into the Diamond's arms. He had thought, in that split second, that she was the one had screamed, that Bella had been shot.

In his haste to carry her from the midst of the fighting he had given not one thought to the feel of tears trailing down his cheeks or the great ache of emptiness chilling him and making him shiver. He had given even less thought to whether or not another pistol was pointed at his back or a blade making to sink into him. His only thought had been that Bella, his Bella, had been shot and well might die, and by the time he had reached his own coach with her in his arms, the Diamond had been sobbing. Now, as she gazed up at him, her lips tilted between smile and pout, he feared he might well begin to sob again.

"It is almost over now, your grace," Bella heard Miss Davies's voice state bracingly from across the way. "You have survived your memories and the battle and thinking Bella shot."

Is it truly Diamond playing his fingers through my hair? Bella thought, bemused. I cannot believe it. Oh, but I think I shall pretend to faint again so that I may stay just as I am all the way to Derrinham House.

"Now all you need is a moment or two alone with the girl in a nice, quiet place—is that not true?" Miss Davies continued. "I would suggest the morning room. The moon will be shining directly through the morning room windows when we reach home and that sight alone must help you to say the words."

"Wh-what words?" asked Bella with a tiny gulp.

"I know," whispered Emily into the shadows. "The exact words I wish to hear Mr. Farraday say one day, and what Jane will soon wish to hear from Lord Barrington."

"Jane," murmured Bella then, sitting up quite suddenly. "Where is Jane? She is not here with us."

"She offered to ride home in Lord Barrington's curricle," explained Miss Davies, "so that his grace might lay you down upon the banquette and look to your comfort. Are you comfortable, my dear?" she added with a hint of laughter in her voice. "Are you feeling better?"

"Quite comfortable and much better," murmured Bella as The Diamond's arm went around her and eased her back against himself until her head rested upon his shoulder. "Much, much better."

Bella glanced into the looking glass above the table in the first floor hall, halted on the spot and gasped. Her hair looked as though an entire army of rats had scrambled about in it. And her face—her face was dirty and there was blood upon it. Dried blood upon her chin. And worst of all, a great, ugly lump rose high upon one cheekbone and by tomorrow, she knew, it would spread into an even greater, even uglier bruise.

"Do not stare so, infant, you have been in battle and look it, that is all. I am even more disreputable than you."

"You are? Oh, Diamond!" Bella exclaimed as he stepped into her view in the looking glass. She turned at once, one finger whispering across an eye swiftly turning black and trailing down an equally bruised cheek back to an ear that was swollen to twice its normal size.

"Got slammed accidently with one of the Runners' staffs, I think," he muttered, grinning painfully down at her. "We make a pair, Bella, do we not?"

"Yes, and not a pretty pair, either. We shall neither of us be able to show our faces upon the street for a week at least."

"And your father will likely call me out and your mama beg to see me horsewhipped if you do not heal by the time they return from Bath. Come, Bella. Enough staring into mirrors. There is something else I wish to stare at."

He took her hand and led her down the long corridor to the morning room where, though not a single candle flickered, the walls and carpeting were bathed in a magical silver light. Leading her to the casements, he stood behind her, his arms about her and they stared silently upward at the full moon. Bella hoped that—well, Emily had hinted that—and Miss Davies as well—but he stood behind her, merely breathing and saying not one word at all. Perhaps she had misunderstood completely. But whether she had or whether she had not, she could not bear to be standing there in such complete silence for another moment.

"Why did you lie to Mr. Winstead?" The words slipped past her lips before she could stop them.

"Lie? To Winstead?"

"About his father. His father was one of the murderers, Diamond."

"How do you know that I lied?"

"Because you tugged at your ear just as you always do when you are telling a regular bouncer. Why did you not tell him the truth of it?"

"Because, infant, his father is just as dead as my own. What would the truth have done but hurt both Winstead and Emily to the quick? A man does not relish the thought that his father has done some great crime. Believe me, I know. At this very moment what Blythe and the others told me of my own father is making my heart overflow with shame. I could not make Winstead feel the same. He is a good man, I think, and he is Emily's brother, as am I. Emily has developed a decided interest in Mr. Junius Farraday."

"How do you know?"

"I watched them together last evening. A definite interest. I expect it will prove a most peculiar match if it comes to be."

"Will you let it be?"

"If Emily wishes it and he as well. Two people who love each other ought not to be kept apart because of what others may think. Bella—"

"Hmmm?"

"Did you—at Almack's tonight—I saw you lead Bar-

rington off the floor and stand speaking to him so very
seriously. Did you—were you accepting his proposal?"

"No. What made you think so?"

"I could not help but think so and it came near to
ripping my heart from my breast to think it, too."

"Ripping your heart from your breast? My agreeing
to marry James could do such a thing to you?" Hope
blossomed again in Bella's very soul.

"Confound it, I find I am in love with you, Bella,"
growled Derrinham into her ear. "I think I may always
have been in love with you, but I did not realize. I know
you have always thought of me as a brother, infant, but
could you, if you tried very hard, think of me as a husband?"

Bella could feel herself fairly quake with happiness.
She had been foolish beyond measure to doubt for a moment that he loved her. He had always loved her, just as
she had always loved him. Had he not just said as much?
How blind we both were, she thought to herself, not to
have known that what we shared when we were young
was prelude to what we will share as we grow old.

"What I said to Lord Barrington was most serious,"
Bella murmured, turning in his arms to face him, to look
up into those most exquisite sapphire eyes, one of which
was at the moment most unromantically swollen closed.
"I told him I could not marry him, Diamond, because
another man possessed my heart."

"Another man? Who, Bella?"

"You, your grace."

The Diamond's arms crushed her against himself as
his lips came down upon hers, softly, tenderly and then
with a rising passion—a passion that flowed directly
from his soul into her own. When at last their lips parted,
Bella laughed and tugged at the wayward curls upon the
back of his neck.

"That was very nice, your grace, and quite wonderful,"

she chuckled, "but now you must say, 'Bella, will you marry me?' "

"Bella," smiled Derrinham, "will you marry me?"

"And what must I say?" grinned Bella.

"Yes," The Diamond offered immediately. "You must say, 'Yes, your grace, I think I will,' and then, you know, we must go on to live happily ever after."

"Yes," said Bella loudly and clearly and with a giggle in her throat. "Yes, your grace, I think I will. But you must kiss me again, thoroughly, so that I may be quite certain."

The duke had not the least argument with that and, in fact, kissed her so thoroughly that neither one of them heard the least sound when Miss Davies tiptoed to the door and closed it softly upon them.